PRIVATE
Mom

ALICIA STEPHENS MARTIN

Year of the Book
135 Glen Avenue
Glen Rock, PA 17327

ISBN 13: 978-1-64649-118-6
E-ISBN: 978-1-64649-119-3

DEDICATION

To JJ, my determined daughter,
and my dear Mother who I miss with
my whole heart every single day!

CHAPTER 1

Cadet Rhya Kennedy clutched her rifle on a slight angle at one and seven against her body. As long as she cradled the weapon tight, no higher than the tip of her nose, she could grip the reins in her left hand as soon as they reached the horses. Rhya brushed her nose—the one she'd inherited from her mother.

"You, princess, have my nose." Her mother, Ava, would pinch the tip when Rhya was young. *"A long line of Italians can be thanked for your crooked nose."*

Rhya would respond, *"Mom, I don't want to be the princess. I want to be the soldier that saves the day when the princess breaks a nail!"*

Rhya's mother claimed they were descendants of famous Italian mobsters, the Garbozzos, six times removed. That invigorated Rhya. To think she possibly had a little grit flowing in her blood, unlike her mother. Rhya believed the Italian inheritance was a blessing. First, her crooked nose was a perfect spot to judge her rifle placement under the wire. *Stay below the wire, stay undetected.* Lifting one inch too high would trigger a series of alarms and explode the booby traps across the massive field that would burst into a firestorm, visible for two miles into town. The mission would be over, with the enemy retaining the secret codes. And Rhya could pretty much kiss any advancement to Battalion Commander goodbye.

The second reason to feel fortunate was those Italian women were bitches! Unfortunately, that trait must have skipped her mom's generation. Her mom was simply a wimp, always afraid to let Rhya go, and constantly trying to dress her in pink freaking sparkles.

The night air was warm and damp, but it was black as hell. A haze loomed so thick that light from the moon and stars struggled

1

to shed even a flicker on the field. Rhya shifted the night goggles carefully with her free hand, barely able to keep her head from rising. Staying low was especially crucial if they wanted to survive and restore the mission. Thankfully all the months of training had her in fit condition. She had to admit, her mother's Hot Yoga class helped with stretching and agility, but she wasn't about to personally commend her. Rhya hated the fact that there was not an ounce of fat on her mother, who could bend and twist in ways even Rhya did not think were possible.

Shit! Here she was in the middle of a vital mission, thinking about her mom again—*Private M,* as all the cadets called her—a constant thorn jabbing in Rhya's head. She focused, repeating her mantra to herself three times. *Forget Mom, only the mission counts. Forget Mom, only the mission counts. Forget Mommy Dearest, only the mission counts.*

Rhya dragged her arm against the dirt to view her Army watch glowing 2100 hours. The mission had to be completed by 2130. Rhya bit her lip, but it wasn't the rich dirt she tasted or the smell of grass ripening from recent spring rains that bothered her. It was the bitter flavor of potentially losing to Cadet Blade, her nemesis. And that was not going to happen. Rhya didn't climb up the ranks because she failed. The highest rank, her dream before graduating, was one mission away. *This mission.* A mission already in jeopardy.

Rhya was well informed about the final mission requirement which was held at the end of her last semester. Only the best cadets were chosen to compete. Two outstanding cadets would lead their teams, on horseback against each other—in a mission to retrieve secret codes—then return safely to headquarters. The leader of the winning team would be pinned as Battalion Commander. A senior JROTC cadet, Rhya had worked her ass off all year as a Second Lieutenant preparing and envisioning the ceremony announcing the award of highest rank.

Cadet Blade, chosen leader of the enemy team, could not defeat her for another reason. Her promise—a bet she shook on. A date with Cadet Blade had to be broken. What the hell was she thinking to agree to such a demand because Rhya's team of two, Cadet Dent and Cadet Maddy, were right now in jeopardy of failing.

Rhya never anticipated something would go wrong, something like one of her troops being kidnapped with the secret codes in hand. *Damn Cadet Dent for getting kidnapped!* The mission focus now included rescuing Dent. Time was running out and snatching a piece of paper undetected was a lot simpler than a piece of paper connected to the 160-pound Gomer Pile of a cadet.

Rhya learned early on after her father's death to never give up, no matter how many mistakes you've made. Even when she was a terrified little girl touring a haunted house, her mother had taught her to keep moving forward. That's what she would do now. Soon the secret codes had to be out of the enemy's wretched control and back in her possession. Cadet Blade and his team of pathetic cadets would see that in under twenty minutes and stand defeated. All would be restored and Rhya and her team would soar in the thrill of glory. Thank St. Joan of Arc, her chosen patron saint at confirmation, for her crooked nose now! Besides she should never have handed the codes to Cadet Dent for safe keeping, let alone allow him to be captured!

Rhya curled her head to the side, her cheek scraping the dirt, stopping for a minute to check on her other battle buddy.

"You okay, Cadet Maddy?"

Her third partner wasn't always the sharpest tool in the shed, but Maddy followed orders to a tee, and looked up to Rhya with respect, wholeheartedly believing in her. Not to mention Rhya had not been allowed to pick her team of two, Cadet Maddy and Dent; they were assigned by the colonel. Unfortunately, when Rhya heard Cadet Dent had been captured, she thought about asking her remaining partner, Cadet Maddy, to be relieved. She knew Maddy's feelings about him could put a glitch in their entire mission. Why did some women let feelings interfere? Rhya had learned that a long time ago when she lost her father. *Don't let your emotions control you like Mom's do.* There she was again. Thinking about Private M.

"Forget her... Forget her... I am everything she is not. My mother is afraid of everything. She just wants my dad back so she can live her happy little hairdressing life in hometown USA."

3

After Rhya thought about it, she decided maybe Maddy's feelings might spur the girl on with extra drive to save the person she was head over heels in love with. Something Rhya would never be—in love!

"Maddy," Rhya growled. "Are you okay, cadet?"

"Yes ma'am, I am. I mean, sir." Rhya could see Maddy try to wiggle her hand up in a salute, her head almost touching Rhya's combat boots and worse yet almost slicing the wire.

"Goddamn it, Maddy. Get your hand down. And you know in the Army they don't use *sir* in that context!" Rhya grumbled in a low order. "You almost hit the wire. We have to reach the horses and we only have thirty minutes left."

"Sorry." Maddy dug her mask into the dirt. "Please don't swear. It makes me nervous... and you know how Private M hates swearing."

Rhya snapped. Just the mention of her mother lit a fire to her soul making her want to swear—just like the mention of Cadet Blade. "We aren't in Kansas anymore, Maddy. This isn't a Friday night movie. A man is about to be blown to smithereens. Who cares about swearing? Now stay low. We're almost there."

Rhya knew horses and loved them as much as JROTC. She picked up the familiar odor of sweating hair, oats, and leather—they were near the tether. The horses were the most important part to complete the mission. Speed would ensure reaching Dent in time.

"Yes, ma'am. I mean, sir. I mean... what am I supposed to call you? I forget. It's kinda like Army time, so messed up." Maddy's voice was now barely audible, her lips avoiding movement below the wire. Rhya swore she heard Maddy mumble, *"Why so serious?"* making her cringe and bite her lips harder, reminding herself there was another reason she'd brought Maddy. The girl had been a gymnast since she was three, light in weight, so catapulting her over the wall would be easy. Maddy had been the best choice.

"The colonel is counting on us."

"I know how much you want the rank of Battalion Commander before we graduate, Rhya."

Maddy was right, but she had no idea how much the mission meant, or how painful the feeling was to lose your father. Maddy had the perfect little family—mom, dad and a brother. Rhya, since the loss of her dad, had searched for a father figure all her life. Someone strong, someone who could save lives. She found that in Colonel Pendleton. Rhya respected the colonel like a father. He was how she imagined her own father, Tyler Kennedy, would have been. Well, almost. She couldn't let Pendleton down. Rhya had to prove to him she was the best person for the job. It would be the greatest honor to be recognized as the top cadet of the program—not to mention she was a girl.

Sure, this wouldn't make Private M proud, but it was what Rhya wanted more than anything. The title, Battalion Commander, would also secure her scholarship and placement as CO of the Cavalry on the Jefferson Washington Military College Equestrian Team. Plus, the triumph would catch the eye of the Army two-star general who for some unknown reason had shown up to observe the mission tonight. The goals only made her shimmy harder and faster along the dirt.

Rhya slithered her free hand up above her head. The yellow tape would be lying horizontally several feet across the ground. No way to miss the six-inch width of plastic. The marker had to be somewhere. She continued, hand patting the ground as if investigating a drug suspect in a bust... and that's when she touched a familiar surface. Her fingers scaled down the rivets in a hard hoof squished deep into the mud. It was Mojo. She could tell by the special metal-wedge shoe. Mojo didn't startle at much unless it was a flashing strobe light in complete darkness. This kept any rider on their heels... another reason not to trigger the wire. All the horses at the school had been gifts, and most had a few bad ticks. That didn't bother Rhya. She actually liked horses better than people.

Mojo stretched his neck down and snorted warm air on Rhya's cheeks. "Hi, buddy," she whispered. Rhya knew all the horses on the farm, having spent her childhood there after school.

She and Maddy made the marker. Once clear, Rhya jumped up, swung her air rifle around to her back and grabbed both of Maddy's shoulders while the other girl was still struggling in the dirt to stand.

Rhya yanked her hundred-pound body up. "Okay girl, let's go."

She glanced at her night watch. There was only fifteen minutes left. Definitely trouble. Not much time to reach the shack, rescue Cadet Dent, and secure the codes. And there was no way to know if Cadet Blade had made it to his horses yet.

"Mojo? But he doesn't like a sudden flash of light," Maddy questioned, staring at the reins.

Rhya slapped them in her hand. "All the reason not to trip any wires, girl. The horses are the luck of the draw, Maddy." Rhya took a breath and thought, *Just like our team of three.* "Would you rather have Superman?"

Maddy slumped her shoulders, shaking her head no.

"If a flash of light comes near him out of the dark, just turn him into himself in a circle. You can ride. Otherwise, he's kind as a puppy. Now get the hell on."

"Rhya, don't swear..."

Rhya ignored the girl and mounted her own horse. As soon as she clenched Superman's reins, his legs started highstep prancing, the sound of mud sucking in the air with each powerful march. Superman was a retired barrel racer and ever ready to tear up the dirt. The steed responded best to a gentle hand—someone who didn't panic and could hold the hell on with their legs. Plus he was a monster to mount. Luckily Rhya had practiced leaping on bare backs since she was a child, her mother cringing every time.

She could see the dilapidated shack beyond the barbed wire course resting on a slope as she catapulted her leg around the beast. The slope was littered with potential landmines marked with orange tips. "Stay on course, Maddy, and you will miss the mines. Just follow me."

This would be a challenge. The colonel's words echoed in her ears. *"Tonight we have a two-star general overseeing this entire mission."* Rhya had heard about this man named General Remy Minosa and his tours. He was feared and respected throughout the Army for his accomplishments and service. *Why had he chosen to come observe this mission?*

"Let's see what you have as your last year students..." she'd overheard the general say to the older retired Col. Pendleton before the mission.

"... This one, she is a possibility," Pendleton answered in an extra gruff voice. Even Col. Pendleton seemed intimidated. "Rhya Kennedy is the best we have in this division. I mean, the best female, sir."

That was the one trait that irked Rhya about the colonel. *Female.* He was slightly chauvinistic. Another reason she had to prove herself against Blade.

Col. Pendleton had pulled her aside minutes before the mission. "Listen, Kennedy. Not only is this mission crucial to your future placement at the JW, but the big guns, Gen. Minosa, is here watching. Our program is small, so your good display could mean more funding. The battalion is depending on you!"

"Yes, Colonel," she remembered saying with vigor, noticing the shadow of a taller leaner figure a step behind him.

Rhya spurred her horse into a swirling 180-degree turn, dug his hind quarters into the dirt and loped off, while Maddy simply turned Mojo and trotted behind. That's when Rhya heard a thundering sound encroaching from their rear-right flank. It wasn't Maddy. *Blade, for sure.* She knew it would eat him alive to have to call her "Battalion Commander" so he was surely attempting to surpass her.

Rhya tasted the thrill of victory when she caught sight of the first orange-tipped marker. She squeezed Superman harder, jiggled the reins lightly, and he leaped off his powerful back hips, galloping into a race.

"Maddy, stay in my tracks," Rhya recommended over her shoulder. "You'll be fine. It'll be like a course of pole bending at our last competition. We've run them hundreds of times!" This was her dream, all she wanted. *JW, here I come!* This mission would secure her college and her position in the Army so she could potentially save lives. Rhya might not have been able to save her dad, but she would spend the rest of her life saving others. Starting with Cadet Dent, retrieving the codes, and being awarded Battalion Commander.

She could hear Maddy wincing behind her, narrowly avoiding the markers. Rhya glanced around and eyed Maddy's gun banging her back, her helmet bouncing, cocked to the side. Rhya pulled Superman to a sliding halt and into another circle. He was breathing heavy and boxed with his front legs to continue. But they'd reached the knoll below the shack.

Rhya made a hand signal to stop Maddy and Mojo beside her. Maddy checked once with the rein, and Mojo simply stopped with no sign of anticipation to take another step.

Rhya grabbed Mojo's reins, moving her closer. "Maddy, you have one minute. That will give me enough time to break in and free Cadet Dent. Now swing over Mojo, onto Superman's back, and I will slingshot you over the barbed wire in one toss. You flip, land on your feet, open the gate, and I will be able to get into the shack." Rhya stared at Maddy who appeared to be worried.

Maddy was tiny—she barely made the height requirements to enter the program. Private M loved her. She was everything Rhya wasn't.

Maddy was reaching for her phone.

"What are you doing?" Rhya asked.

"I'm going to text Dent to tell him we're here and I love him."

"He screwed up and got captured. Now put that away!"

"Well, I don't feel very confident about your *slingshooting* me over the fence," Maddy exaggerated the word. "I might never see him again and you know prom is..."

"Goddamn it, Maddy, it's 2120!" Rhya interrupted, tapping her watch. "We have less than ten minutes."

Maddy shook her head. "I love ya, Rhya, but sometimes you are self-absorbed. And I really get confused about that Army time, too."

That ticked Rhya off. She was fed up. Rhya wedged her bottom behind the saddle onto Superman's rump. She reached over and snatched Maddy's air rifle, shoving it in the case for her. Maddy attempted to say, "Hey wait," but Rhya did not heed the pleas. She gripped Maddy's almost weightless body by the waist.

"Let's go!" In one sweeping motion, she forced Maddy to transfer to Superman's saddle, then stand. "Up... up... stand on it!"

Maddy barely stabilized herself, and Rhya catapulted her up over the barbed wire.

Maddy was so agile she flipped as ordered over the fence with a light scream, landed on her feet from all her years dismounting the balance beam, and opened the gate, all while Rhya was egging her on in a low whisper.

I'd like to see Blade do that! Rhya thought with a grin.

She met Maddy at the gate and handed her the reins. "Now wait here and hold the horses."

"Yes, sir," Maddy said. "I mean, ma'am. I mean whatever I'm supposed to call you." Her voice petered out as Rhya already jerked past, and headed for the shack lit up by a faint lantern.

Inside, sitting patiently on a wooden chair, was... Cadet Dent. Rhya checked her watch: 2128. She was just in time! Rhya rushed Dent and reached out her hand. "Come on, let's go. Hand over the envelope."

Just as the paper envelope that encased the secret codes touched her fingertips, a firestorm of light erupted outside beyond the doorway.

Rhya snapped her fingers like a lobster claw and snatched the envelope. She forgot about Dent and raced to the door. A brilliant light pulsated over the entire field, sirens screeching. The once pitch black area was now a carnival of lights. Rhya could only watch in horror as Maddy's horse sidestepped, colliding into Superman who then reared up, causing Mojo to yank hard and rip free of Maddy's tether. The commotion of strobing lights, bells and distant voices left Superman dancing, Maddy screaming, and Mojo tearing off in a rotating buck when his reins ripped from her hands.

In the distraction, a figure suddenly appeared plastered in the doorway blocking her view and her exit—lit up like the shadow of a devil with a flashing halo. He snatched the envelope from Rhya's hands. *Cadet Blade!*

Rhya yanked off her night goggles and lunged for Blade, but it was too late. Almost clobbered in her forehead by the heel of his black boot, she landed in the dirt. His last words were, "You owe me a date!"

CHAPTER 2

"Oh my!" Ava Kennedy threw her phone in her purse, hopped in her car, and headed toward the edge of town. "Something has to be wrong!" The high school certainly wasn't far. Ava lived in the middle of a town consisting of a mere six blocks. However at a time like this, the drive felt like hours.

The tracker she had placed on Rhya's phone showed her location at the extra fields behind the high school. When Rhya hadn't answered a text, Ava continually dialed another twenty times. She always became possessed when her daughter did not respond in some way to her texts.

This especially made no sense today, because Rhya was late for a long planned truck-driving lesson—something Rhya had been waiting a decade for because she wanted to drive her father's truck. A truck that sat in the driveway since his death. The promise had been made when the girl was eight, then dated and sealed. Ava wished Rhya had thrown the paper out, but sure enough it appeared on her sixteenth birthday.

"Mom, you promised."

"Says here you must be eighteen." Ava re-read the crinkled paper. *"Don't you remember? Graduation present will be lessons from a professional."*

Rhya had screamed and stormed from the kitchen. *"I can't wait until I move out!"*

Ava never thought Rhya would be sixteen, let alone eighteen and about to graduate. Luckily, Ava held off as long as possible with the truck. Yet, now everything was coming to an end. Life would be so different without Rhya in the house.

John Mason's driving school had a waiting list, and John the owner was none too happy when Rhya missed the lesson. The only saving grace was Ava had styled his wife's hair for twenty years, since they were friends in high school. So she reminded John not to hold a grudge with his wife's hairdresser.

It made no sense that Rhya didn't show up. The lesson was all she'd talked about for a month—driving her father's old Ford F250. Ava had made the truck a graduation present, with one stipulation—lessons, the only way Rhya would be permitted to drive the vehicle.

Ava knew Rhya thought the signed promise was the force behind leaving Tyler's truck sit in the driveway for twelve years. Ava certainly had no desire to drive the oversized behemoth, although sometimes she would sneak outside with a glass of wine and drown her sorrows in the front seat after Rhya went to bed. Ava had offers from townsfolk and Tyler's friends to buy the vehicle admired by most men in her country town. But the truck was stationary for one reason... and not the promise. Ava had fallen head over heels for Tyler Kennedy the moment she eyed him zooming around town on his motorcycle wearing a leather jacket. The Army officer was still the love of her life. As long as that truck was parked in the driveway, Tyler would be coming home. That was the reason she kept it.

Dang girl, so headstrong. Like her father. Ava headed for the school in search of her daughter. Something was truly wrong. Ava even tried reaching out to Col. Pendleton. No luck. She punched the gas harder.

The man from the trucking school was still back at her hair salon. He had been waiting for over an hour and a half. She'd left him happily conversing with clients after she offered him a free haircut with Jeffery, her assistant. Ava had paid dearly for that truck lesson—even threw in free hoagies from the JROTC sub sale—and if Rhya kept up this behavior, Ava would not let her drive the truck even if she was eighteen.

The sun was setting and darkness eased in by the time she arrived in the lot next to the outer fields. In the distance a low light beamed over a makeshift shack. Ava made her way toward muffled voices, definitely men. She could hear their whispers and was quite frankly a little confused.

Ava saw dark outlines of figures in the distance, but the area was pitch black. Her stilettos made it difficult to tread in the springy ground which almost sucked them off. She began to walk on the balls of her feet. Rhya, not to mention the colonel, would be so upset. *"No heels on the turf or fields, Mom. They destroy the ground cover!"*

Ava was searching through her purse and trekking at the same time. If she could just find her cell phone, it would make a good flashlight. She picked up the faint smell of manure, most likely from the Potter farm. They had generously provided the use of their land and horses as a gift to the school for kids with different than typical interests.

Ava wobbled as she neared the shadows. At first, she presumed it was the colonel's low grumble, but now she wasn't so sure. The figure was giving no indication that he knew her. She abruptly stopped and continued to rummage through her handbag for her phone with more intensity.

The larger figure, definitely a man, seemed to be creeping in her direction, but he still didn't answer her call or announce himself in any way.

Fumbling inside her purse she nervously called, "Colonel, is that you?"

Concerned, Ava stepped back, relieved to finally finger her keys. She squinted while the silent ghost lurched toward her with outstretched arms like a zombie. *Why doesn't he say something?* Ava thrust backwards, her heart beating faster, just as one of her stilettos sucked into the dirt like quicksand, sending her off balance.

Her other foot searched to stabilize her body but managed only to hit an orange pyramid-shaped object glowing in the dark like the reflectors on the interstate. In fact, a row of lights weaved a wavy pattern in the distance, their visibility blocked until the figure moved closer.

The shadow hastened and was within steps of Ava. She wrestled her imprisoned stiletto, to no avail. *Oh no, he's about to lunge!* Maybe he had kidnapped Rhya. Ava stepped harder on the glowing pyramid, gaining her foothold. Suddenly, a high-pitched sound pierced the air like an endless alarm clock for the entire county. Within seconds a domino effect of lights lit up the field, strobing over the distant shack as if it were the year-end car sale at Merv's.

Fueled with adrenaline, Ava yanked her foot twice to free herself, but her shoe was captive and sucked her back. His arms were almost snaring her shoulders. Ripping her foot forward, the heel released with such force her body flew into the air, along with her pocketbook, its contents and her phone strewing about the field.

Her body slammed directly into the figure full force, landing on him with a crushing blow, keys still clenched in her hand as protection.

"Ahhhhh!" she screamed, her new pink fuzzy sweater shuffling above her midriff. Thankfully the other body had cushioned her fall. Her left hand was pressing against a uniform full of medals, and her keys slammed under the man's chin. "I've had self-defense classes, I warn you."

Ava's hand was shaking as the pointed end of one key pressed into the soft flab under his chin.

The swirling lights in all directions showered his face with colored rainbows. "Colonel?" The rainbow of lights made him anything but happy. Instead he appeared like a monster, a fury of prisms crossing in his eyes.

Voices were echoing as bodies crisscrossed the field. But the colonel had no trouble hollering over them all. "What the hell?"

Col. Pendleton lay flat out beneath Ava's petite body. His hand touched the fleshy part of her waist, while a distorted expression on his face revealed a deep-seated shock.

Ava heard something squish as he attempted to lean up, but the key jabbing in his throat prevented him from raising too high. Some material that had softened his fall was oozing out from beneath his side... she could smell the familiar odor—several large piles of greenish manure where the horses must have been standing.

"Colonel..." Ava tried to stand, but she only slid harder on top of him. His Army cap was lying deep in a pile of horse sludge above his balding head which most likely had a green stain on the back where he landed.

A boy in uniform tethered a horse on the side, watching out of the corner of his eye and snickering under his hand.

"Cadet Roman, help this woman up and off of *me!*" the colonel ordered. "And wipe that shitty grin off your face."

The boy's smile vanished like chalk on a sidewalk in a gushing rainstorm. He began to step toward them in a nervous shuffle.

"And Mrs. Kennedy, could you take the key out of my neck?"

"Oh my gosh, sir. I'm sorry! Please calm down. Swearing doesn't—" Ava silenced when he raised his finger at her.

"Colonel, I am sorry. Why didn't you say it was you?" Ava apologized.

"We're in the middle of a mission here!"

"Colonel, Rhya was to come home..."

This time he sliced the air with his entire hand. Pendleton appeared to be alerted to some sound.

Ava stopped talking, but then perked up. "I know there's a lot of commotion, but do you feel that vibration?"

He offered no response. Ava began to hear a rumble as the earth's vibration transferred through the man under her. The echo appeared to be closing in.

"Colonel, is that a train?" She noticed that the boy felt it too, because he halted in his tracks. Even the horse was frozen, raising his head at full attention, erecting his nose in the direction of what sounded like an approaching freight train.

The retired colonel flung his head up, bumping into Ava's with a clunk as he tried to catch sight of whatever was racing toward them. Pendleton positioned his head and shoulders to look beyond them from behind.

"Colonel? What is it?"

Ava too elevated her head, dropping her keys onto his chest when she grabbed both his shoulders with her hands. She scanned the field. The crisscrossed runners were all now headed in one direction, toward her. Some cadets were frozen dead in their tracks, and others grabbed and tossed friends from the path of what appeared to be a rogue horse. The crazed animal was trampling anything in its path. Ava helplessly watched in horror as the beast plowed over another horse which flayed out in a double split and leaped back to its feet.

"OMG. My God, Colonel…" Ava blinked, blinded by the multitude of flashing lights. She caught sight of four scrambling legs headed directly for their horizontal bodies flattened on the dirt. *A runaway horse!*

"Mojo!" the boy yelled. "It's Mojo. He just took out the sign-up tent! He's headed right for us!"

Mojo had flattened a table and chairs with a raucous clang of metal. The steel tent poles were now bent like toothpicks from the powerful impact. The red canvas tent latched onto Mojo's rump for a brief second until his buck kicked it off with a swish so loud she heard it over the magnitude of noises across the field.

"Mojo, whoa. Whoa!" The colonel waved an arm in the air frantically, hoping to divert the possessed beast who was on a crazed gallop, his saddle now rolled beneath his belly, whipping him into mad hysteria. In seconds the hooves would be churning them like butter.

"There's a second horse too, Colonel!" yelled the boy who was already wrestling his own horse for control.

Ava clenched the colonel harder as she witnessed more legs cutting the air like a serrated blender on puree. She screamed, "There's a… a man on the other horse!"

The stranger was trying to race along Mojo's side and snatch up the reins. His body hung, dangling over his own mount, his free hand outstretched and bopping between the animals to grasp Mojo's bridle. Mud and dirt spun in swirls through the air under the rapidly pounding hooves. Both rumbled toward them.

"Colonel, they aren't going to stop." Ava dug her nails into him. "We're going to be mincemeat pie!"

"Prepare for impact!" The colonel encircled Ava's head and cupped it with his elbow tight, protecting his own with the other.

"We're going to die!" Ava shrieked, burying deep into his chest. "Sweet blessed Mother!"

The horses' hooves were so close the mud splattered and pelted her fluffy pink sweater as painful as darts. The scraping sound of heavy metal shoes narrowly missed their bodies, whistling with a force of air that whisked her ear like rockets.

It seemed an hour passed, suffocating in the rise and fall of the colonel's chest, until the thundering slowed to stomping and snorting. The heavy breathing of horses, clanging of bridles, and chomping at bits sounded under another man's voice. "Easy boy, easy."

Ava was numb except for her racing heart knocking against the colonel's.

She peeked out through the crook of his elbow to see the man on the other horse. He had managed to nab Mojo and bring him to a stop just before they would have been trampled, split apart like a watermelon at a picnic.

In one leap the hero kicked a leg over his saddle and dismounted. He backed up both horses, then reached his free hand up to stroke Mojo's face. The horse's nostrils were flared, rimmed in a pink, puffing air, and foaming with sweat.

Once both horses had settled, the uniformed gentleman handed the reins to the stunned boy whose mouth almost touched his collar. Suddenly enamored, the cadet's trembling arm started to raise in a salute.

"At ease, son. Let's try to untether this saddle quietly before this horse startles again and all three take off."

The man's uniform was decorated with stars across his shoulders as he leaned in to unleash the girth, his strong hand gently unlatching the buckles then sliding the saddle to the ground.

Mesmerized and focused on the man who miraculously charged in on horseback and saved their lives, the sounds of the field seemed almost nonexistent to her. Ava's fingernails were still embedded into the colonel like daggers. Her sweater was up over her abdomen and her mini-skirt had slithered above her thighs. She kissed the colonel's cheek three times with a hard peck. "We're alive! Alive!"

The younger officer stepped over their bodies spread eagle, his heavy boots planted almost directly at Ava's face. Reaching down he touched Ava's arms. "Let me help you."

He raised her up with one swoop, placing her to his side. Ava went rigid, maybe sickened by the thought of nearly being trampled or perhaps at the sight of him. He was tall and dark, about her age. His cropped-close hair was feathered with flecks of grey sparkling in the lights from the field. His chiseled face spurred her knees to wobble.

He stepped back over the colonel, and Ava was now facing him, almost touching his chest with hers. She must've gripped his shoulder because she suddenly became aware of the stars across his uniform. Ava noticed two stars, or perhaps four, on his shoulders, or was she simply seeing stars? Everything was a blur. She raised her head and met his chestnut eyes. Something moved in her, a rush of warm air. Or was it cold because her sweater was shoved up to her chest? Afraid he saw the shiver, she covered her embarrassment by smacking his shoulder.

"We could have been killed," she said.

Ava bent to aid the colonel, but she only had one shoe remaining and lost her balance. The strong arm of the other officer wrapped her naked waist this time. "Forgive me, miss, but I did just save your life."

Ava tried to shimmy her pink sweater, now speckled in mud, over her visible flesh—flesh he was touching with a firm touch. *Two men in one night.* He glanced down at her bare foot, and she watched his Adam's apple move in his throat as he followed her shapely legs to the rim of her mini-skirt.

Thank God for hot yoga. Her worry eased until she remembered the tattoo on her inner thigh. Ava shimmied her skirt, tugging it lower, and cleared her throat.

CHAPTER 3

"What the hell, Mrs. Kennedy? You did it again!" The colonel was now on his feet. He scarfed up his hat, holding it between thumb and index finger to avoid the residue. Never mind that his whole back was smeared with manure.

Ava took a deep breath and sighed. Honestly, the colonel didn't smell too good either. She scanned the field, now crawling with hysteria like a crowded summer carnival where the lions escaped.

"I'm so sorry, Colonel. But Rhya was supposed to meet me at the salon. She had a truck-driving lesson scheduled at 7:30—"

"Mrs. Kennedy, first off that was two and a half hours ago. It's now 2200 hours. Next year that girl will be driving Hummers and carrying an AK16. She doesn't need damn driving lessons... or your helicoptering!" Then he grunted. "Just look at me." He held his arms out, his hat dangling from his hand.

"I don't like Army time, Colonel. It just gets me confused. I think Maddy agrees. Sort of like the address of *sir.* There is an entire textbook on using *sir* in the Army, right Maddy?" Ava glanced at the cadet for help but knew by the colonel's scowl she better quit talking. She could almost see the steam puffing from his ears yet she was compelled to explain. "I just wanted to be sure Rhya was okay." Scouring the ground, she eyed the contents of her purse scattered everywhere. She tried stooping to gather her things, but realized the hero who'd stopped Mojo still clutched her arm. His steadfast grip restricted her movement.

"Am I being held prisoner?" she snapped, then realigned with the hero's eyes. He didn't smile. This man was muscular and next to him, her tiny body felt as if in a cocoon.

He swallowed and she watched his Adam's apple hit his tight shirt collar. The stars and stripes, like soldiers in formation across his shoulders, were perfectly aligned. Just as her husband Tyler's had once been.

When her eyes fell into his, a vacuum switched on and sucked all the air from her lungs. Ava couldn't speak. She was like a fish out of water. She tugged hard on her sweater, then shimmied at her skirt again. Breathless, she could only flinch when his free hand shifted toward her. The man brushed some crusted mud off her shoulder, suffocating her even more.

His touch muffled her voice because her words were barely audible. "My purse?" Ava pointed down, not breaking sight of his eyes which had captured hers.

The officer released his hand, then bent to pick up her purse and several items.

Ava swayed unbalanced in her one stiletto and one bare foot. Or was it her head spinning as she ogled his nicely shaped rear? Even as he rose and held the purse out to her, she remained hypnotized. She examined the chiseled shape of the fingers on his outstretched hand. They both stood, awkwardly holding the purse, until his gold wedding band flickered in the lights and brought her back to earth. Embarrassed, Ava slicked a strand of hair back into her pigtail.

Ava blinked when he cleared his throat. Once again aware of the commotion and the colonel's grumbling, she looked up upon hearing another familiar voice. "Hey, Mrs. Kennedy... I mean Private M?"

Two figures approached in the glaring lights. Dent and Maddy were limping across the field toward them arm in arm. Maddy waved her free hand holding a pair of night goggles.

"Maddy, is that you? Is Rhya with you?" Ava held a hand over her forehead. "Colonel, these lights. Do they have to be so bright? I can hardly see." Ava noticed her sunglasses case and stooped to nab them. When she stood she took in the taller officer's intimidating stare, still penetrating.

Ava teetered from one bare foot to one stiletto. Fiddling with the case, she said, "These lights are just too bright." She slid the sunglasses on even though it was evening.

"Hey, Private M. You need my night goggles?" Maddy frowned. "It's a little wild here right now. But Rhya's coming." Then Maddy let out a gasp when she noticed the colonel in his manure-covered uniform and stained head.

"Will you two love birds separate?" the colonel blurted. "Cadet Maddy, pick up Mrs. Kennedy's things. Cadet Dent, go to the maintenance shed and turn off the strobes and alarms. But leave me some light. We have a mess to clean up."

"Yes, sir... I mean Colonel." Maddy saluted both officers and reached for Ava's keys and other scattered items.

"Jesus Ch—" Pendleton slapped his side and reached for his whistle as another JROTC cadet tried to brush him off. He then pierced them to attention with a sound of the gym whistle. Everyone jumped except the two-star general. "Troops, disband. Report to the center now," he screamed. Ava wondered why her daughter was so enthralled with the man.

"Mrs. Kennedy, you are going to be the death of me. If you didn't raise so much money for the cadets and JROTC..."

"The kids like me, too." She shrugged and then looked at the mysterious general. "They call me Private M." She quirked a smile to cover her discomfort.

"Gen. Minosa, this is the infamous Ava Kennedy," Col. Pendleton said. "Rhya Kennedy's goddamn mother."

Ava hooked eyes again with the officer who continued to imprison her bag. "Could I please have my purse?" His nod was chilling as the officer finally released the bag.

"Colonel, please. I have tried to teach Rhya not to swear. These kids respect you." She shook her head, again wondering what Rhya relished in this program. "Please try saying something like 'Jezoooo' or 'Holy Smokey from Bethlehem'."

"How is this?" The colonel took a deep breath. "*Thank God Almighty*. Somehow Gen. Minosa leaped on a cadet's horse and was able to stop the runaway animal. A little thanks, maybe?" He stared at Ava. "God only knows what we would do without Ava." He mumbled the last statement, as if speaking to himself.

"Better language, Colonel." Ava reluctantly faced the handsome man illuminated in the backdrop of lights. "And yes, thank you."

Her *thank you* was dry, almost callous, even though the officer had saved her life. She herself wanted nothing more than for Rhya to go to college and forget about serving her country and "saving the world." Ava had already lost the first love of her life to the Army—Rhya's father. She wasn't about to let them steal her greatest. At least not without a fight.

Trying to be a stellar mother, Ava had controlled her urges to deter Rhya for the entire four years of high school, praying her daughter would come to her senses. But since receiving a full scholarship to the Early Commissioning Program, the inevitable was lurking too close for comfort.

The cadets, all seniors at Stayman High, were starting to file in and line up in a confused disarray. Some laughed, others seemed nervous, shaken by the event or some even nonchalant. Ava heard one cadet lean into another and say, "Oh my gosh, look at the colonel."

Another chuckled. "Is that Private M?"

"Looks like her. Dang, she's smoking hot."

Frustrated, the colonel inflated his chest and released all his air out the gym whistle in one blow. "Line up. That's an order."

Maddy handed over the items from Ava's purse then hugged her. "Private M, Rhya's going to be pretty mad. She almost won and you know how serious she is about the program."

Ava hugged the girl hard. She loved petite little Maddy. Always such a good friend to Rhya.

Maddy continued backing up and pointing toward the field as two cadets rode toward them on horseback.

"Rhya?"

Maddy nodded.

"Cadet Maddy," the colonel addressed. "Now."

"Maddy, honey," Ava whispered. "You better line up with the others before the colonel has a coronary." Ava gave her a little tap. "I've been in trouble with Rhya before."

Two more horses were trotting across the field. Ava recognized her daughter's voice. "Blade, I had the codes in my hand!" Rhya spun her horse around and returned to the other boy's side. "Give them back."

"No way. A deal's a deal." Cadet Blade smiled and loped away toward the others in formation. "Rhya Kennedy, you are going to prom with me," Blade hollered back.

The colonel closed in on Ava. "Mrs. Kennedy, this was to be an important test for these kids, your daughter especially." He pointed toward the oncoming horse. Ava could see the two riding and arguing as usual. "Goddamn—" Then the colonel broke, appearing to melt when he met Ava's motherly glare. "Dang nabbit, we have a two-star general here."

"That's better, Colonel," Ava clapped.

The man rolled his eyes and mouthed, *"Why me?"*

When Rhya caught a glimpse of her mother, she increased the trot as if to plow her over, then halted her mount a foot away, although Superman continued to prance. Rhya and Superman were a monument in front of Ava. Rhya's hair, in a military bun with rarely a strand out of place, now spidered all over her face.

"Mom! Why?"

Ava attempted an innocent princess wave, knowing her daughter was going to be highly perturbed. Rhya was so covered in mud except for the area around her eyes where her goggles had been. Ava softened from the crystal sea-blue stare—Tyler's eyes. Ava saw his soul every time. The past eleven years reeled up like a movie in her mind.

"Don't start with tears, Mother," Rhya ordered. "It's not going to work this time!"

Ava couldn't contain herself. She teared up. Rhya always wallowed in disgust, furious when Ava was sappy, which equaled over three quarters of the past decade.

The colonel moved in front of Ava to block her view. "You two... Blade, Kennedy... dismount and up front now."

Rhya mouthed something to her mother. *"What are you doing?"*

Ava mouthed back, *"Driving lessons."* Ava held her hands as if turning the wheel of a car.

But the colonel pointed for Rhya to steer Superman away, toward the others, avoiding a maternal confrontation.

Then he turned back to Ava. "As I said, Gen. Remy Minosa and I are running one of our most important drills of the year. This mission could put our high school on the map! These JROTC cadets have worked all semester, including your daughter, who may have just lost her promotion to company battalion leader, not to mention her advancement as CO at the Jefferson Washington Military College for the equestrian team."

Ava ignored him, watching Rhya take her place next to Blade.

"Your daughter is quite determined and quite the equestrian," the general quietly inserted.

Ava barely acknowledged him. She loathed this all. "Colonel, stop. We haven't totally agreed to that. Rhya has signed nothing."

"She's eighteen," he said. "Plus, this is why the general is here."

"I'm her mother," Ava stated and jammed her purse up on her shoulder. Standing taller she reeled away from them, looking back at Pendleton with tears welling.

"No matter. At eighteen..." The colonel stopped. "Jesus Ch—" He stopped again. "Jessie of Nazareth, Mrs. Kennedy. It's what your daughter wants!"

"Thank you for not swearing. I remind you, I have rank as Private M."

The colonel scratched his bald head in exhaustion. "Mrs. Kennedy, it's just a nickname. You have no rank. Only the kids call you Private M."

"I remind you, Colonel, this display of lights and alarms was not cheap. My little salon bleached a lot of heads and sold a ton of hoagies every season to pay for that. Not to mention, Mrs. Potter is a very good client. They own these horses you ride, as well as this field, and all I have to do is put a bug in her ear." She turned toward the general who moved to retrieve an object from the ground a few feet behind her. "I... I am in control of Rhya's decisions."

The colonel turned to examine his cadets, seemingly lost for words.

"Well, thank you for your service." Ava looked at the man approaching her holding something in his hand. "I am sure we will not meet again, Gen. Mimosa."

Ava turned to walk away. She would deal with Rhya later. This whole idea of signing was finished, over, *finito*. There would be no signing for the ROTC scholarship.

Ava's bare foot squished into the mud, and once again she wavered like a rocker and tripped backward, directly into the general's hard bicep. He stabilized her tiny figure with his other hand, standing her up like a Barbie doll. Once more he captivated her. *What in the world was she acting like this for!*

He held up her other silver stiletto. "It's Minosa, ma'am. Not Mimosa. And I believe this is yours."

Ava snatched the heel and did a 180-degree turn, huffier than Superman. Keeping the shoe in her hand, sunglasses on, she began to limp away, not even passing a glance to her daughter who was still mounted and covered in dirt. She imagined the girl shaking her head in disappointment.

From a distance she could hear the last words of the general in a low voice ask, "And what exactly does the M stand for?"

"Mom," the colonel responded. "Private Mom."

CHAPTER 4

Ava ripped another picture down. The photos were tucked under the large half-moon mirror above her cutting station. That way, she could admire her daughter Rhya every day she styled hair. It wasn't just for her. Her customers had shared in Ava's raising Rhya single-handedly after Tyler was killed in a convoy accident in Afghanistan. Her clients were like family and her assistant, Jeffery, like a second mother.

Jeffery was folding the white towels, his bleached pompadour dipping down across his forehead. After each fold he would run the side of his hand along the crease three times as if to iron it. He placed the towels in the cabinet in perfect symmetry, as impeccable as sheets on a bed made at an Army base.

"Oh, Ava," he said, placing another towel into the cabinet. "You did it again. Rhya is never going to forgive you one of these times."

"I hate that she joined ROTC." She brushed a photo with her thumb—Rhya at the tender age of six, a year before her dad was killed. "She wants to crawl through dirt, jump out of helicopters and ride motorcycles! Can you even believe it?"

Ava waited for a response. No one in the room spoke except Jeffery. "So? If I'm not mistaken, you once were a fanatic about motorcycles at one point in your life." He appeared to touch on the subject gently, even looking away at the towel on his lap.

Tula, the nail artist, let out a gasp and muttered to her client, "I can't believe he has the nerve to bring that up."

"Jeffery, I dabbled with riding and where did it get me?" She glanced at the room of eyes staring at her. Ava took a breath as if on the witness stand. "I went through a short time in my life, when

I wanted to be exciting, go against the grain of everything. Where did that lead me? A broken leg!"

"And a tattoo," Jeffery blurted.

"Jeffery, really. Shouldn't Rhya learn from my bad experience?"

"But wasn't that how you met Tyler?"

"You don't meet your soulmate because you are wild and dangerous. It's a good way to die. She should listen and trust her mother," Ava snipped.

Clearly when Jeffery erected his chest taller, he was hurt. "I want to fold towels. Is there an issue?"

"Jeffery!" Ava knocked down a dish of bobby pins, which scattered across the floor. "Rhya's smile was never the same after Tyler died," she whispered. "I just wanted a happy family. To mind my own life, grandkids on the playground, fifty years of marriage." She was tearing up and scanning the room for sympathy, oblivious to Jeffery picking up the bobby pins. He always cleaned up after her.

"Neither was your smile the same," said Gwen, the manicure client whose voice was raspy from too many years of Virginia Slims.

"I did what I had to do," Ava blubbered. "Ran this beauty shop and raised my daughter."

Nothing new. She had been crying all night. Maybe every night for the last eleven years. "Rhya grew up a serious child. I made her that way. Gosh, I'm sorry about that." She flung the picture in a shoebox with piles of others. "I hate the scholarship and I hate the Army." Ava could almost hear the roll of ten eyes in unison behind her back.

"It's what Rhya wanted from the time I first met her." Jeffrey stooped over for another towel. "I am right, aren't I?" His chin poked in the air. Ava hated when he was right.

She looked at all the pictures around her mirror, telling the two ladies under the dryers about each one, then slowly ripping them down and tossing them in a shoebox. She never noticed Jeffery sneak behind her and rehang them on the other mirror next to hers.

"Do you know how many people would be so proud? How hard she works!" Patricia leaned out from under the dryer directly behind her.

"Everyone I know," Patricia's elder sister Gwen affirmed wickedly.

"Ladies, ladies," Jeffery said to the women under the dryers, one eighty and the other fifteen months younger. "How many times have we been with Ava, ripping down those pictures? She'll paint and revamp the whole place and everyone will be happy again. Now who wants fresh coffee and cookies?" he asked. "Tonight is a gala. The last prom. And we're all going to put on smiles for Rhya. It's bad enough she can't stand her date, let alone not talking to her mother." Jeffery threw his hands in the air then looked directly at Ava. "Smile!" he ordered, and planted an oversized grin on his own face as if snapping a photo.

"You think I'm not proud? That's not it at all. Rhya might lose her life!" Ava swung around and stared at them all. "She could be killed just like Tyler." She grabbed another picture then tossed it in the shoebox.

The beauty shop fell silent except for the rolling hum of the two head dryers over Gwen and Pat. Even Tula the nail tech stopped filing Gwen's nails.

Finally Jeffery broke the silence. "Two coffees," he said, flipping his hip on the way to the coffee bar like a hula dancer, zipping past the large St. Francis statue. Because Ava was Italian-Catholic, statues were everywhere.

Discreetly he reached into the shoebox behind Ava, but she turned just in time to see the picture in his hand. She ripped it free before he could tape it back up.

"Jeffery Paul," Ava said, shooing him away. "Don't you have an appointment?"

"I do, but she's running late!" He winked at the ladies under the dryer.

"It's fate," Gwen asserted and Pat nudged her with an elbow. Gwen was the older and always overstepping boundaries.

"No one wants to die," Tula said, "but what your daughter wants is to live her passion."

"You need to be proud. Again, accept this!" Pat gently added. "That school was a blessing. To have an ROTC program with retired Col. Pendleton? Not to mention the equestrian program? How many schools have that? It's why your daughter soared. I went through my whole life working in a sewing factory. Hated it," Pat tried to console. "Look at the opportunity she has."

"Not to mention you can get on with your life. When was the last time you had sex?" Gwen hollered louder than necessary.

Marian, a woman sitting in the corner styling chair, with bleached strands encased in over eighty aluminum foils, looked over with wide eyes.

"Gwen, let the woman start with a date, for gosh sakes," Pat said.

"Listen ladies, I never want to see another man," Ava asserted. "I'm done. My heart can't take it."

"Okay... a woman then," Gwen said, but Pat only elbowed her harder.

Tula giggled. "Well, anything, right? She needs someone."

"Or something? Maybe Yandy.com has a special item," Jeffery joked, his eyes widened. The ladies all snickered, enthralled with him.

"Shh!" Ava, on the other hand, evil-eyed Gwen and pointed the scissors in her direction. "Need I remind you, I am cutting your hair?"

A young girl peeked around the corner next to the mixing room. "Jeffery, I think I'm dry." It was Rhya with a head full of rollers. She had been sitting in the other room under the extra dryer the entire time.

"Let me feel," Ava said, stepping toward her to tap the rollers.

"No, Mom. I want Jeffery to do my hair for prom."

Ava stopped as if a knife had pierced her heart.

Jeffery flagged Ava and touched the rollers. "Now Rhya, your mother loves you. We know how she is." He shuffled Rhya back to the other room and brushed a backhand toward Ava to calm her down. *"It will be okay,"* he mouthed. *"Give her time."*

Rhya kept talking. "You would've liked this general who came to observe us, Jeffery. He was so handsome. Well, for an older man. Of course, Mom did her usual and made a scene."

"A man in uniform heats me up. You know it, girl!" Jeffery slowly shut the door and glanced back at Ava. *"It's okay,"* he mouthed again. *"I will make her gorgeous."*

Ava stood motionless except for a tear streaming down her cheek. *Why am I such a ditz?*

Finally Gwen spoke up, almost a sensitivity in her tone. "Honey, you want me in your chair? I think I'm dry." Gwen didn't wait for an answer. She plopped in the hydraulic.

Ava nodded and the two sisters exchanged glances with Tula.

"This is going to be one rough summer," Tula whispered to them.

"I feel I can't go on without Rhya," Ava said quietly to the picture in her hand. She laid it in the shoebox.

"You've been doing hair here for twenty years. We practically raised Rhya. She will only be a few hours away."

"A few! I will never survive." Ava was now combing and brushing Gwen's hair after taking out the rollers. She very deliberately massaged as she daydreamed.

Ava had attempted mastering motorcycles to meet the handsome boy named Tyler Kennedy who worked at the Harley store her dad often visited. It was one time in her life she was proud of herself... until the incident. On the best summer of her life, one of their adventures across the state, she collided with an elk crossing the road in the small northeastern Pennsylvania town of Benezette and broke her leg.

But Ava's ditziness did not deter Tyler, he had asked her to marry him just before he left for boot camp. He was the love of her life. The salon had been Ava's passion for twenty years—this little reverted five-and-ten-cent soda fountain store had sat vacant, but she and Tyler converted it into a three-chair styling salon. She raised Rhya upstairs in the two-bedroom apartment. They were a staple in the town of Logan, right on Main Street, a block from the square. Even the mayor was a client, and the colonel tanned in the back sunbed room. *Ava's Tint and Tan*. But it all seemed meaningless now without Rhya.

The sisters were looking at each other, concerned. Ava was seemingly in a trance, brushing more rigorously with each stroke. "What about your magazine work in Bethesda, dear? Right outside Washington. Near the military college," Pat suggested. "That will be knocking at her back door. When you work on the *Hair Bloom* layouts, you can visit her!"

"Yes, you can go on the weekends and visit." Tula had to shake Ava's arm because now she was ramming the brush into Gwen's hair, almost yanking it out by the roots.

"Girl, I'm going to get whiplash," Gwen hammered.

"Remember that last photo shoot you did on the blonde model?" Tula held up a magazine. "Right here in *Hair Bloom*. Front cover even. 'From Black to Pastel in an Hour!' No one can do it like you, Ava. You are the blonding queen!"

Ava stopped brushing and stared at the magazine cover. Yes, that was her talent. She ignored the timer that had been blowing up.

"I think I'm done," the lady in the corner called again. But no one answered her.

"Clients have all watched Rhya grow up," Ava said. "Eighteen years down the drain. Can't remember life without her, can't remember life with Tyler." She was chanting to herself, seemingly in a trance.

Gwen grabbed a brush and whacked her rear. "Wake up, silly, or you'll be a dried up and lonely hag. You aren't your daughter. You have a life."

Jeffery suddenly hollered through a crack in the door. "Hey, are you ready? The princess is here."

His hand ushered Rhya in and the room filled with shuddering deep breaths.

Usually there was nothing shy about Rhya. Ava had raised a strong, independent woman, until it came to dressing up—unlike Ava who loved anything in heels, pink and sparkly.

Rhya arched her neck, batting her eyes. "You guys."

"Oh, my lady, you are going to be the bell of the ball," Tula said pressing her hands in a prayer over her lips. "Thank goodness we painted those nails in Bashful Pink. Looks perfect."

Rhya held up her hand to the two older ladies.

Ava stopped and left the blow dryer dangle by her side, still running. "Rhya, you look stunning."

"Mom," Rhya said. "Do not cry! Jeffery, she'll blow a fuse again. Tell her to stop the blow dryer." Suddenly with a loud click, the room dimmed and all electricity shut off.

"Someone get Ava tissues! How in the world did that just happen. Rhya, you are like magic!" Jeffery yelled. "This place is always blowing fuses. What beauty shop doesn't?" He headed to the fuse box mumbling in a low voice.

"How can you go from a military mud-infested uniform to this Cinderella?" Gwen groused.

"Jeffery, you are amazing." Pat shook her head.

Jeffery headed back after he snapped the fuse. Rhya met him with an enormous bear hug, and Ava felt her stomach ache deep in the pit. She loved Jeffery. He seemed to always save the day. She would be lost without him, but it still hurt that Rhya respected him more.

Tears streamed down her face. The dress they'd bought at Stewart's fit Rhya like a glove. Ava couldn't remember the last time her daughter dressed up, nor when she would possibly dress up again, so she was glad Rhya lost her bet with Cadet Blade. What mother didn't want to savor her little girl in rhinestones and dresses?

Jeffery had styled Rhya's brunette hair half up in the front and the rest cascading down on her bare shoulders. The dress was short, but not too short, and sleeveless. Its pattern was a beautiful white with simple spring flowers. Rhya was in top shape, taller and curvier than Ava, more like her father.

"That's a body they have never seen before at JROTC," Gwen announced. "Those boys are going to drop and roll over seeing you in *this* uniform."

"Gwen!" Pat hit her sister's shoulder.

33

"Rhya, you are gorgeous." Ava smiled and her daughter tilted her head, seeming to forgive her for the episode at the field the night before. "And your makeup is beautiful."

"Mom…" Rhya hugged Ava but tenderly. "I know you always mean well."

Jeffery clasped his hands, then in his signature style, fanned his cheeks. "I need a tissue now," he said.

Ava turned and reached for a key on the counter. "Here," she said, offering it to Rhya. "Take the truck. I know you and Blade are meeting at the school." She tugged on her apron straps. "You don't need lessons."

CHAPTER 5

Ava waited only a second after Rhya shut the salon door, then whipped off her apron. "Jeffery can spray Marian's hair and ring you out. No time to explain. Got to run!" She quickly ripped the cape off the blonde client she had just colored with a mosaic of highlights.

Gwen and Pat were perplexed why Ava was in such a hurry, but finished checking out and left. Tula seemed to be lingering, taking her time cleaning up.

"Marian," Ava insisted. "You can pay Tula. I have to go!"

"Wait, Miss Ava. Why the rush?" Jeffery put his hand straight in the air blocking the door.

"Because I'm a chaperone, if you really must know."

Jeffery raised an eyebrow. "Does Rhya know this?"

"I am still her mother, Jeffery. Now out of my way."

"No." He stood firm and held his hands up like boxing gloves.

Ava glared at him. "Really, Jeffery. You know I'm small but mighty, so stay out of a crazed mother's way. I don't care if she likes it or not."

Marian was clearly not happy to be pushed out of the chair early. She sat fiddling with a brush.

"You will never learn," Jeffery said and clutched her by the arm.

Ava stomped. "Let go!"

"You are not chaperoning wearing that..." He pointed his index finger up and down Ava's body. "*Tsk tsk*..." Then he swished her down into the hydraulic chair and said, "Jeffery the magnificent is ready. Cinderella is going to have nothing on you!"

"You two fight like an old married couple," Tula said as she shoved Marian onto the sidewalk and locked the door. Marian was still staring back inside as if confused.

Tula yanked all the blinds down across the front, waving at Marian as she did, then ruffled her pastel pink bleached bob and reached for a hairdryer, saluting. "Tell me what you need, Jeffery. At your service. Let's do this!"

Two hours later, Ava walked up the steps to Stayman High School in three-inch, clear Lucite heels with freshly painted toenails rather than a sweater and black pants. Her light brown hair had fresh blonde highlights. Jeffery had done a marvelous job. Ava shifted her strapless dress and shivered slightly when she reached the door, setting her shoulders back with a deep breath.

Darkness was just settling in. She could hear the music resounding from the gymnasium as she stepped through the double glass doors. She was late, but Jeffery had taken care of that too, phoning the head of the PTA, Ruth Stevens, to explain there was an emergency color correction at the salon.

"Tell Ava no rush!" she'd said. "We're thankful to have chaperones."

Jeffery had everything planned—hair, makeup, even a dress.

Unlike Rhya, Ava loved to play dress up. But it was over twelve years since she wore rhinestones, glitter and a cocktail dress above the knee with Tyler.

Ruth's husband Ben was at the door taking tickets. "Ava Kennedy!" he said, standing up from his metal chair, screeching it back. "How lovely you look."

Ruth came around the corner with a plate of food for her husband. She was slightly overweight. She owned the bakery across from the salon and loved to sample her own goods. The plate trembled and almost dropped from her hands when she eyed Ava. "I didn't even recognize my own hairdresser! I never see you without a smock! You look stunning. I'm so glad you made it to chaperone... especially with the big announcement tonight."

"Big announcement?" Ava touched the curls cascading over her shoulder.

"Yes, the announcements on who signed?"

"Signed? That's funny. Rhya never said a word about anything like announcements."

"Oh, she probably wanted to surprise you."

"But she didn't know I was even going to be here... chaperoning. I wanted to surprise her. Signed what?"

"You don't know they're announcing the seniors who signed on..."

Just then Millie the librarian wrapped Ava in a huge hug from behind. "You look gorgeous, woman," she said. "About time you dressed up again. You look as beautiful as your daughter."

Ava blushed, then for a brief moment a bad feeling rushed over her. Hopefully, Rhya would not think her mother was trying to steal the limelight. That was not her purpose. She just wanted to spend every minute possible with the girl.

Ava proceeded to the gym which was decorated like a weekend in Venice. She caught sight of Rhya immediately, drawn by Blade's obnoxious laughter across the gym. Rhya, seemingly unhappy, perched at the table next to him. His arm was over her chair, a proud peacock with his latest conquest. Although handsome in his suit he was laughing too loud, with a bunch of fellow cadets at their table.

A slow song played softly and the food and punch table was littered with a crowd of both seniors, adult chaperones, and staff. Ava heard some whispers as she entered the room. She noticed Ruth already making her rounds across the gym floor, probably announcing Ava's arrival because everyone she spoke to glanced her way and either waved, smiled, or stood in shock whispering to their neighbor.

Within minutes, the entire room of gawkers seemed to be turning in Ava's direction. She shimmied her dress down an inch again. Jeffery had followed them shopping that day in Stewart's, and Ava remembered remarking about this dress. *If only I had an occasion.* Jeffery told her he went back the next day and purchased it, knowing full well she would be on the chaperone list. The elegant cocktail dress was gorgeous with its sequin white top and black bottom. Short but not too short, revealing her very shapely legs.

Ruth made her way back across the gym and snatched up Ava's arm. "Honey, there's someone I want you to meet."

"Ruth!" Ava blistered.

"Oh, stop standing frozen in time. You look as nervous as some of these prom girls." Ruth tugged her across the dance floor toward the punch table. That's when Ava caught sight of the back of Col. Pendleton's shining bald head, manure stain removed, standing at the edge of the drink table. He had on a clean crisp uniform, slightly hunched over, talking to the handsome officer she'd met last evening. A rush of heat zipped up her spine.

"Ruth, no. Please, I already know..."

But Ruth was not letting go, and before Ava could resist, they were planted next to Col. Pendleton who was in the middle of a conversation.

"I am telling you, that girl's mother is a pain in my rear, but she's always on the frontline ready to serve. Selling hoagies, volunteering... And pink. She loves pink. Every time we decorate for an event, it's pink... and glitter. What do you do with that in JROTC? What do you do with a volunteer like that?"

He hadn't noticed the two women scoot next to him. Ava wasn't really paying attention to the colonel's words, just his voice. Instead she locked eyes with the taller officer she'd met the previous night.

The colonel, oblivious, kept talking. "You have no choice but to use her to help the program. Dang beauty shop. Has her fingers everywhere. But time to get that daughter of hers away from her mother. Lots of potential, if you ask me. Babying these kids is not right. You got to give them guts, make 'em tough. Tough love." He shoved his cup in the air.

"Losing your dad might be tough enough, Col. Pendleton," Ruth intercepted in a soft but firm tone.

Ava was still not connecting to his words, too captivated by the chestnut stare infiltrating hers.

"General Remy Minosa," Ruth said. "This is Rhya Kennedy's mother, Ava. The general is a graduate from the Jefferson Washington Military College and a two-star general. We are honored he has come personally to assess funding and give out the Cavalry award of CO, company head."

Remy reached his hand out to Ava. "I believe we met last night." His eyes maintained a lock on Ava's. "It's Private Mom, right? I see tonight you are fully dressed." He glanced down at her heels. "Both shoes." His lip curled quickly on one side.

Ruth lifted an inquisitive eyebrow.

"Yes. And you, sir, actually smile." Ava took his hand. Then she turned to ask Ruth to inquire about what sort of signing, but it was too late. The woman had already dashed off, leaving Ava alone in the dust.

Ava checked out Remy's hand. He had still not let go of her from the introduction. She thought this was an appropriate moment to thank him for saving her life, but a student hollered from the dance floor, "Hey, Private M, you look flaming."

Ava gasped and scanned the gym. Her hand slipped from the general's. The disco ball in the center created light speckles across the walls, and the ceiling mirrored her rhinestone top and earrings.

That's when another student blurted, "Hey Rhya, your mom sure looks good."

Ava eyed her daughter who was glaring fire directly at her. Still sitting with elbows on the table and her chin cupped in her hands, she now appeared disgusted with Ava as well as her date.

Ruth stepped to the podium and tapped on the microphone. "Okay, alright. Let's stop acting like we are in junior high. You are seniors about to enter the real world. Time to get serious. You worked all year to pay for this beautiful dance... the food, the decorations... and you did such an incredible job, you have enough money left over for prizes and a donation to a charity of your choice."

The room cheered.

Ava felt a presence draw closer to her shoulder. She could smell his woodsy aroma as he brushed her arm.

Ruth continued. "Let's have fun and donate some money."

A heavy set DJ with sunglasses did a spin frontwards and backwards on the turntable with a vinyl record making a funky noise. They all cheered again.

"Here's how it works," Ruth said. "You pick a dancing partner and when the music stops, everything goes dark. The DJ will spotlight three couples. These couples will dance and the crowd will vote by cheering. The last couple standing wins half the kitty, and the other half goes to the charity of their choice." Ruth paused then added, "Now, pick your partner."

The lights dimmed and the room fell into darkness except for the white twinkle lights on the cardboard gondolas and houses of the pretend Venetian setting.

Ava glanced over and traced the outline of the general's chiseled nose, down his jaw and across his shoulders. His muscular arm turned her toward him, and for a moment she thought he was quite forward. But she enjoyed the tingles that needled up her body.

"Ava, would you like to dance?"

Ava paused for a moment saying nothing, shocked he'd addressed her by name. His hand enveloped hers again. He wasn't waiting for an answer.

The DJ played Kenny Chesney's "On the Tip of Your Tongue," and the muscular man led her a few steps onto the floor. All she could think about was his hand encircling hers. It had been so long since a man touched her in such a way. Even longer since she'd felt warm sensations from a man's touch.

When he stopped, picking their spot on the floor, he faced her and placed his free hand on her waist. Ava stumbled toward him as if drugged, not knowing where to place her other hand as it dangled like a puppet, unsure what to touch—his shoulder, his waist, his hand.

Remy released her waist momentarily, then took her other hand and gently placed it on his massive shoulder. She felt motivated to say something, anything to fill the awkward air between them.

She tilted her head down, blushing. "I wanted to say thank you for saving my life."

"My pleasure," he smiled, twinkles of light bouncing off his velvet brown eyes. Silence lingered between them again. Neither moved until he stepped closer. "Mrs. Kennedy, let's just dance. It's been a busy week for me and this feels nice."

She nodded and he inched even closer. *It's been a long twelve years,* she thought.

He began to sway and Ava's limp body drifted into him like magic, as if like her hand, she belonged entwined to him. All along. The arm around her waist swept her in tighter. Ava fingered the broadness of his shoulder. Her head nestled against him, almost preventing them from moving. Then the room went dark.

Ava's thoughts drifted... his body pressing tight, thigh to thigh, his strong abdomen cupping her curves. He tucked his head over hers.

She never expected the spotlight to zoom in on them as one of the three couples. She was still dreaming, not even about Tyler, not hearing the music, just melting in the arms of this man she barely knew, feeling his chest rise with each breath.

The *oohs* and *ahhs* of the audience brought her to her senses, not to mention the blinding glare of a bright light. Ava scanned the room for the other couples. Rhya and Blade were glowing under another spotlight. She saw Rhya mouth, *"What are you doing?"* from across the floor.

Ava realized her head was still lying under the man's chin. She flinched to free herself from his embrace. The general returned to a stern demeanor as if he was stunned as well, straightening the front of his uniform. Ava tucked a hair that had fallen, and he eyed her hand still encased in his other, again sending a rush of heat to her cheeks.

"All right, everyone else off." Ruth scurried around with the mic, placing the spotlight pairs back on the floor. Ava tried to resist. "Oh, no," Ruth commanded and shoved them together with both her hands. "You are one of the couples," she blurted into the microphone when she returned to the pulpit. "DJ Dan, hit it."

The music started again and he played musical chairs with the spotlight. The seniors recklessly screamed and raised an octave louder every time it hit Ava and Remy. "Go, Private M," she heard them cry, while under her breath praying for them to stop.

Remy did not pull her close this time, and they sidestepped slowly, just smiling at the room of students.

The song seemed to go on an hour until Ruth finally yelled, "I believe we have a winner." She stepped off the platform and headed in their direction.

Ava stepped back completely the instant Ruth made the announcement. Both she and Remy awkwardly clapped with the crowd, and she heard him clear his throat.

Ruth hovered over them with the mic saying, "You are our spotlight couple. You split the pot with your favorite charity."

"No," Ava shook her head. "No. How about you pick Rhya, or another senior?"

Remy's strong hand reached up and took the microphone. The room went silent. Ava knew Rhya was staring at her, and she read the anger smeared across her face.

Then Remy's voice broke the glare. It captivated the audience with a calmness Ava admired. "Cadet Kennedy, I agree with your mother. Besides, this is your night."

Ava smiled and joined the clapping. Rhya changed her attitude when the general spoke and refocused the room on her. She awkwardly smiled and acknowledged the crowd with a flick of her hand.

"Rhya, you pick the charity. Tonight I am accepting your signature to the Jefferson Washington Military College... and your position as CO of the Cavalry." Then he turned to the colonel, the room silent as he completely took charge. "Col. Pendleton, I am awarding your program $10,000 in funding. The U.S. Army thanks you for making a fine group of men and women."

The crowd roared.

Ava stepped abruptly away from him. She had been taken, infiltrated. He'd known all along why he was here this evening and that she would be horrified by the announcement. His way of keeping her at bay until Rhya signed. Quite the plan. As for Rhya, she stood motionless when Ava met her eyes across the room, a standing ovation around her. She'd never spoken a word to Ava, her own mom, not a word. Ava wondered for one minute if Jeffery knew. Or Tula, the clients, and the town for that matter?

"Ava. Mrs. Kennedy," Remy called, handing the microphone back to Ruth. "You should be very proud."

"Proud?" Ava snapped. "You have no idea how I should feel. Clearly you are one of those cold-blooded military men who steal daughters and cheat on wives." She pointed to her ring finger. "You have one, if you need to be reminded."

Ava took another step back, unable to control the words jetting from her mouth. Feelings that had been drowning deep inside waiting, locked up behind a thick cement wall cut with cracks, years of cracks. Now they poured out like a dam that had broken.

Remy tried to reach for her.

"Don't you touch me," she said, wobbling in her sandals and losing her balance when her clear glass heel caught the edge of a flowered archway around the dessert table.

Ava soared backwards in a snow shower of petals, crashing into the colonel who had been about to shove a piece of cake in his mouth. The dessert smashed against his face. Then he reached from instinct to grab and catch Ava midair, tearing the side of her sequin top. Once again she found herself lying on top of the colonel, this time with icing and the entire senior prom cake oozing from his back.

The room fell silent once again. Except for a few flowers whispering to the floor.

"Stealing daughters and cheating on wives?" the general responded standing above them. "Is that what you think?"

"That's what you're doing." Ava rose, not caring she was once again missing a shoe.

"Mom, please," Rhya tried to intervene.

"Oh, don't you worry, Rhya. We shall talk. You never said a word."

"She doesn't have to, Mrs. Kennedy. She is eighteen and already signed."

"Well, that might be what you think, Gen. Mimosa!"

"I warned you," Col. Pendleton whispered in Remy's direction as a student helped him up, icing plopping to the floor. The colonel patted his coat down until he found a silver flask from one of his pockets. "She's the reason I drink." He raised an empty flask upside down, almost in tears. "And it's Minosa, Ava. General Minosa."

"Mrs. Kennedy," the general spoke softly, with a penetrating stare. "I give you my regards. Have a nice life."

"You as well, General," Ava remarked. "I pray for all the mothers whose daughters and sons you steal, and I pray for Mrs. Mimosa."

Ava headed out, limping through a path that opened between the students and adults like the parting of the Red Sea. The crowd whispered and some stood open-mouthed. Ava searched for Rhya, hoping to find her, to apologize, but the girl was nowhere to be found.

Ava held her nose perpendicular to the ceiling, trying to appear confident. One heel clicking, her bare foot quiet with each forward step. Quiet then click, quiet then click, a symphony as she stomped toward the gym door.

"It's Minosa," the colonel hollered behind her.

Ava pelted a look over her shoulder in time to catch the colonel point a finger at the general. "She infiltrates your head. I'm warning you."

CHAPTER 6

General Remy Minosa pinched the last button shut and pressed his hand down like an iron on his coat. Scarlett stayed sitting by his feet. The Olde English Bulldogge wagged her bump of a tail against the floor repeatedly, adding a whimper. She must have suspected he was leaving for summer training. What Scarlett didn't know was that she was going too.

He examined himself in the full-length mirror. Fanatic about perfection, his uniform was perfectly pressed, shoes always polished. He still had a full head of hair at forty-two, trimmed each week, every line a precise razor edge. Most barbers on the bases knew him well by now. He smiled slightly, thinking of Abe at his alma mater Jefferson Washington Military College. That barber had to be approaching eighty years old. It would be good to see him again as they had become quite the friends back in the day. This mission to his old school where he was once CO of the equestrian team and cavalry would prove interesting, and he actually felt an enthusiasm for life he'd been missing. God knows the last decade had been painful as hell.

He studied a clear sandal on his dresser, resembling Cinderella's glass slipper. He'd had every intention of returning the shoe to Ava Kennedy when he picked the heel up off the gym floor that night at the Stayman senior prom. But events happened so quickly. He was furious after she'd spouted off at him. In fact, he found it hard to believe she could hurt him as she did. No one affected him like that anymore. Not on three tours of duty or while running entire regiments around the globe. Yet, she'd wounded his self-esteem.

Little could she know her words rang true.

He knew nothing about her, or what she had been through herself. Until the day Ava danced with him, nothing or no one had touched him, broken the barrier he built. Until her cute little figure soared through the air. Until he caught sight of her walking into the gym, flat out gorgeous, her skin soft, her hair cascading across her shoulders. Her olive eyes piercing. And her sweet aroma, even her shoes smelled of sweetness. Not to mention, the dark little secret tattoo etched on her inner thigh. He'd caught a glimpse of an image when her skirt drifted up both times. But everything flashed so quickly he could not decipher exactly what it was, though he would like to find out. Remy found himself dwelling on the thought several times a day, allured by Ava's perfectly defined body.

Remy loathed these feelings. The colonel was right. She was a flake—a helicopter mom like his wife, no doubt. This didn't change the fact she stirred emotions in him he had caged long ago. Besides, one thing he was positive about... he would never see her again.

A two-star general retaining a glass slipper. Really? *Forget about her*, he commanded himself. She loathed him anyway, so he couldn't return the shoe. He liked admiring the article on his dresser. He laid the heel reverently in his suitcase on the top.

Remy had made the decision to bury himself in his career, and his wife couldn't have cared less, drinking herself to oblivion. Once he'd attained two-star status nothing could stop him or his love of country. He touched the picture of his son and placed it next to the shoe in the suitcase. His heart was broken. His son's death haunted him—a constant torment that voraciously drove him into his career.

Remy zipped up his duffel bag. Hopefully Ava's daughter held all the honorable characteristics documented in her file and displayed during their brief interview. She definitely fit the bill with her ability and knowledge of horses. He needed the best on this mission. A vital mission. His cover story would be overseeing the regiment of cadets—highly unusual for someone of his rank. There was evil lurking and infiltrating deep inside the walls of Jefferson. The equestrian program appeared to be at the center of illegal activity, but he knew the program was the scapegoat, a front, and he needed two class-A cadets to scour to the bottom of illicit activity.

He scraped up his house keys as the car beeped outside his condo on a side street of Kent Island. Washington was only an hour away. He eyed a picture of his son in full uniform with his wife in happier times, then slipped it in the side pocket with his keys.

Scarlett was lying at the door now, her eyes drooping.

"Ah, what's up, girl? Come on." He held out the leash. "You get to go this time."

Scarlett rose, her tail banging the door. Remy bent over to clasp the leash on her, and Scarlett tried to kiss his cheek.

"Hey, no softy stuff. You're tough just like me, so act it! Come on. Just you and me, girl."

The drive seemed short. At least to Remy, who last remembered combing through the files on his lap regarding the case. Scarlett was next to him in the back seat. He must have drifted off to sleep. The next time he heard the driver call his name they were passing the entrance sign at the Jefferson Washington Military College. Scarlett was sitting in a new location as co-pilot up front, next to the driver and panting between her smiles.

"Love your dog, sir."

"Traitor," Remy kidded at the drooling bulldog.

The school was nestled in a quiet area near Bethesda, a combination ROTC training center and military school. The driver pulled the black Mercedes onto a side street directly across from the main gates. "This is it, sir." He pointed to an older, brick, two-story house with black shutters and double black doors. "This is where the officers and staff live on campus. Your name is already painted on the top step. See it?" The driver pointed to the riser of the last step. In black against a light beige was his name, *General Remy Minosa*. "They do this for all the staff. Your wife won't be joining you, sir?"

Remy shook his head, not making eye contact. Scarlett perked up, her tail beating the seat. The man seemingly knew to drop any more questions about his family, perhaps because Scarlett was about to lick his cheek.

"A beautiful old brick house."

The man patted Scarlett. "Indeed. And right behind your house, sir, is the barn and arena. Just inside the gates to the left is the chapel. See the steeple?" The man pointed. "And the mess hall, well that's—"

Remy interrupted. "Just where it was twenty years ago. Glad to be back." He tossed a tip to the driver on the middle console.

"Thank you, and I like your Scarlett there." The driver nodded.

Remy answered with a nod, and the two stepped out of the car. He planted himself on the sidewalk for a moment and took a deep inhale. The two-star general eyed the house and campus, remembering how decades ago he'd dreamed of teaching here one day. He remembered returning for his son's graduation. The thought caused his heart to ache with a pain so intense it reminded him of his vow never to come back. Yet, here Remy stood, ready to bring the school back to what it represented, fully aware his manhood had been guided and shaped in every corner of the establishment. Today, the June cadets would parade in, leaving their weeping families' arms as children. Eight weeks from now, he would have reshaped some into commendable adults, while others would relapse home. But that focus was not his top priority, just a facade. His true concern was two cadets and an infiltration to discover whatever corruption some higher-ups were delving into at his alma mater.

He glanced at his watch. He was scheduled to be present on the arena field at 1300 hours. It was already 1200. Just enough time to get Scarlett settled, lay his suitcase down and eat some lunch.

Remy was thankful a welcoming meal was waiting on his kitchen counter, labeled: *Welcome, from the staff and Dean Amy Ironside.* He let out a puff of air with a quick smile. That was one woman he was anxious to see. Old Ironside. He unzipped his suitcase on the large table of the connecting dining and living area. While he chewed the sweet bologna sandwich, he placed the picture of his son and the Cinderella slipper on the mantle above the stone fireplace. He gripped the mantle for one moment, swallowed and bowed his head momentarily. Standing tall, he observed Scarlett already curled on the leather lazy-boy.

"I can see you think this is home already. Hey, and don't move on my account. Here. Gotta go." He fed her the last bite of the sandwich and placed his cap on securely. He was confident she would not move a muscle until he returned.

It was a beautiful sunny afternoon as he waited in the center of the arena field with Col. Pendleton by his side. Remy had invited the colonel to help this summer, knowing he could trust the older man completely without revealing his true intentions.

The cars started in waves at exactly 1330, alphabetically by the first initial of the cadet's last name. The comforting trait about these incoming cadets was their desire to be here. They'd endured a grueling application process to be selected, although he knew some would not be able to finish their commitment.

"We're almost at K, sir," the colonel announced.

Remy tilted toward him. The other man was about the age of his father if he were still alive. He noticed the colonel glancing around nervously. Minosa raised an eyebrow.

"Just making sure there's nothing soft I can fall into. Cleaning these uniforms is not cheap."

At first Minosa acted confused, not wanting to reveal he too was waiting for Rhya Kennedy.

The colonel appeared fidgety. "That woman will be with her, you know. She might bring her assistant, and maybe even some clients!"

The colonel's dry sense of humor would have been like his father's too. Remy thought as he suddenly connected the dots. He had been so concerned about the mission he really didn't anticipate seeing Mrs. Ava Kennedy again. Funny, he almost had an intuition about the twinkle in the colonel's eye. Anyway, the hundred-pound woman had crushed him, and she was a major flake. Her presence wouldn't have a morsel of effect on him.

That's when he recognized her, in two-inch wedges walking up the steep incline following Rhya Kennedy with an entourage behind her. The woman was trying to keep pace with the new cadet. Her memory was stained in his mind, her tiny frame, her waves of blonde streaks blowing in the summer breeze, and those bug-eyed sunglasses. Something inside him stirred, the same weakening he'd experienced that day he wrapped his arm around her waist and touched her soft flesh.

Remy was aware of Rhya Kennedy's father's death—he had studied the background on this cadet. But why her mother, a beautiful woman, had spent twelve years alone was unimaginable. Then he observed a man skip-stepping along behind, turning his head to look at every uniformed male officer. And trailing several lengths after that were three women, a younger one with pink hair and two older ladies stopping to breathe every few feet.

As they neared, the three women lagging in the back stopped in the middle of what was called Suicide Hill. Remy had climbed that baby millions of times at a run, a walk, with weights, with half the Battalion throwing up in hundred-degree summers, not to mention in shorts in sub-zero weather. The three were clearly not making the arena field at the top where the cadets gathered. They plopped on a bench blowing kisses. The pink-haired girl yelled, "I'll wait with these two. We love you, Rhya!" All held tissues to their noses or waved them in the air.

Cadet Kennedy forged ahead among other families and cadets with two shadows behind her, one in three-inch sandals. Remy sighed as the colonel elbowed him. He tried not to peek in her direction, but those white capris fit her shapely figure just right as she marched after her daughter.

"Here we go, General."

The last problem Remy Minosa needed was becoming involved with a flaky helicopter mom. He arched taller and puffed out his chest, securing his own dark sunglasses, telling himself this lady didn't motivate him one bit.

Rhya Kennedy approached and he could see the JROTC colonel had already well prepared her. The girl's hair was precisely pinned back in a military bun, and she saluted with proper form and hand formation. She was one of the few cadets with no tears welling in her eyes or shyly sticking like glue to her family.

"General Minosa."

He didn't even have time to acknowledge Kennedy before a small arm slid between him and Rhya Kennedy. "Mr. Mimosa, I remember you. Do you remember me?" He briefly glanced down, her glittery pink t-shirt sculpting her chest and flickering in the sun.

He followed the extended hand, tipped in pink manicured nails, ignoring the fact she wanted to shake, refusing any display of emotion to the little woman below him. He was an expert in the art of intimidation.

"Mom, please. It's General... General *Minosa*," Rhya grumbled.

"Yes, Ava Kennedy, better known as Private M. I do recall." Remy thought his dark sunglasses and stern manner would ward her off. Wrong, dead wrong.

"No matter. I just have a few questions. If I could speak to you directly." Then she turned and acknowledged Pendleton. "Colonel, I am surprised to see you, but glad to know you will be watching over Rhya." She didn't wait for a response. Ava proceeded to push the general out of line, off to the side of the sign-in table. "I know we started off wrong. So I'm sorry. Okay?" She didn't wait for him to respond either. "If Rhya doesn't like it here, this is my number." She held out a piece of paper. "And here is a list of food she likes, and please make sure she wears a helmet when riding. I had a heck of a time with that." The skip-stepper gentleman was behind her nodding, nudging her forward. "Call anytime, and we'll be here," she added.

The man stepped forward. "I'm Jeffery, sir, and I've heard so much about you." He flicked his wrist in the air then looked up and winked at Remy. "I think this is just a phase she's going through. Rhya, I mean. Maybe even Ava. A long phase, come to think of it. She was seven or eight when she—"

"Jeffery, Mom..." Rhya executed her body toward them, but the colonel shouldered her back.

Remy Minosa stood speechless. *Are these two for real?* He thought it best to ignore these idiots. He could not allow such a silly display to get under his skin like the colonel complained. *Do they know where on this globe I have been? The remote places, the bloody attacks?* Remy shifted and raised his voice. "Kennedy, in line at the front, now. Cadets, let me introduce your CO of the Cavalry. Yellow Flag Platoon, it's yours. Go now, Kennedy." He gestured to a yellow flag on a six-foot thin pole. "The rest of you boys and girls fall in when you're signed up to the flag color connected to your platoon. Now!"

Ava and Jeffery jumped at the harshness in his voice.

"Parents on the side, at the stone wall, please. And no one is allowed to sit on the wall. That's a privilege. This includes you two," he directed to Ava and Jeffery. His heart skipped a beat when he saw a tear stream down under her bugged-eyed sunglasses. He inhaled a small breath, not to be noticed, and refused to acknowledge her pain. "To the wall, please."

Ava stared him down. "You are heartless." Then she shook her head and stomped away, raising her hands in the air to the ladies on the suicide hill as if confused.

Jeffery swung his hips around and tagged behind. "I know he's heartless, Ava," Remy could hear Jeffery say, "but I do love a man in uniform."

Remy took his place back with the colonel. *Those two.* In a matter of an hour, the cadets would be boarding a bus for their eight-week officer boot camp in Fort Knox. And Rhya Kennedy would finally be separated from her mother.

Remy could still see the woman out of the corner of his eye as he gave his speech to the lined-up cadets about to board the bus. Most were a disheveled mess except for a select few like Kennedy and his other choice who had arrived early with the B group. Ava was already disobeying his direct order, right off the bat, sitting on the stone wall, but she was grappling with such large sniffles that if she wasn't sitting she might fall over, so Remy made no comment.

"You can all share one last hug with your family, and after that, on the bus. You are now the property of the United States Army. And parents, there will be no contact for the first two weeks." He heard a huge gasp from the direction of the wall, knowing full well who it was. "And after that, cards and letters only. Cadets who receive any type of package, be it food or what, will share in more ways than one. Keep all mail at a minimum. This is a time for your child to become an adult!" After a final inhale, he ordered, "Now file in. Kennedy, next to me at the bus door."

General Remy Minosa stood beside Rhya Kennedy as cadets climbed single file onto the bus. He wasn't sure if he preferred to stand next to her observing the cadets, or to eye Ava one last time. He caught occasional whiffs of her light perfume, the one that lingered on his coat from the night at the prom at Stayman High. Unexpectedly, Remy observed an elderly man coming nearer in a golf cart. He didn't recognize him at first. The man was much older than he remembered, now bent over and using a cane as he stepped off the cart. His hand reached out to Remy, slipping in behind Jeffery who was hugging Rhya.

"I just want to congratulate you on your promotion," the older man said. "The last time I saw you, you were just a general. Now look at you."

Remy knew the voice instantly. "Abe? The best barber on campus?"

"The only barber on campus. You better remember me." The older man clenched Remy's hand in both of his. "I heard you were coming back this summer as a commandant. Luckily my replacement fell through. Broke both his arms in a skateboard accident, go figure. I guess I should be happy to cut your head of hair until they find a replacement." He pointed to Remy's head. Then Abe nudged Jeffery standing next to Rhya. "Hey, you a barber?"

"Funny, you should ask. Yes, I am."

Abe lit up. "Are you kidding? You're kidding, right?"

Jeffery nodded with a huge grin.

"Wow, that is ironic, you be standing here." Abe laughed. "Hey, you want a job?"

Jeffery shared in the amusement, pointing at Ava who was in a bear hug with her daughter. "I already have a job. She couldn't live without me." Jeffery winked again and Remy felt uncomfortable because the wink seemed directed at him. *Lord, these two!*

"How lucky I am," Remy concentrated on Abe. "But you? What would you do in retirement?"

"Enjoy life. Seems like you should, too. Don't wait to be eighty like me." He tapped his cane on the ground. "Me and the missus have a place on the beach down south. You should come visit one day. There are horses not a mile from my place, and I know how you love horses. Best rider this place ever had go through the program."

"Well, that might never happen for me, Abe. You know I love the career."

"Well as for me, I have Parkinson's," Abe confessed. "I need a replacement fast or there will be some crooked buzzes around here. I can't do the things I love anymore. Maybe you need a break too, Remy."

Remy looked at the final cadets boarding the bus and Ava Kennedy being shooed away from her daughter.

"Mom, I'll be all right," he heard Rhya affirm. The girl waved a flick of her hand at the three women on Suicide Hill causing a commotion.

"I'll be all right" had been his son's exact same last words to Remy's wife before being killed. The colonel nudged Remy with an elbow, bringing him to attention. "Kennedy's mom is headed your way."

Remy remained staunch as the petite Ava faced him. Her makeup had smeared lines where tears streamed under her glasses down her cheeks.

"Gen. Mimosa, please give her an office job, and go easy on her," Ava begged. "She's all I have."

He hoped she didn't see how hard he swallowed. Her statement cut him. "Mrs. Kennedy, we don't put our best in the office. And it's *Minosa*."

The colonel shot Ava a snub of air as if to say she had been defeated. Remy remained motionless while Ava backed away softly into Jeffery's arms.

"General Remy Minosa," he repeated and immediately boarded the bus so as not to let her see he shared in her pain.

CHAPTER 7

R emy stood behind glass that appeared to be a mirror from the other room. Arms folded, the sergeant offered him a coffee. He declined and Col. Pendleton snatched it up instead.

The weather at Fort Knox was hotter than normal, which added to these two weeks of hell for the cadets. But the group was impressive. So far he'd only lost one to dehydration. In six more weeks they would change so drastically, both physically and mentally, that their parents would not even recognize them. Afterward though, parents would cry again but this time from being damn proud—just as he had been of Jason, his son, when he'd graduated. The parents would attend graduation, this time grinning ear to ear. *"Say, that's my daughter... that's my son."*

But these first two weeks were physically and mentally draining on them all. Alone, trekking the Kentucky wilderness, no contact with home. Everyone, including staff, would lose at least ten pounds, returning horribly rank and in need of a warm shower... or any kind of shower... starving for a good meal and letters from home.

The cadets were gathered for the two-week reward in this room. They would receive their first contact from the outside world, then could go to their barracks and cry because they still faced six more weeks of hell to go. PT test at 3:00 A.M., twenty-mile marches carrying thirty-pound rucksacks, studying for exams, shooting practice repeated until precise, gas chambers until one could survive for a full song without a mask, and more days in the field, male next to female, no showers, and eating only mess hall grub.

So far Kennedy had not entered the room, but Remy saw the other cadet, Blade. These were the two he had chosen for his mission once they returned to Jefferson Washington. Kennedy had the fever—a fever to succeed. Something drove that female and Remy knew at her deepest depth it was most likely her father's death and her flaky mother. He had searched the archives to read about Tyler Kennedy. Enlisted right out of high school, a good soldier and man, he'd died in a Humvee accident while rescuing a group of civilian families. He'd crossed enemy territory, leaving the Humvee behind and earning a Medal of Honor. Remy felt the pain not so much for Rhya, but for Ava. He had read about her, too. The report sat on his coffee table below her sandal in his new residence at the JW.

Remy stood straighter when Cadet Rhya Kennedy entered the room. Blade was already seated. That was the current problem. The two hated each other. Remy needed them to work together if this mission was to succeed. They both had the will, but not being able to work together would put the mission at risk.

He leaned closer to the glass to observe Rhya. She filed in, found a desk and slapped an evil eye on Blade.

Emotions must be contained, and now he wasn't completely sure these two could accomplish the task. All of the cadets appeared dirty, tired, hungry and completely exhausted. The excitement of receiving letters uplifted them, even if a minor reward. They would only have one day off. *So enjoy*, Remy thought to himself.

For a second, he wondered how Ava was doing. Missing her daughter, he was positive. He sensed an ache in the pit of his stomach, thinking about her soft skin and sweet smell. How she made him feel, how she loathed and blamed him for Rhya signing onto the scholarship and the Army. *Damn*. Ava was in his mind again like a bad dream.

Thankfully, a remark from the colonel made Remy shove thoughts of her aside. "I never saw so much mail!"

"What?" Remy asked.

"Sir, they are still carrying in the boxes." The colonel whipped off his hat and scratched his head.

Remy counted the mail crates. "One, two, three…" he looked puzzled at the sergeant. He never remembered receiving so much mail in one sitting, even for an entire troop stationed overseas. And he was positive he'd made it clear there would be no gifts or food when he explained the details to parents at Jefferson Washington Military College. Somebody didn't understand the message.

"No sir, I have never seen this much, and all regiments have about the same number of cadets."

Remy left the mirrored room and walked in to join the cadets. At that moment, one cadet in the front rose and vigorously saluted. "Room attention. General Minosa."

The room resounded instantly with squeaking desks, chairs and cadets leaping to attention. "General." All saluted.

Rhya watched the general position himself at the head desk next to a cadet named Meridian. Like everyone else, she only knew the other cadets by last names or code names. She pictured this cadet's first name as "Gerald," because his code name was Weasel and he was a known brown-noser. *Probably an only child.* Spoiled to the rim and a straight-A student, Meridian was larger than normal both in width and height, but he too had lost weight the last two weeks.

Fort Knox was brutal and Rhya's body ached from head to toe. She was one of five females, but gender didn't count for anything. Everyone was expected to perform equally, although Weasel was an oversized pencil pusher.

Two weeks ago they would have been a weak disheveled mess when Weasel announced the general's presence, but today the entire room rose simultaneously with a swooping salute. No one flinched, chin up, back arched. A pin could drop and be heard.

"Have a seat," the general said. "I have some announcements and the names of cadets I want to see personally after Meridian divvies up the mail."

Everyone relaxed as Rhya drifted off thinking about the ten years that brought her to this point. She tried to stay erect knowing she was not going to be chosen for anything special, and that she wasn't in trouble. Before she realized her thoughts had wandered from her exhaustion, a muffled familiar voice touted her name. "Kennedy?"

"Kennedy!" This time a rush of hot air filled her ear cavity, and she was staring crossed-eyed into General Minosa's eyes, his nose almost touching hers. "Kennedy, stand up."

Rhya scanned the room, then yelled in his face, "Sir. Yes, sir. I mean, Gen—"

"Well, stand the hell up."

Rhya's desk screeched as she stood and saluted him.

"I want to see you personally at 1400 hours, immediately after this mail call."

Rhya was flabbergasted. What could she have done?

"I didn't hear you, Kennedy?" he prompted.

"Yes, General."

Although Rhya respected Gen. Minosa, even if he ordered her to scale the Empire State Building she couldn't imagine what caused her to be singled out. She had tried to be a stellar cadet. Her stomach shook feeling his eyes penetrate her.

"Now, sit down."

Meridian started calling names, flipping through the envelopes. "Kennedy. Kennedy. Kennedy." Rhya wanted to crawl under the desk. Her name seemed to be echoing. Then there were larger envelopes—pink ones, and boxes with sparkles. She could even smell her favorite sugar cookies. *MOM*, she irked.

Minosa made her open the first box. The aroma was delicious and her stomach growled. Pink glitter fell on the floor when she opened the card. Her heart dropped.

"Well, Kennedy, isn't that nice your special someone sent you sugar cookies? Pink cards with glitter... who wasn't listening?"

"We can only speculate, sir," Rhya answered in a low, disgusted voice.

"*Sir* is for those who don't work. We don't use that around here." He watched her nod then went on. "Cookies for the office staff who work very hard. They will enjoy them."

Glitter fell all over the desk and floor, not to mention Weasel's hands. The sparkles had also rubbed off on all the other cadets' mail.

Col. Pendleton snatched up the cookies and handed them to Weasel. "Have one, then send these to the office." He nudged Minosa and grunted quietly. "I warned you. Ava Kennedy, she finds a way into your head. Drives you crazy, a lonely helicopter mom! Lunatic."

Remy held his hand up. "It's okay, I understand." He inhaled. "Meridian, stop the mail."

Weasel obeyed with a formal salute.

"Alpha Company, First Platoon—Kennedy's entire platoon," the general called. "You now have a new exercise to master. Push-ups. Let's call them *Cookie Push-ups*, because I believe you will be performing many Cookie Push-ups until these remaining six weeks are over. Now, half right-face, front leaning rest position. Move. Gimme ten."

Rhya was absolutely sure she was in massive trouble. First, her comrades were going to loathe her, all because of her mother. They were sure to have Cookie Push-ups until their arms fell off, because her mother was out of control. Second, she knew the rule about the word *sir*. Officers should be addressed by their title. And third, this was only the beginning of a rough six weeks. She'd been singled out.

Weasel Meridian was pissing her off even more, rolling his eyes every time her name was called. More heart shapes, teddy bear stickers, pink and glittered. Some smelled like her mother's perfume. There were enough care packages for the entire platoon. Weasel seemed to enjoy ogling her performing the so-called Cookie Push-ups. When the last piece of mail was distributed, her entire platoon had glitter all over their arms.

Searing from pain, the room of cadets grunted, breathing heavy.

"Dismissed. Fall out," the general commanded. "Rhya, get the broom. There's a lot to clean up."

The chairs squeaked and scratched the floor again, all eyes burning holes through Rhya as they exited.

"Meridian, wipe that smug look off your face and fallout, or you will be blowing cookies instead of pushing them."

"But sir, I mean General..." Weasel was still sitting in front of the box of mail. Voice quivering, he said, "General, it's another card. It's pink with a teddy bear sticker."

Rhya held her broom and dustpan, watching Col. Pendleton shake his head. "Hate to see the platoon suffer like this. That woman!"

Remy called Rhya sharply, "Kennedy!"

"No, General," Weasel said softly. "This one's not for Kennedy."

Everyone stared at Meridian. "Then who the hell is it for?" Remy snapped.

"You, sir. I mean, General." Weasel held up the envelope, his hand visibly shaking.

The room fell into unendurable silence. When Rhya had first stepped off the bus in Fort Knox she missed her mom, Jeffery, and the beauty shop. She even missed her days with Col. Pendleton back at high school. Though she'd never admit this, she liked having her mom in her brain and didn't need the mantra. She truly missed her. From age seven she'd been raised single-handedly after a crash killed her father. She'd felt the Army would be a way to connect, to remember him, carrying her on his shoulders. She recalled how people had respected him when he was in uniform, and she was a princess when they had been together. But here she missed her mother.

Until now. Why she had sent Gen. Minosa a card was unfathomable.

Rhya watched in horror as the two-star general's eyes studied the card. The man of one of the highest commands said nothing for at least a minute.

"What the..." the colonel muttered, breaking the silent barrier.

Minosa squared his shoulders back and eyed Weasel who now practically hugged the card.

"Should I give it to you, G-general?" Weasel asked softly.

Col. Pendleton glared at the boy. "No, throw the damn card—"

Remy stretched his hand out slowly. "Let me see the name?" His voice rose in a way he had not planned.

The cadet extended the pink envelope, passing it slowly under his nose with a deep sniff.

"It's from her," Weasel said. "Kennedy's mother. And she spelled your name wrong."

"I swear she does that just to get under your skin," the colonel grunted. "I warned you. She makes you nuts…"

"Colonel," Remy stopped him. "Meridian, why are you holding my card under your nose?"

Weasel was still savoring the smell of the pink envelope. "Sorry, General. Just, it smells good… like… like home."

Minosa bent his eyebrows together in question. Weasel dropped the letter on the floor in front of him like an empty cartridge shot out of a gun. Remy looked down and tried to appear nonchalant as several silver sprinkles trailed behind.

"I'm sorry, General," Rhya said, moving closer with the broom and dustpan after seeing Weasel drop the card then stand at attention, too nervous to retrieve it. She intended to pick it up.

"Aren't you supposed to be dismissed, Weasel?" he said. "On second thought…" He checked his watch. "Kennedy and I have a meeting. Take the broom and clean up for her."

Serves you right, Weasel. Rhya smiled inside as she reluctantly handed the general the card. *Yup, his name is spelled wrong. Why, Mother?*

Gen. Minosa locked eyes on Rhya and she instantly knew to gather her belongings without a minute to spare to meet him in the next room. Occasionally she glanced up at him as she packed. To her horror, she observed Col. Pendleton standing behind the general. The older officer was about to sneak an enormous bite out of one of the sugar cookies her mother sent.

When the general turned to dismiss him, the man was already devouring the cookie. Flushed with guilt, he immediately confessed. "Well, they *are* good. You might want to try one." Pendleton held the half-eaten cookie in the air and snatched another in his free hand, right before marching from the room.

CHAPTER 8

The day Rhya left for Fort Knox, Ava had not experienced such an ache since Tyler's death. Her heart went missing, lost its place in her chest, and was now floating somewhere in the pit of her stomach. This ache may have been worse than when Tyler died. Not only did Rhya's leaving resurface all those feelings from after his death, but left Ava's life completely empty. She found herself at the same spot where she had worked for two decades. With nothing and lonely.

For a week the beauty salon was a dismal environment. Jeffery and Tula tried their best to make Ava laugh. They decorated the salon with the best pictures of Rhya from the prior decade—to their disappointment, it only made her cry more. Customers stopped by with cheery trinkets and cards, even people she hadn't seen for a long time. Every day she would lay a stack of cards filled with sparkles and pink hearts on the reception desk. The mailman would poke his head in. "Wow, that's a lot today," he would say with a wink at Jeffery. "All to Fort Knox. I can almost smell sugar from these boxes."

But Ava gave no response, just kept working. She could hear the clients whisper while under the dryer. "I've never seen her like this."

Gwen even said, "I know what she needs, but she's not going to find that here. Maybe she needs to go back where those soldiers are... you know, Jeffery... that general you told us about."

That was just before her sister Pat hit her. "Gwendolyn!"

Ava thought about the general, the handsome man who stoked her dreams. She wanted to send him dark notes in black envelopes, but decided to send him one card instead, with a gentle note thanking him for his service and for watching her daughter.

A week later at midnight on Saturday, Ava was still awake, weeping, stretched across her bed, clutching a pillow that was soaked with her tears. Ava's own mother would be proud; she knew nothing else to do except fiddle with her rosary and repeat a novena to St. Joan of Arc. Suddenly, as if the Blessed Joan spoke directly to Ava, a small statue of the Saint toppled from her dresser.

Joan!

There was no question on Rhya's confirmation which Saint she would emulate. Ava shuttered. Joan of Arc… a saint, a soldier.. *Is this a sign? Is Rhya okay?* Ava could almost have thrown the statue across the room, but there would be too much Catholic guilt.

She touched the figure, setting it gently back in place, then studied the painted sculpture. Seemed a piece had chipped. "Now your hair is even shorter," she whispered. Well, Jeffery the barber was amazing with barbering as well as art. Maybe he could fix Joan's hair, too. *That's what we do.* Ava wiped her tears, then stopped. *Yes, that's what I do! I'm a barber!*

She kissed the statue hard on the lips.

"Thank you, Saint Joan." Holding it in the air, Ava spun around. "Meet the new barber for Jefferson Washington Military College. Private M will officially be working on a military facility."

Besides, it was time to move on. It would only be temporary until Rhya's four years were up, then maybe she'd barber as needed wherever Rhya went. A traveling military barber. Private M's *Snips and Shaves.* She'd dreamed of a career change, and with this idea she could also be near her daughter.

The next morning she phoned the school. If her idea came through, then Jeffery and Tula could manage the salon while she was away. They would be excellent bosses.

The following day Ava received a phone call, and her scream could be heard across town. "Can do. See you Monday morning!"

The commandant of the college advised her there was a contract to sign. They would need to see her license, but she also needed to examine the facility and meet Abe who'd been there for over fifty years. He'd be hard to replace. Most importantly, she would need to demonstrate a fade haircut.

Now, she had to break the news to Tula and Jeffery who she knew would be a complete mess.

Jeffery plopped in a hydraulic chair with a pile of tissues splayed on his lap, catching a breath between sniffles. "No. I can't work w-without you. I love Tula, but you and I... we're a team like Lucille and Ethel. Well... maybe Will and Grace. But you, you'll be lost."

Ava held his hand, her heart broken already. She couldn't bear to see Jeffery cry. He was like a second mother to Rhya. Ava hadn't even considered how shattered he would be if she left him, too.

"I heard Abe, the barber at the school, talking about retiring..." Jeffery blew his nose. "I even stopped by and visited the barbershop before we came home that day. There are two chairs. You could make the establishment really sweet. Take me... please," he begged. "Tula can hire a hairdresser for the time being to help her out. Let me come."

Jeffery stared into her eyes like a sick puppy. He was a master barber, Ava told herself. No one could whip a straight razor in seconds without one nick or slip. He was an artist at designing initials and lightning bolts while Ava was better at color. Her specialty was bleaching, like on the cover of *Hair Bloom* magazine.

"Well, the condo I'm supposed to be provided does have two bedrooms..." Ava dragged the thought out loud.

Jeffery held his breath and rose, as if waiting.

"And really," she continued. "I could never have made it through the last twelve years without you." Tears puddled in Ava's eyes. "You're the best partner anyone could ask for."

Jeffery gasped for air, let out a heavy sigh and wrapped his arms around her as if to never let go.

"I knew you'd miss me before you even left. Okay..." he said, releasing her. "Now where do we start to pack?"

The two agreed, the quicker Ava and Jeffery could make the move, the better for all. An extended goodbye would only be more difficult on them, not to mention Tula and the clients. Besides, Ava wanted to be settled in by the time Rhya and the regiment returned.

Plus, Jeffery informed her that Abe's Parkinson's was creating real issues. "The doctor," he said, "already advised him to retire somewhere sunny and relax, because the work was stressing his health. We need to move before someone else signs up for the job."

Two weeks later, they unloaded the Jeep and carried boxes into their new barbershop. Located next to the bookstore on one side, there was also a military surplus store open to the public on the other. A snack and gift shop stood on the far side of the surplus store, and on the bottom floor was the huge gym facility that housed a shooting range, indoor pool, some classrooms and the auditorium.

"Jeffery, I must say you look handsomely dressed for the first day on the job." Ava pivoted toward him as they carried the last boxes of equipment in the back entrance. She was side stepping in tight black capris, a sleeveless white top with rhinestones across the collar, and high wedged sandals.

"I am wondering how you walk in those shoes at such speed, girl."

Ava stopped and melted. "I love you, Jeffery. Thanks for coming."

"Are you kidding? We're like an old married couple." He passed Ava and laughed, dressed in his creased jeans and crisp white shirt. "Well, you know what I mean. Besides, this place is crawling with men. After working with those ladies all the time, it will be a well-deserved break. Could be a new *Officer and a Gentleman* story." He howled at his own innuendo. "Get it? I'm the gentleman. I kill myself!" When he turned back he must have noticed Ava was about to back into a man loading a van from the surplus store. "Ava, watch out."

Too late. Jeffery stepped in their direction. Ava's tiny figure plowed backwards, ankle overturning ankle in the three-inch wedges, timbering into a bulky man carrying a wooden crate.

Ava's box flew in the air, spewing contents all over the sidewalk. The man in fatigues caught himself, but his crate landed in front of the van door and its lid slid off.

"Oh my gosh, I'm so sorry." Ava tried to touch the man's muscular forearm. He elbowed her off, appearing nervous like the rabbit in *Alice in Wonderland*, rushing to retrieve the crate lid.

"Lady, watch where you're going. This is priceless military equipment here."

Jeffery already set his box down by the curb and started collecting Ava's contents—her curling iron, several brushes, a box of combs and a can of spray—but froze at the man's snarky response.

Ava leaned into him with a perky shoulder, ignoring the brush off. The man was stout, but muscular, appearing somewhere in his fifties. Probably a depressed gym head, his body sagging now that he was older. "I'm sorry," she repeated, reaching out to straighten the lid on his crate. "I'm the new barber next door." Ava pointed to the shop's back door which Jeffery had wedged open with a flower pot.

"She's a better hairstylist than a walker," Jeffery said. "Always off balance in those sandals."

"Look, lady." The man ignored Jeffery, moving his crate a foot away on the macadam. "You stay on your side of the building, and I'll stay on mine." He pretended to slice a divide with his hand between them.

Ava noticed the box contained rolls of equestrian gauze for horses' legs. She was familiar with the equipment because of Rhya's JROTC experience. She couldn't help eyeing the inside of the van. Other crates were stacked inside, some labeled MREs, others labeled spurs and Stetsons, and she also caught sight of vet supplies before the man's pumped up body stepped in front of her.

"I said sorry." Ava held her dainty hand out. "Let me introduce myself. Ava Kennedy. You might recognize the last name. My daughter Cadet Kennedy is the new..." Ava kept rambling, pretending not to hear Jeffery whisper for her to stop. She usually had her way with bullies. "...the freshman CO of the Cavalry. Seems like you have supplies for horses?"

He slammed the van door shut, nearly missing the tip of her Italian nose. Then he blew her a huff and mumbled, "Wouldn't know her from Adam." His forearm muscles bulged as he shoved the last box across the front seat to the passenger side. He said no more, fiddling for his keys, then sighed and jumped in to speed away.

"Gym junkie!" Jeffery sneered. "Have you ever seen the commercial, *I pick things up, I put them down?*"

"I hope most people are friendlier than that." Ava watched the white van roll away, noting the black number in the back—a large 2—and a dented bumper with a twelve-inch red scuff.

"Oh, don't mind him," a man called from the back of the surplus store. "That's the football coach. Retired Army. He does some work here in the store for me and sometimes inventory. He's got a losing football team and dates the equestrian instructor. He's also bat-shit crazy, hence the nickname Batman. But I don't like that equestrian instructor either. They fit each other." The man held out his hand. "Shane Blevins," he introduced himself.

Ava and Jeffery sighed with relief. "I guess you heard we're the new barbers in town!" Jeffery pointed to them both. "Ava Kennedy and Jeffery Cortiere. That's Jeff-e-ry."

"We're going to miss Abe," Shane said, "but we're in need of a new barber." He took his cap off and rubbed his head. "Welcome." He greeted them with a warm smile, then helped Jeffery gather their contents.

Ava placed an index finger on her chin. "Shane Blevins?" She inquired. "Aren't you the owner of the school?"

"Why, yes. You've done your homework. I inherited this when I retired from the Army, after my grandfather willed it to my father, Jefferson Washington. He asked me if I wanted it." Shane smirked. "What was I thinking? I said yes. And I worked a deal with the government, so here I am. Always broke from maintenance and repairs. But let's keep the owner thing as our little secret."

"Secrets? What do you think this is, a beauty salon?" Ava kidded. "I've crossed over to barbering. Barbers keep big secrets!" She knew she usually had a way with people, especially men, if she wore heels and sported a peek-a-boo of leg. "And I have my own."

"What might that be? I mean fess up if we're telling secrets." Shane flirted with a wink.

"My daughter is the CO of the cavalry..."

Jeffery interrupted in a low tone. "It's not going to be a secret if you keep telling everyone on campus."

"She doesn't know I'm the barber yet. We," Ava pointed to her and Jeffery, "are going to surprise her."

"Mum's the word. I promise." Shane winked again. He was quite handsome, not to mention charming as he carried her box in the door and set it down. Ava and Jeffery followed. Shane faced them and ran his hand through his thick waves. His hair was not buzzed like most men on campus. "Well, I will need a haircut as soon as your doors open. Guess I shouldn't complain since most men in their sixties are going bald." Shane shot his cap back on and flicked a wave goodbye.

Tuesday morning at precisely 07:00 A.M.—after Ava set the Joan of Arc statue sporting a pixie with a picture of Rhya on her station—she nodded her head to Jeffery. He switched on the barber pole to start its twirling up and down motion of red and white, flickering in the morning sun. Ava flicked the Closed sign to Open and stepped outside to take a picture of the new sign Jeffery painted and surprised her with. She decided to keep the name simple.

Private M's Barbershop

Ava scanned the arena field where regiments were already marching and exercising, including the football team in the center. Even though the military junior college was small, a commotion stirred on campus every day from regiments who had already completed the Fort Knox bootcamp or others that hadn't left yet. In addition to summer school students, the football team and the band were already present as well.

The campus consisted of only select students—about 1000 handpicked cadets. Ava's condo, although outside the gates, was only a short walk away. It overlooked the stables on a lovely side street near Officer's Row which was a string of large stately homes.

She was excited because Rhya would be able to visit on weekends without leaving. In fact, Ava could see her every day.

Earlier that morning, around 6:00 A.M. before Ava and Jeffery walked to the barbershop, a trailer unloaded a stunning ebony thoroughbred. Full of energy, swinging his muscular neck in circular motions, he had a high-step prance. As soon as the groom released the lead inside the gate, the majestic beast bolted, running and leaping as if freed from a year in solitary confinement. Screaming and hollering, he galloped across the field then rotated back, streaming the fence line, letting the other horses know he'd arrived. Although Ava never actually rode much when Rhya was growing up—she was too tired from working to pay the bills—she loved being able to see the stables, delighted to think she might see Rhya ride again like the old days.

"First clients. Here they come!" Jeffery declared, disturbing Ava's thoughts.

Her assistant manned his position behind the chair, cape in one hand, clippers in the other. A little bell on top of the door announced Shane Blevins, who came in with one of the Cavalry cadets who helped at his store. "Told you I'd be first!" Once again, he sported a welcoming smile.

Over the next weeks the two were busy shaving, cutting and styling regiments and battalion leaders. And just like at home, blowing fuses. The old school simply was not quite ready for Jeffery and Ava's high tech tools.

"This was just what I needed, Jeffery!" Ava told him. "Something new in my life."

"Yes, the girl from the same hometown, afraid to leave for forty years. Not to mention afraid to ride horses or fly, afraid of her own shadow since the wretched bike accident when you were eighteen. Oh, what love drives us to do!" Jeffery confirmed. "Next you'll be jumping out of airplanes! Or maybe driving motorcycles again!"

As soon as the professors, office staff and other employees who lived on campus discovered Ava and her talents had been featured in *Hair Bloom* magazine, she was all the rage. They began peeking their heads in the door inquiring about appointments.

Cadets were in and out of Jeffery's chair in minutes for fades and military buzzes. Jeffery always added a signature statement, saying, "Oh, live a little. Hair grows back. How strict are the COs in the summer? What are they going to say? You'll have a hat on anyway." Cadets left his chair sporting racing stripes, initials, and a few blonde tips.

"This campus is beginning to look and smell really good. Unfortunately, the electrician is getting a real workout. Thank goodness he likes his new haircut," Jeffery touted as he powdered each cadet with a dash of cologne and Clubman powder. "*Voila*, you smell divine." Then he would ogle their tushes swaying out the door. "Hmm... I love tight buns," he'd say with one leg cocked, hand on his hip, admiring his own work and more.

One day, in between clients, Ava needed a break, and leisurely walked around the gym watching the calisthenics. She cringed when she observed the football coach, Batman. He was reaming out the team who was sweating and scattered on the floor in exhaustion.

"I've been here ten years and I've never had a team I was proud of. Not once. Look at you all! You're supposed to be the Army. We've lost every scrimmage so far, and it's going to be another bad year if you don't loosen up." He blew his whistle. "Now, hit the deck and give me a hundred sit-ups."

Ava passed the stable arena that same night and observed a woman issuing orders to a team of riders. Tall and thin, blonde hair streamed down her back as thick as a horse tail. She was actually stunning except for her oversized jaw which was filled with too many oversized white teeth. The thirty-something woman was hollering at the equestrian team just like Batman had screamed at the football team earlier that day.

"You need to loosen up, and reach for the target. We're leaving for the first show in a few weeks. Soft hands! Quiet eyes."

"But Miss Pam, I'm so uptight worrying about the pattern for Class 3—" one of the students tried to confess.

Pam interrupted. "Sit straight and ride. You're in the Cavalry." Then she gritted her teeth with a fake smile. Or maybe it just looked fake because too many teeth jetted from her mouth like an old horse.

Ava empathized with the students. If the body was not stretched properly, then it could not respond with ease and elegance. That was Ava's motto. She shook her head. "They all need yoga," she said under her breath. And then it hit her. She would visit the so-called Dean Ironside first thing Monday morning to propose her plan.

Ava slipped on her kitten-heeled sandals. They were usually a persuasive tool, especially when worn with a jean mini-skirt and a pink t-shirt with a little lace right between the cleavage. She'd worked hard to keep shapely legs even at forty. A runner since high school, Ava jogged three miles most every morning down Main Street before work at the beauty shop back home, plus she was an experienced Hot Yoga instructor.

The campus dean's office was in an old brick building on the third floor with no elevator. The day was a whopping ninety degrees already, and the air conditioning was not working. So by the time Ava reached the third floor and opened the stairway door, she was blasted with a fog of stuffy thick air.

Taking a deep breath, she tugged on her top just for a little lower placement then tapped the door labeled *Dean Ironside.*

"Come in," a woman's voice ordered. *Must be the secretary.*

Ava shifted her skirt and peered in with slightly curved lips. A wall of heat hit her. It was hot in the hallway, but a sauna upon entering the office. The label on the desk read *Sergeant Amy Ironside.* The woman behind the desk was dressed in fatigues, fanning herself with a magazine. Ava could understand the frown on the woman's face. Obviously, her mini-skirt wasn't going to be much help with this dean. She might as well have worn a turtleneck.

"Yes?" the woman asked bluntly, as if suggesting Ava should turn around and leave.

"Hi," Ava said, clearing her throat. "I'm the new barber... Private M," she added, trying to lighten the mood.

"I know who you are. I have a copy of *Hair Bloom* right here. You're the talk of the campus." She was curt as she tapped the magazine she was fanning herself with. "And you want what?"

The woman's hair was fifty percent grey and a wiry mess of curls springing from a hopeless bun in humid weather. She waited and flicked the magazine for another rush of air.

"Sorry about the heat," the woman said. "Damn circuits have been blowing the last two weeks. Not that the place was a hydro plant before, but something is not right lately. Maintenance can't keep the air running long enough to cool things off."

"Oh my, that is awful to have to work in this heat. Must be some high-tech pull on the electric panel or something..." Ava's voice faded. She hoped her face did not reveal a line of bull. She knew what the problem was... the barbershop.

"Well, when they figure it out, I'm personally taking care of the problem myself." The woman wiped some wiry grey hair from her forehead, to no avail, and rolled the magazine tight in her bare hands.

Ava gulped. *This isn't going to be easy.*

"So, what's your problem?" Apparently Ironside was in no mood.

"Well sir, I mean ma'am... I was wondering... if I could offer yoga classes the rest of the summer? Free, mind you."

The woman rolled her eyes. "Yoga?"

Ava cut right in and sped up. "I'm licensed and yoga would loosen everyone around here. Limber this place up. I could do the 5:00 A.M. slot on the athletic field, maybe." Ava's voice mellowed, because she could see the dean wasn't exactly receptive, pushing her chair back from her desk with a lingering loud squeak.

"Yoga at 0500 hours? I was warned about you."

When the woman stood, she was much larger than Ava. Her outfit appeared so confining and heavy. No wonder she was hot. Ava began to picture cute little Army yoga attire. But maybe another day to address fashion. Right now her idea was in jeopardy. Ava swallowed. "I could help you with your hair, too?" She said it so fast the dean blinked. "It's Sergeant, right? I can help you have beautiful hair."

Ava stood paralyzed. She watched the woman limp around to the filing cabinet, perhaps digesting what Ava had just presented.

"You can?"

"Yes, I might run the barbershop, but deep in my veins, I'm a cosmetologist, the one from *Hair Bloom*. You should have seen that model before. That's our little secret." Ava pointed at the crushed magazine.

"Really?"

"That and no one can know I'm Cadet Rhya Kennedy's mom, okay?" Ava nodded and left the dean's office with a handshake and a new client, knowing every woman longs to be beautiful.

Ava didn't tell Rhya the news in any of the many letters or short phone calls she was allowed. She only longed to hear her daughter speak, not upset her. Ava was sure Rhya would miss her so badly by the time she arrived back on campus, her daughter would not complain about either her or Jeffery being there. She wanted the shop to be the grandest of surprises.

CHAPTER 9

General Minosa sat at his desk waiting for Rhya. He held her file and leafed through the pages although he'd already read her bio thoroughly. He studied the picture of her winning the state title in JROTC. The young cadet had been quite impressive this summer also, loyal to a tee, even vowing to work with Blade if that was what she was called to do.

Her safety was of utmost importance because the woman in the next picture had made that clear to him. He touched the photo with his finger. Something about the woman made him smile, which he hadn't experienced in years. According to the colonel this woman was a major nutball—a helicopter mom who loses everything, falls everywhere and causes commotion. Remy certainly had a small taste of her attributes. Everything in Remy's life had been structured, completely rigid. Yet his heart pounded every time Ava Kennedy was near.

Rhya tapped on the door and peered in. "You wanted to see me, General?"

"Yes, come in." He motioned her to a seat across from him.

He followed Rhya's stare as she noticed the picture of her mother on his desk forcing him to close the file. "Sorry about my mom," she said. "The pink envelopes, cards, cookies, glitter..."

He raised his hand. "Relax, Kennedy. This is not about your mother... although she has been a catalyst in causing the regiment to dislike you." He stopped, realizing that actually helped with his plan of examining Rhya under pressure. Imagine, Ava Kennedy aided his plan and she hadn't even tried. "You've proven yourself capable of dealing with the pressure of being in command and not the most popular leader."

Rhya shifted in the chair, still remaining as erect as possible.

"This is about something else I have in mind for you. A mission I've been sent to JW Military College to investigate. And I'm about to call on you for assistance."

"Me, General?"

"If the Army called you to serve your country as a spy at the school, would you?"

Rhya sat even taller. "Yes, General."

"I was reading about your father, Kennedy," he said. "I don't know what you remember or have been told, but he was quite the hero. Do you remember him?"

"Yes, General. My mother was sure to tell me. I do remember the day he left. He placed me on his shoulders, and we walked and he said..." Rhya hesitated.

Remy knew she was a young cadet missing her family. He thought he'd help her. "I would have liked to meet him." When he studied her, Rhya Kennedy didn't flinch. She didn't even blink. The young cadet clammed up tight, as a good soldier should.

"I would like to make him proud. To finish what he represented." She swallowed and appeared to harden even more. "I promise I'm not goofy like my mother. My mission growing up, General, was to be everything she's not." Remy sensed she immediately felt guilty for her last remark, then added, "In her defense, she was as devoted to my father as he was to his country."

Remy let out a little nasal breath. "Kennedy, again, this isn't about her. You already have the job. Seems some illegal activity is transpiring at the military surplus store expanding to the equestrian division. I need someone on the inside, a cadet, someone not worried about popularity, and not afraid to get her hands dirty." He tapped the file in front of him. "I see you want to be in the FBI one day. Well, this is your chance to see if you like this stuff."

"Yes, General."

"Illegal sales of military items have been showing up on the black market, which of course is unlawful, and the distribution appears to be directly coming from the school. Exactly how, I'm not sure. I need an insider," he said. "Actually, two. One at their equestrian division and one at the store. My suspicion is someone is rearranging inventory numbers."

Rhya tapped her head to the back of the chair. She clearly raised an eyebrow on the thought of two cadets. "Let me guess. I'm your Cavalry cadet and Blade will be your contact at the store."

"You learn quickly." Remy stood. "That's the first part of this operation, and the only part Blade will know about. You two aren't going to be friends. In fact, he's going to believe you're the bad guy."

Rhya tilted her head. "But everyone knows I've tried to walk a straight and narrow tightrope in my life."

"Well, maybe it's time Cadet Kennedy can't take being a goody-two-shoes anymore."

She focused on his stare. "What do I need to do, General?"

Immediately, Minosa briefed her on the situation. "When you return, we'll review all the details, but what I need you to do is to be the dirty player. There is a piece of the puzzle that goes beyond fudging numbers and selling black market military goods. Of course, most pertinent of all is your promise of silence, especially not to any cadet... or family. No matter what I ask of you. I understand this may hurt people you love, like your mother and Jeffery."

Rhya took time, clearly pondering her response, then replied, "*Especially* my mother. I understand. Besides, she won't even be near me at school. I would never share with her, and I won't have the opportunity to care what she thinks."

He sensed the frustration in her voice. Perhaps she questioned his intentions and values. Why should she trust him? He knew he had to reinforce the good before he could fully tell her the truth about the mission.

"My parents died when I was young, Kennedy. According to this file, your mother, from what I can s-see..." he stumbled, wondering what had come over him to be so empathizing, "...is that she unconditionally loves you. She's done everything in her power to guide you, and quite amazingly, she did it as a single mother."

Rhya said nothing, only saluted, waiting to be dismissed.

Why the hell did he just soften? He cleared his throat and lowered his voice an octave. "So, that being said, even if you have to disappoint her, could you still fulfill the mission I am about to give you? Do what I ask? Are you sure?"

"Absolutely, General," she answered emphatically.

He opened another file and leaned across his desk. Afterwards, when Rhya left, Remy repeated a mantra to himself, because as much as he wanted to fulfill his own duty, what he was about to do would crush a woman who stirred his soul. "Nothing matters but my career. My son died for his."

Remy repeated that mantra on the flight home four weeks later until he reached in his pocket and pulled out the pink envelope. Even though the school had its own landing strip, he'd taken a commercial flight so he had an uninterrupted moment to open the card and reread it. He'd actually read it a hundred times. He found himself smelling the envelope, like Weasel the day the cadet had handed out the mail. Remy opened the top and slid out the card, a few remaining sparkles falling on his lap. He read the inside one more time.

General Mimosa,

Remy shook his head, absolutely sure Ava Kennedy had messed with his name on purpose, just like Col. Pendleton suggested.

Please, be easy on my daughter. She is a remarkable woman and has conquered some life events with incredible resilience. Mostly, she is all I have and I love her with all my heart. Just a thought.

Please enjoy a sugar cookie when you have a break, and let them sleep in on Saturdays and go to church on Sundays.

Remy caught himself with a slight smile and tried hiding it with his hand, hoping no stewardess or passenger noticed.

Sincerely, Mrs. Ava Kennedy
P.S. Thank you for your service.

He quickly shut the card when the stewardess leaned over him. "Sir, would you like something to drink?" she asked. "Nice card. Bet you can't wait to see her. She must be pretty like those sparkles."

Remy glanced down and smiled again. And this time he didn't try to wipe it off.

Minosa and Col. Pendleton had both flown back a day early. One day of peace and deserved rest. Minosa threw his bags over the sofa and eyed Scarlett who had been well loved by the Dean, Sgt. Amy Ironside, with whom he had been friends for over twenty years. Scarlett was lazing on the cushy rocker, her tail banging the arm.

"Well, General. She was a spoiled good girl, and it was an honor watching her for you," Amy greeted him. "Your place is lovely... well, maybe a little lonely, if I might say." Then she headed for the door.

"Sgt. Ironside," he called. "Thank you." He eyed her. As an MP she'd been nicknamed Old Ironside, later losing a leg in combat. But nothing stopped her. Since his son's death and his wife's obsession with the bottle, Amy always showed concern for him. But there was something different about her today. Maybe it was the civilian clothes, although he'd seen her like this before. She looked refreshed, younger. "Call me Remy," he said. "We are good friends."

She looked at him seemingly surprised. "Okay... Remy!"

"And Amy," he said, stopping her at the door. "You look nice. Something has changed."

She actually blushed. "Thank you, Gen... I mean Remy. I changed my hair. You know we have a new barber here at JW?"

"Well, it looks very nice on you." He wasn't sure why he'd even remarked about it. This was so out of character. "Well, maybe he can do something with this mess. I need a cleanup." He nodded, took off his cap and rubbed his head.

She smiled. "I am sure *she* can, but besides, you look great. And so does that Col. Pendleton. How is he?" She winked. *Ironside winked*. Definitely out of character for this sixty-year-old sergeant.

"And she's awful cute too, Gen... I mean Remy."

"Well, then I look forward to a haircut. And I'll let Col. Pendleton know you asked about him."

"Something's different about you too, Remy," Amy remarked as she shut the door.

He looked at Scarlett. "Want to go for a run?" The dog just wagged her tail and rolled over, sticking her oversized belly out as she nestled in the recliner.

"I see where I rate." He patted her head. "Guess I'll go visit Diesel. I heard he arrived with quite the scene."

Minosa headed to the stable for a long awaited visit with one frisky thoroughbred. Diesel was on loan to him from a good friend who served in the stables at Ft. Myers near Arlington Cemetery. Selected for his beauty and prestige, Diesel had been a parade horse for funerals and ceremonies for the Unknown Soldier. But he proved a bit too feisty. They called Minosa, known throughout the Army for his riding abilities, to work with the horse until he could calm down. Remy quickly accepted the challenge. The steed would clear his mind, causing him to focus on something outside of work and his personal life. Honestly, his friend had probably thought they both could benefit each other.

Remy headed to the barn and was saluted at the second stall. The cadet's hat was crumpled in his pocket while he cleaned the stall. Minosa noticed the freshly shaved head and squinted at a strange zigzag scar in the back along the cadet's occipital. The cadet flicked his hat on fast upon seeing the general. Minosa decided it must be a strange injury.

Remy rode Diesel for two hours. The horse pranced around the arena like a combination dressage horse and barrel racer. Remy concentrated on Diesel as he quietly handled him, asking him to move forward, or to come back, until finally the steed was side-passing with the least touch of a leg in either direction.

There were two jumps in the center of the ring, and out of curiosity he commanded the three-foot like a pro. Remy eyed the five-footer next, then circled Diesel and nudged the steed forward. Diesel approached with more vigor. An unexpected bang from the direction of metal bleachers chased Diesel forward with a jolt.

Remy slowed the lope into a circle and scanned the direction of the stands normally filled with an audience. The bleachers were hidden behind a black curtain. He traced the crease where the curtains could divide and reopen, closed at the moment to keep them free from too much arena dust. From years in combat, Remy had a good intuition. He side-loped Diesel toward the curtains and something alerted him to the presence of another. Watching.

After a few moments, there was nothing other than the sound of someone walking with light taps beyond the curtain. Remy loped Diesel several circles until the horse quietly changed leads when asked. Then he again centered him toward the higher jump. Diesel pricked his ears forward like radar and lined straight for the center, respecting Remy in every step.

They cleared the jump with plenty to spare. Like champions. Remy rubbed the soft neck of the beast now damp with sweat. His hand mingled with the horse's mane. Other than Scarlett, he had not felt such solace since his son's death. And Lord knows Scarlett was easy. Diesel utilized every effort of his patience to ride.

He wondered what had changed inside himself. Perhaps meeting Ava and keeping that glass slipper on his mantel. She stirred emotions in him he hadn't experienced for years.

When finished, he led the horse to the grooming area. The tack room door was slightly ajar, and he could smell the aroma of leather. He reached his hand up to peer inside.

"Good afternoon, General." A tall blonde with a thick ponytail greeted him. "I heard you had returned. Can I help you with something?" She shut the door fully behind him. "Your tack can stay in your private stall area at the back. No need to put it in the common area. I'm sure you like peace when you ride."

"Just looking," he said, reaching out his hand. "Pam, right?"

She was a civilian instructor hired by the school to run the equestrian program. He knew he had the authority to be here, but for the sake of the mission and Rhya Kennedy as CO he bowed back.

"Yes, sir. And I keep everything in A1 top condition. No need to worry about that." She seemed defensive.

"I can see you do. I wanted to re-introduce myself and tell you I look forward to seeing you work with the new Cavalry CO. I believe you will find her very proficient."

Pam nodded. "I hope so. I need an outstanding CO to make this unit top-notch. By the way, your horse has been very spicy. He needs to be ridden... often."

"Well, that's my intention now that I'm here," he said. "Plus, I thought my new CO could ride him also."

"That's a lot of animal. She better possess the skill needed." Pam tilted her head in concern.

Remy noticed her hair was much lighter then when he'd first studied the staff pictures before arrival.

A cadet passed by with his hat off and dodged into a stall.

"I'll be here to ride Diesel in the mornings," Remy said. "I want to exercise him on the arena field."

"I'll warn you, sir. It's very busy down there in the mornings. Lots of sport practices, band practice and now the stretching class."

He acknowledged her concern. "Well, Diesel needs to be desensitized. But stretching classes?" Remy eyed the hatless cadet kneeling on the ground wrapping a horse's fetlock. Minosa stopped and examined the cadet's head. Another scar? A strange line zigzagged the occipital area ear to ear. He was about to question the cadet, but a ruckus in the direction of the office grabbed his attention first.

"Are you all right?" Pam called down the barn walkway.

There was no answer, so Remy took a step toward the door.

"Yes, ma'am," a cadet answered.

Remy waited, seeing Pam was satisfied with the response.

"Here," she said, reaching out for his horse's lead. "Let me have one of the cadets bathe Diesel. You look exhausted. Go take a break. Maybe we could meet for a drink at the local officer and staff hangout on Friday? The Bulldog Den. I heard you have a fetish for bulldogs... and you are the new kid on the block."

Remy thought to answer with a quick no. Socializing wasn't his style. He had no time for dating or flirting.

He hesitated, then realized for developing trust with the woman in question, a night out might be the perfect setup. "Give me the address, and it's a date."

The following morning, Remy entered Diesel's stall. He examined the magnificent horse who looked especially shiny. A sweet orange aroma lingered in his clean stall. Remy led him out and brushed his silky mane and tail, realizing the scent was emanating from the horse.

"Cadet?" he called to a passing student.

"Yes, General?"

"Why does this horse smell fruity?"

The cadet shifted twice from one leg to another, hesitating. "I was ordered, General... the new barber brought a gallon of shampoo down for Ms. Pam. Makes the hair shiny. I was instructed..."

"I guess," Remy acknowledged. "If you like fruit salad."

Diesel glanced back at Remy as if he understood and stamped his hoof on the ground. The metal shoe sparked against the concrete. A brief thought of Ava Kennedy brushed Remy's mind... her Lucite high-heeled sandal sparkling on his mantel.

Then Diesel whinnied.

"Okay, boy. Let's go."

Dawn was just breaking as they headed to the field to walk the outer rim. Remy and Diesel could both hear the upcoming commotion of whistles, marching regiments, and music. Diesel responded in his prancing demeanor, but this time he listened to the hand that asked him to wait.

Remy waved at the football coach and the band master, then stood on the outer rim watching the track team.

Asking Diesel to remain at attention and watch even after he'd been ridden out was a challenge for the steed. He clearly would've rather engaged in forward motion.

Remy heard the football coach, Batman, blow his whistle, gathering the team in the circle on the far edge, their workout jerseys all in a huddle around someone.

Batman then drifted to the sidelines, hands folded as the team spread out in rows and started stretching maneuvers, led by quiet music that Remy only heard when the band stopped practicing the school's fighting march. He could tell the leader was a woman only by her tone because the rays from the morning sun obstructed his view with a vibrant glare directly in his sight.

He squeezed Diesel to move forward for closer examination as he noticed the team's odd stretching maneuvers.

A track cadet was standing on the edge of the field. "What exactly are they doing out there?" Remy asked.

"Looks like Downward Dog, General."

"Downward what? Since when did we start yoga at my alma mater?"

"Everyone is taking a yoga class for stretching, General. The football team won their first scrimmage in years, and Batman... I mean Master Sergeant... thinks it was the yoga."

"Because of yoga?"

"Sure. See?" The cadet pointed to the field of jerseys. "That's a Camel," he said, "and now they're moving into Rabbit pose."

A passing cadet whispered to the boy Minosa was talking to. "Look at Cadet Drew with his rear in the air!"

Remy began to ask another question but noticed something in the back of a passing cadet's head. "Who's teaching y—" He halted, seeing another strange scar. And was that blue-tipped hair? "Cadet, cease."

The student stopped dead in his tracks.

"What is this etching all the cadets have in their head?"

"General, Dean Ironside approved the haircuts for the summer," the boy blurted, simultaneously saluting. His hand shook nervously above his eye.

"She approved? So they're not standard?" He side-passed Diesel closer. "And what's that smell?"

"General, I just received a haircut." The cadets both straightened up. "The barber, he doused me with cologne."

"He? I thought the new barber was a woman."

"It's the Blowing In Form now, General. Maybe you can see the woman barber who's teaching the yoga class." The cadet pointed again to the field where the football team was engaged in a complicated yoga position.

Confused, Remy scanned the area. Suddenly a thunderous rumble released from the outer edge where the landing strip was located. Within seconds a Chinook hovered amid the sunlight, and a force of warm wind whirled around them. Every muscle in Diesel inflated. The horse attempted to leap forward as if triggered to race toward the immense roaring machine.

"Fall out, cadets." Remy was busy holding back Diesel as the rumbling almost pulled the horse like a beam from *Star Trek*. The cadets scattered in seconds. "Never met a horse like you, Diesel. Guess that's because you were raised on a practice battlefield."

Once back at the stable, it was obvious to Remy that he needed to talk to Amy Ironside... and then go check on the barbershop for a haircut.

Chapter 10

By chance, Ava had observed Gen. Minosa riding in the indoor arena the previous afternoon. She'd never expected to see him. In fact, she had doused him from her mind. On a break to visit the stables, she intended to reintroduce herself to the riding instructor, Pam Waverly, and offer a gift of shampoo to thank her for attending a yoga class. She'd noticed Pam had hair as thick and coarse as a horse's tail and was in desperate need of a good detangler.

Ava slipped in the side of the barn, her hands loaded and struggling with a basket of wet brushes, conditioner, and the gallon of coconut-grapefruit shampoo for the horses. Of course, she hadn't thought to change out of her kitten heels to visit a 200-year-old barn built of mortar and stone.

Ava had been walking across the arena stands, hidden behind a black curtain drawn from the pole building ceiling to the arena's dirt floor to keep the bleachers clean. Through an open flap between two curtains, Ava caught a vision of a magnificent ebony horse.

The steed appeared to be the same one she'd admired when released in the field earlier. She had been admiring him for several days as he paraded in the summer sun and green pasture.

Ava inched her shoulder into the open edge of the curtain, splitting it slightly wider, hoping not to alarm the animal or alert the rider. She shuddered and arched back when she saw him, nearly dropping the gallon of shampoo and one of the brushes cradled in her arms.

The General. General Remy Minosa had returned.

Inquisitive, she inched one eye toward the crease, not being able to resist. It was the first time she'd seen him in eight weeks, and the first time in civilian clothes. He wore an Army green t-shirt and a pair of jeans. His concentration was alluring, and his body in top physical condition—broad shoulders rolling into a firm chest, muscular thighs bulging in the jeans. His forearm muscles tensed and released as he exercised the reins with his fingers.

The horse responded to his legs, deep seat, and most of all quiet hand. She had studied those hands before. They were sculpted, chiseled like his jaw and cheek. Strong from work and maneuvering equipment and weapons. Hands Ava found herself longing to touch.

She was drifting forward, not thinking, lost in a dream. The horse's canter created a steady methodical beat, as they approached a three-foot fence. Both horse and rider cleared the fence with ease. She was ogling as the general arched the horse around, changed leads and aimed for a double-rail, five-foot jump when the loose brush slid from between her elbow and chest, falling to the concrete with a ridiculous amount of noise.

Suddenly, the steed dipped a shoulder, stumbling as if scared. The general drove him in a tight circle, regaining respect. He momentarily touched the horse's nose almost to his calf with a check of the rein, glancing up in the direction of the stands. The general was clearly aware of a presence. Ava dove back again, retreating.

What am I doing? She froze, knowing he would investigate any movement of the curtain.

God. Had he seen her ogling? Quickly she grabbed the brush off the ground and tiptoed off so her heels barely pitter-pattered across the cement walkway. Head down, once off the platform and in the barn, she ducked into a tack room, only shocked to interrupt Shane Blevins with Pam in an awkward tête-à-tête.

"I'm sorry," Ava apologized. They must have heard the uncertainty in her voice.

"Oh, Shane and I are friends," Pam defended. "We were just chatting."

Funny way to chat. Ava noticed Shane was snuggled so close his thigh brushed against Pam.

The three stood for a minute, no one uttering another word. Ava broke in and juggled the jars and brushes to show Pam the shampoo and conditioner.

Shane cleared his throat and dipped down and skirted out between them.

Pam hurriedly agreed to try the products. "Yes, sure. Put them in my office. Cadet Bracket will show you the way."

The female cadet led Ava to an office and pointed to the shelves. The two laid the items down and were about to walk out, when Ava heard the familiar voice of the general. She sucked back into the doorway too fast, colliding into the cadet behind her.

Once again her heel snagged, this time in a missing section of mortar at a broken area between two bricks. This caused her to fumble sideways onto Pam's desk, knocking a bag to the floor and creating a crashing noise. Several MREs in green and tan packages tumbled out. Ava stopped and stared at the cadet who was trying to help her up, but Ava placed a finger to her mouth. "*Shh.*"

Pam Waverly's voice called from the aisleway where she stood with the general. "Is everything okay down there?"

The cadet froze, her eyes as wide as saucers. Ava cued her by making an OK sign, asking the girl to respond while simultaneously nodding her head like a hammer so the girl would say yes.

The cadet answered, then stared at Ava for another command. Ava motioned her to stuff the MREs back inside the bag. The girl saluted, then picked up the meals.

Ava tried to press the cadet's hand down as she peered out to the walkway and noticed Pam distracting the general. "Go... go..." Ava directed with her hand. The cadet seemed confused, however luckily she saluted again and obeyed.

The last thing Ava wanted in the already strained relationship with her daughter was for Rhya to find out the truth from someone else—the truth that she was the new barber and yoga instructor. Now cadets were saluting her, so returning to a low profile was top priority. Jeffery was right, as usual, and Rhya needed to know straight from the horse's mouth before the information was breached by someone else. Ava just wasn't sure how she was going to break the news the next day when the bus arrived.

The bus from Fort Knox was coming in at noon, so Jeffery placed an early closing sign on the front door. Ava glanced up at the clock at 11:00 A.M. *One hour.* Her heart skipped. She hadn't seen Rhya for almost eight weeks. She'd thought nothing could interrupt her excitement... that was, until Jeffery announced, "We're in big trouble now."

He stopped cutting as the bell on the door rang and a familiar gentleman walked in.

"Colonel," the cadet in the chair acknowledged the newcomer.

Col. Pendleton stopped dead in his tracks. He was evidently shocked to find both Ava and Jeffery styling hair. He ignored the saluting cadet and reversed out the door as if he'd entered a bad dream. He examined the building front, eyeing the sign that read Private M. Ava read his lips saying, *"What the hell,"* as he rubbed his chin between his thumb and index finger. Then he busted back inside.

"What the hell is going on?" He placed his hands on both hips, proceeding to order the cadet, "Face off."

"But my haircut," the young man questioned since Jeffery was only half done.

Jeffery whispered, "Come back in fifteen, and I'll put a free racing stripe in the back."

"Face off!" the colonel reiterated. "And don't come back. There will be no more racing stripes." He waited for the cadet to leave. "First, l thought to myself, what are all these assholes running around here with strange zigzags in their hair and blue tips... can you imagine? Then goddamn yoga on the practice field?" He paused.

"Colonel, please don't swear. I can—" Ava started.

"I knew something was strange."

"Colonel, you lost weight." Jeffery tried to change the atmosphere.

Pendleton blasted at him, "There is no way you two are staying here. Who the hell is behind this?"

"Colonel, please stop swearing. We've rented the barbershop and we are staying!" Ava screamed so loud it even stunned Jeffery.

Silence invaded the room, and the three stared at each other in a standoff.

The sound of a bus pulling to a screeching halt with a piercing release of air brakes was so loud in the field below broke the silence.

"They're here!" Ava yelled, ripping off her cutting smock. "Jeffery, let's go! I am sorry, Colonel..." Then she changed her tone instantly to her sweet demeanor. "But see Dean Ironside. We have her approval." She brushed by the colonel, blowing him a kiss. "Now, unless you need a haircut, we have a bus to catch."

Ava raced down the field almost turning her ankle from the unstable wedged sandals. Thank goodness she'd changed from her spiky heels. Jeffery loped behind, his arms swinging in circles, until they reached the waiting crowd.

The two of them filtered in with the other parents who were permitted to see the returning cadets for one evening. Little did Rhya suspect Ava could see her everyday now if she wished. Ava was positive her daughter had completely missed her. *She said so*, Ava reasoned, from the few letters she received back.

The driver yanked opened the doors, and they slammed against the metal rim with a loud clang. The first cadet off was Blade—Rhya's least favorite person. Jeffery and Ava were huddled among other parents who had come for an overnight stay that was permitted to briefly congratulate their son or daughter. Ava's heart was pounding through her chest to see Rhya, as one by one the cadets popped off the bus, all dragging, ordered to line up by the master sergeant.

"Cadets, in formation for inspection before you are released."

Ava could see her own least favorite person—General Remy Minosa—walking up the hill toward them for inspection. He'd changed into full uniform from his riding attire that morning. Now even more handsome, but stern, his chiseled jaw pressed deep into the neckline, not the quiet relaxed man on the horse.

Ava could see other parents tearing up, clapping, yelling names. Someone called, "That's my son. That's my boy!"

Ava kept eye contact on the colonel who had strutted onto the field, beelining straight for the general. He placed two fingers to his own eyes and then motioned at her and Jeffery. *"I am watching you both,"* he mouthed. Ava prayed he would not tell the general, or worse Rhya, so she held up her two hands to demonstrate prayer and blessed herself with the sign of the cross. *"Please,"* she mouthed back to the colonel.

At that exact moment, Jeffery sucked in air and cupped his mouth with both hands, nudging Ava with his shoulder. "It's her, it's her." He was jumping up and down in little hops like a bunny, then fanned his face and raised the other arm. "Rhya, Rhya, over here!"

Ava cupped her hands on her mouth, too. The sight of her daughter immediately swelled tears, especially because she looked exhausted and about fifteen pounds slimmer, her hair back in a military bun but disheveled from the arduous trip. To Ava's dismay, Rhya was waiting by the storage area of the bus with other cadets, about to carry a pack three times her size.

"Oh gosh, Jeffery. I am not sure when to break it to her that we're here running the barbershop."

"Well, I thought about that. It might not be well received."

"Jeffery, you are my rock. Please be my support. Please advise me," she begged.

"Hmm..." was all he said, too busy waving at Rhya.

Ava was pushing into a father next to her as the cadets threw on their rucksacks from the bottom of the bus compartment. All of them appeared tired and in need of a hot shower. Ava elbowed the man. "Those sacks appear so heavy, don't they? Especially when they are all tired." Ava balanced on her tiptoes in her wedges, securing herself with the man's arm. "These cadets deserve dollies, don't you agree?"

"Dollies? This is the Army, lady. What do you want, a bunch of wussies?" The man frowned. "You want to hold their hand and let them wet themselves like Baby Alive?"

Ava eyed him hard. *How grumpy.* Then she began to reminisce out loud. "I gave Rhya a Baby Alive one year for Christmas, mister."

"How'd that go, lady?"

It was like he had ESP and knew the answer, putting her on the defense. "That was the only doll she ever had as a little girl. She always wanted bows and arrows or cap guns." Ava was almost chatting to herself, disappointed. "I was so excited when she asked for Baby Alive. But that was the one and only doll."

The man shot her an eye roll, realizing his son was stepping off the bus, and attempted to yell the boy's name.

Ava interrupted, placing her finger in front of him. "Not dolls... I meant the dollies that help you carry stuff, like when you move, or at the airport. You know, those sacks are way too heavy. Don't you think that has to be hard on their backs?"

"I knew what you meant, lady." His eyeballs did a somersault again, and he scurried to the front.

The company formed several perfect rows, standing at attention as General Minosa examined them. Rhya caught Jeffery's wave and curved her lip almost unnoticeably on one side.

"I don't think she saw me, Jeffery. Do you?" Ava stood on her tippy toes again and rocked forward. She was so tiny she almost tumbled.

When the cadets were dismissed, Ava and Jeffery rushed like tight ends to Rhya before she could even pick up her duffel bag. Ava reached out and pinched the tip of Rhya's nose first, then wrapped her arms around the girl in a bear hug. Instantly, she caught sight of the colonel bending in to converse intently with the general. One hand chopped the palm of his other as he spoke.

The general immediately scanned the crowd until his sunglasses made contact with hers. Ava momentarily felt like ducking his view as she had twice that morning, but instead she just locked on him as she hugged Rhya. She let go of both Rhya and the deep brown eyes at the same time, the ones she knew were masked under dark glasses.

He headed toward them, so Ava tried to lift the rucksack in a panic to escape, but she stumbled forward from the massive weight of the bag landing on her knees.

Jeffery tried to help but only landed on top. By that point the general and the colonel were hovering above them both. "Go ahead. Tell her," the colonel insisted. He pointed at Rhya.

Everyone remained motionless as Jeffery struggled to rise. "Oh, boy. Here we go," he moaned in Ava's ear.

"Tell me what?" Rhya questioned and easily swung the sack over her shoulder.

"As you can see, your daughter can carry that sack by herself, Mrs. Kennedy. She has been trained." The general's eyes were not visible, but Ava thought she read a curve in his lip. His freshly shaven face had been tanned from Kentucky sunshine.

"Your mother here..." the colonel began.

"Colonel, I think there is some difficulty over there," the general interrupted. "Seems there's confusion with the rucksacks. Could you go see?" He pointed in the direction of the bus.

The colonel didn't have a choice. He squinted at Ava then obeyed.

She heard Jeffery exhale the huge breath he had been holding, finally opening his eyes to see what might happen next.

"Your daughter is very impressive," the general said to Ava. "You can be proud. Remember that, no matter what happens. Now, enjoy the evening because I am sure you have a lot to discuss." He turned his head down, and Ava saw her reflection of fear mirrored in his glasses.

Jeffery grabbed Rhya. "Come on, let's go," he said, and Rhya followed him like a zombie, unsure what had just transpired.

Ava's petite frame couldn't move. The muscular body almost levitating over her had captivated her. She touched a loose piece of her ponytail and tucked it behind her ear.

Jeffery backtracked and looped her arm. "Let's go," he commanded and started bowing out like a servant. "Thank you, thank you, sir. Come stop in the... well... you know where... for a you know what. We owe you a free one."

The general pointed at his head. "I do know where and I do know what... but no racing stripe."

Ava's mouth opened slightly. *He knows!* But he never told Rhya. He was leaving that up to her.

Rhya did an about face to address them both, asking Jeffery, "What's wrong with Mom?"

"I'll let her tell you."

The general had shoved the file in front of her with a picture on top. The image showed her mom and Jeffery hugging in front of their so called new barbershop.

"She rented the barbershop." He was frank.

"Are you kidding?" She knew she was better off not showing too much emotion in front of him, instead demonstrating how in control she really was able to remain. She'd always been told she was mature for age. Now she had to prove it, sinking deeper in the metal chair. "*Private M.?* Sounds like a boudoir, General. Really, can I ask why did anyone allow my fruity mother to do this?"

"Part of the mission," he said, standing up and walking around the desk. He was handsome for a forty-something, the way she thought her dad might be. He barely sat on the edge of the desk in front of her, his two hands gripping either side.

"You knew my mother and Jeffery... knew she was going to open a barbershop?" Rhya was having trouble digesting.

A light smile etched his face, as he let out a faint blow of air, seemingly trying to refrain. "No, of course not. But when Dean Ironside reached out to me, I initially responded with an emphatic no. Then I realized it would be icing on the cake for your cover. The 'good' little girl wants to break all ties with her flighty, helicopter-ing mom. *Boom*, you have the perfect storm to walk on the edge. Plus, the commotion on campus will put eyes in other places. Just a little campus drama to take the edge off. Especially if everyone is enrolling in yoga."

"Let me guess," Rhya said. "She's teaching yoga, too."

"I've also made sure that when things look sour during this mission, or you have to leave, your mother has signed a contract to stay at JW and fulfill her duties. My promise to you."

After hearing the mission, Rhya knew he was right. The only problem now was that she had to be herself. Really show displeasure when her mom surprised her with the barbershop news. Of course, wanting to hug them both because she'd whole heartedly missed them for eight weeks would be difficult to control. Rhya also understood the days and events that followed would be crushing for her mother. But it was Rhya's duty, what she was called to do. Rhya would have to avoid her mother at all cost because her heart actually ached watching her mother's excitement and anticipation fall into the abyss.

The most difficult would be the firestorm she had to perform on the athletic field the next morning when her mother was teaching yoga to the equestrian team. That was going to be the real judge of Rhya's acting ability. After the morning production, the stage would be set for the break-in and bust.

Rhya headed to the stables to meet Pam Waverly and this horse called Diesel. Rhya had read about Pam in the file the general had handed her. A civilian hired by the army as an expert equestrian—a former Olympic hopeful—who ended up pregnant by an officer. She hoped to make a comeback, until a rogue horse she was training at the base in Fort Hood busted out her knee when he crushed her in the stall. Pam wanted compensation from the Army. *Bitter* was the best way the general could describe her.

Pam greeted Rhya at the office door, introduced herself and set out as her tour guide through the barn. "So your mother is the new barber? She is very nice. She supplied us with shampoo, and tomorrow we will have her yoga class on the athletic field."

"That's her, but I'm not happy about it. She's like a monkey on my back."

Pam said nothing as they entered the tack room. Rhya noticed all the saddles and pads appeared in brand new condition. "Nice tack. Did you just receive a shipment?"

"Yes, I am a fanatic with our equipment."

Several crates in the corner were marked "wraps," "vet supplies," and "MREs." Rhya thought it odd to find MREs in the equestrian tack room.

Pam eyed her. "Just empty crates." Quickly the trainer led them down the stone aisleway toward Diesel's stall. "Since you are the new CO, you and I will have to have a tight relationship. This might be hard with your mother on campus. Quite frankly, I need your one hundred percent devotion." They were nearing the stall located at the far back of the arena.

"No worries," Rhya said.

"Well, from what you just told me, we should be fine."

"I've been trying to break from her for years. I thought this was my chance. Boy, was I wrong. I would do anything to escape from her bondage."

Rhya was not only in awe, but overcome with privilege that the general would allow her to ride Diesel when she reached his stall. Clearly a thoroughbred, the steed was fully black with a tan muzzle, and his nostrils rimmed in black. He was elegant, standing over sixteen hands, sculpted refined legs, muscular hips and powerful neck. His mane and tail were coarse, wavy, shiny and... "Fruity?" Rhya whispered aloud as she studied his immense body.

"He should be somewhat blown out as the general rode him this morning." Those were Pam's famous last words.

As soon as Rhya swung her leg over the English saddle, Diesel pranced like a caged beast.

Pam stayed by the rail cautiously observing. Rhya wasn't nervous until Diesel eyed the black curtain in the stands moving, being pushed open for a few observers. This stole his concentration, and Rhya had to reaffirm to him she was in the saddle.

When Rhya noticed Gen. Minosa climbing the bleachers for a lonely seat at the top corner, she posted Diesel into a forward trot to calm both their jitters. They trotted for what seemed like an hour. Diesel's energetic style felt as if they were floating. With each extension he flicked his fetlock, almost freezing in air for a second. By the time they were loping as one, Pam cued Rhya to attempt a jump.

Rhya aimed for the three-foot jump, quivering herself, his neck and head pointed to the top of the arena in a blast of excitement she almost could not control.

They soared a foot higher than the jump in a sloppy mess, Diesel throwing Rhya up out of the saddle onto his neck, leaving her grasping for rein.

"I'm okay." She popped up, regaining her control and arcing him to a small circle. "Thanks for embarrassing me, Mr. Diesel."

"He takes every jump higher and longer than he needs," Pam instructed. She had opened the gate and stationed herself inside the arena. "Just keep talking to him. Not too much hand, ease him back."

Rhya approached the jump a second time, letting her hands ask quietly.

"Beautiful!" Pam clapped.

Rhya sat deep, stopped, then patted his shoulder and rubbed under his mane, permitting him to stretch his neck as he tugged at the reins. His neck arched and his nose reached for the earth, snorting some dust with his breath. Rhya smiled and searched for the general in the stands to thank him. But he had disappeared.

The following morning reveille bugled over the intercom, the cue to rise. Rhya swung her legs over the edge of her bunk and meditated. She had to be at the athletic field for yoga and to execute a defining scene with her mother. She would have to gather all her strength to create a scene that was believable... because for sure, Rhya's actions were going to damage her mother.

The equestrian team was already in a huddle on one side of the athletic field. On the other was the football team and Coach Batman. He was chumming up on the bleachers with Pam Waverly. She wore a tight spandex outfit, which was indeed sealed to her body like saran wrap. Waverly was not tiny like Rhya's mother, and the stretching flowers went from daisies to poinsettias on her thighs. Her t-shirt was cut low and suctioned to the curves.

Surprisingly, Jeffery was there, too. His Nike shorts revealed skinny white upper thighs, and his fitted matching spandex shirt pointed over his hard nipples. He always wore white bobby socks to his shins, no matter how Rhya and her mother tried to persuade him to change it up.

Her mother was in front stealing the thunder. The football team ogled her tiny frame, everyone fussing how cute she was in her little yoga outfit and rhinestone earrings. As soon as Ava saw Rhya, she rushed over.

"Mom," Rhya said. "If you don't mind, I would rather pretend to disassociate."

Her mother looked at her. "Disassociate?"

"Maybe I mean just plain disassociate. Yes, from now on we don't know each other." Then she repeated her words, accentuated and loud. "I do NOT... hear this... NOT know whooo yooou are!"

Rhya leaned in her mother's face and yelled again, making sure both teams on the field witnessed the revelation.

Batman and Pam ceased conversing. Her mom's cheeks flushed. Ava blinked several times and backed away to her boom box on the turf. Rhya could see her hand shaking as she flipped the switch, turned on the music, and asked the cadets to line up.

Pam Waverly rose to mediate, but Rhya raised her hand. "Sorry, Ms. Pam. All good."

Pam halted and drifted backward to the bleachers.

Rhya took a position in the middle, two rows between cadets and didn't utter another word until Ava called for a Downward Dog maneuver.

"Wow, Mom. Look at you," Rhya interrupted the solemn music. She heard Jeffery gasp, his mouth open as if to question her boisterous actions.

Everyone froze again, whispering slurs among the rows.

"The forty-year-old helicopter mom had to come show off her ass to all the college cadets. Stick it up in the air, why don't you? Higher," Rhya yelled.

"What's come over you?" Stunned, Ava could barely speak.

"Oh, I am sorry. Did I swear, did I say ass? Wow!"

"Rhya, that's enough," Jeffery snapped, moving off his mat to stand above Ava who was staring in disbelief at her daughter.

Rhya glanced over at Pam Waverly. "I can't. Miss Pam, I need to be dismissed. Wouldn't you be embarrassed if she was your mother?" Rhya stormed off the field and Ms. Pam tore after her.

Ava attempted to follow. "Rhya, wait."

Rhya stopped, a nauseous feeling rushing over her. *Oh Saint Joan, please forgive me.* "Go home, Mom. I've wanted to say this for a long time... I hate you."

Rhya knew those last three words stopped Ava like a cement wall.

Ava said, "Rhya, you don't mean this."

"Oh yes, I do." Rhya forced every facial muscle to play along. "With all my heart, I do."

Rhya raced to her dorm and collapsed across her bed, aware her mother would be doing exactly the same. Crying, praying to St. Joan. But her mother had no clue the worst was yet to come.

CHAPTER 12

Ava knew Jeffery was not the yoga instructor the cadets dreamed of in front of the class, and he couldn't quite maneuver Downward Dog without her. But he'd learn. She pictured him in his white bobby socks, lanky legs, and spandex shorts with those nipples protruding through his tank top. The cadets would adjust just like the clients when Jeffery couldn't seem to bleach or color hair like she could. Her phone had blown up for months with complaints and comments from clients, but they eventually fell into his chair, when they realized she was just too busy to style them all.

Ava even asked to see Old Ironside to request moving back home. "Sorry, Ava. Your name is on the lease."

"Please, I made an enormous mistake. Jeffery can stay."

"Well you signed. Besides, your assistant, Jeffery, wants nothing to do with the barbershop here without you because I have already inquired. Sorry, Mrs. Kennedy." This sent Ava into a week of depression knowing Rhya was right outside the four walls of her condo—on campus somewhere and Ava couldn't see her or go home. She was now a prisoner at the JW.

Jeffery had been up to visit Ava in her room several times a day, usually with a treat—hot tea, cold tea, red wine, or chocolates. All which she declined. "Ava, everyone is asking where that hot looking yoga teacher is. And there's your appointments—the list of bleach blondes and color keeps growing. You have to come back. I can't style them like you. Please..." he whined, as she laid across the bed the entire week.

On Saturday evening he laid down next to her. "I can't do it alone," he said. "I just can't do one more Camel yoga pose without you."

"I'm going home. I went to see Ironside, but I'm going to have to call an attorney." Ava blew her nose.

"Now, look," he said. "I'm over your moping stuff. You are coming to have a drink at The Bulldog Den." He rubbed her back. "You know Rhya will get over this, too. One day you will be laughing with the grandkids about it!"

"She's never been so horrible." Ava sniffed again "Besides, I don't want to be with a bunch of kids in a bar."

"Kids?" Jeffery laughed. "The Bulldog Den is for staff and adults. The kids go downtown. You'll love it. I've been there twice this summer." Jeffery stood and wiggled his hips. "Big Daddy General might be there," he coaxed. "Come on. Drinks on me!" He wiggled again. "You know us, we can sit there and have a few glasses of wine and devise a future plan."

Ava sat up and hugged her knees close to her chest, surrounded by a pile of used tissues, then sniffled. "Okay. You know, you're my best friend."

"You can wear this pretty little low-cut blouse," he said, already raiding her closet. "And that satiny wrap skirt that falls above the knee, lined with a ruffle down the side. And your favorite clear sandals—the ones that look like Cinderella's glass slippers." Jeffery was rummaging around like a clothing salesman for a runway show. He was now on the floor crawling on his hands and knees, his butt pointing promiscuously into the air. "Where's the other one? Come here, you little bugger, I know you're in here."

"Jeffery," Ava half smiled. "No, it isn't."

"That is a dang shame! Well, why did you pack one shoe?" Jeffery walked over, balancing the lone heel in the air. "Sure were beauties."

She reached out for it and almost lovingly caressed it. "The shoe... went missing."

"Missing?" he quirked. "Hey, are you stroking that shoe? What's that I see in your eye?"

"The night I fell into..."

Jeffery gasped, then fanned himself. "Oh my gosh, the night you... are you in love with the colonel? Now I know you've lost more than your shoe."

"What? The colonel? Col. Pendleton? Really. Now I know you are crazy, Jeffery." She scrunched her forehead and stared him down. "Oh, you're just trying to make me laugh." She scooted to the bed's edge and he plopped down too, wrapping his arm around her.

"It's the night you met *him.* You like *him.* I see it."

"Jeffery." She smirked. "I liked the shoes." Ava touched the Lucite clear heel again. "I thought the other one would just show up."

"Come on," he said. "Get dressed and you can walk like this." Jeffery rose, arching his back, and limped out the door making Ava giggle.

The Bulldog Den was located outside the gates of the college, luckily within walking distance. Ava heard the live music and crowd as they neared. The end-of-summer smell lingered in the air underneath the sound of crickets and locusts hiding in the trees.

"I never saw anyone who can walk and wiggle in heels like you, Ava." Jeffery was following on the sidewalk behind her.

"I fall too! That's how I lost the shoe." She wasn't laughing.

"This place is packed," he said, scouting the patio.

It was a warm August summer night and the outside bar area was scattered with people as they walked up the steps. Ava felt suddenly ill to her stomach. "I can't do this. There are too many people." She was never good with large crowds, especially if she didn't know anyone. Overcome with fear she swung her tiny body around to plow back down the steps, bumping into a couple behind them.

"Hey, watch out!"

Jeffery gripped her arm and pointed her body back up.

"I can't believe you are making me do this," she said. "Do you know the last time I was out at a bar?"

107

"Yes, twelve years too long. Now waltz up those steps like you own them," he coaxed. "And look who I see."

"Who?"

"No worries," Jeffery laughed. "I brought the shoe."

"What?" Ava froze. He held up the clear sandal. "Jeffery, you didn't!" She snatched the shoe from him and stuffed it in her purse. "You are something. Always could make me smile."

He nudged her on. "I figured we can either find out who has the other one, or we can use it as a weapon. Now come on, let's get a drink."

The live band was playing a country tune. Ava glanced around the bar and patio and found two seats at a tall bar table. Jeffery ordered wine for them both, and by the second glass Ava had managed to relax. She was cocked sideways with her legs crossed, one bobbing in the pathway.

"Don't look now, but someone locked on to your leg swinging in that satiny skirt." Jeffery leaned in.

"What?" Ava tugged on the edge of her skirt trying to cover a little knee, but the material was too short.

Jeffery smirked. "Stop that, you have nothing to hide with that body. Make the general drool." He scrunched his face with another smug look.

"Are you kidding? Stop!" Ava curled her leg down and checked the entrance. "Dang, the general is looking this way!"

"I told you!" Jeffery grunted back. "Why don't you go out on that dance floor and show him what you got, woman!" Ava could tell Jeffery was a puppet to the wine.

"Are you kidding? I want nothing to do with General Mimosa, the man who stole my daughter. And secondly, he is married and look at him, with Pam Waverly by his side this time."

Ava leaned in, almost lying on top the table. "Drink up, it's time to leave." She gulped the remainder of her wine, then set the glass down and snatched her purse, shoving the shoe deeper. But when she swung off the stool, Ava plowed dead center into a chest. His chest.

The general.

"Is this table free?" Pam Waverly asked pointing to Jeffery's seat. Jeffery extended his hand offering her his barstool.

Ava was busy two-stepping, trying to bypass the muscular man in her path. She bumped his arm and the clear heel popped out of her purse. He caught the shoe, but without a second to spare she snatched it and rammed the heel back.

Ava glanced up. He said nothing, graciously stepping aside.

"Mrs. Kennedy, you do not have to rush off," Pam suggested. "Stay, we can get some more chairs."

"That's okay, I have had better company." Ava shot the general a look like a dart. Jeffery inhaled and wrapped her waist.

"Time to go, so sorry. Enough wine for one night." He shimmied Ava forward, but she bent back over his shoulder. "No wine talking, here. Just truth." The patio chatter lessened as some patrons peered her way.

"Ava, time to go," Jeffery instructed.

She could see Remy Minosa was ignoring her, and that infuriated her more.

"Not hiding behind those intimidating sunglasses tonight, are you? Just out carousing."

Jeffery egged her forward, squeezing her waist.

"Have a great night, General Mimosa," Ava barked as the two slid onto the stools. "By the way, where is my shoe? He likes shoes, Ms. Waverly." Jeffery pinched her and Ava winced.

Remy seemingly stared at the menu as all eyes in the bar were on them. Pam Waverly ruffled her napkin, probably embarrassed as she arched into him, her cleavage billowing out.

"I can't believe you, woman," Jeffery huffed and steered them out of the restaurant.

Ava said nothing, swinging her body in her skirt and heels, backlashing the general until they reached the condo steps.

Jeffery unlocked the door and held it open. "No." Ava refused to enter and plopped on the stoop. He disappeared for a moment and returned with two glasses of red wine. He eased down next to her, careful not to spill a drop. "Ava—"

She interrupted, "Rhya has been my whole entire life. She is all I lived for."

He wrapped his arm around her. "I know. Remember the time you wanted her to wear the two braids with pink ribbons on the ends? You tried to douse her hair with sparkles. I don't know who was crying more during that head butting episode." He softened and they giggled. "How do you think I feel?" He wiped a tear. "Every Friday night was movie night. Who will I watch James Bond with, or *Officer and a Gentleman*? We watched that movie over a hundred times, and I still bawl my eyes out!" After an hour of reminiscing, Jeffery squeezed her again. "Come on, Ava. Everything will be okay. Let's go inside."

"Thank you, Jeffery, for a wonderful evening," she said. When he stood and held the door open, she added, "You know what? I'm not ready to go in. I'm going to head to the barn."

"What?" he said with a hand on his hip. "You most certainly are not going to the barn by yourself."

"I need some time. The barn is right there behind us. I have my phone... and a weapon," she said, pulling out the shoe from her purse. They both started laughing. "I can't believe what I said back there. I had to vent!"

"How brave you are becoming," Jeffery said. "Okay, but thirty minutes and I come search you out."

Ava hugged him, then motioned the shoe at him and headed down the walk.

"Use the pointy part," he called. "Right in the eye."

She smiled and stuffed the sandal back in her purse for the second time before heading to the stables. They were practically right out the condo's back door. The barn was dimly lit, and the tapping of Ava's heels on the brick aisle echoed lightly above the munching and occasional snorts. Ava inhaled the aromas of hay, bedding, sawdust, and grain—scents she always associated with Rhya's youth. Memories floated through her mind of Ava, the weekend-horse-show mom.

She tiptoed along the stone and greeted each horse by the name pinned on the stall door. She followed the indoor arena rail to the far corner where two stalls were tucked in, one empty, and the other housing the black steed that was all the talk in the barbershop.

"Well hello, big boy." Ava was feeling quite happy after two glasses of wine and only a few cheese nachos at The Bulldog Den. She fingered the red card pasted to his stall and briefly wondered what it meant.

Drowning in her sorrows, she'd hardly eaten all week, and the wine had streamed right to her head. Ava reached her fingers to the bars to steady her balance. The handsome steed arched his neck and snorted several times, touching her fingertips.

"Oh, you like my Pink Blush nails. Well, thank you. Glad someone does," she kidded. "You sir, are very handsome."

"He says thank you," a man's voice came from behind her. "And do you always come to the barn dressed like that?"

Ava leaped out of her skin when a hand reached up and gripped one of the bars next to hers, almost touching. Realizing it was the general, she relaxed back, almost by accident melding into his shoulder and firm bicep. She wanted to hate the man she had managed to oust in front of the entire bar. But with his body this close, his woodsy aroma set her heart into flutters like a hummingbird's wings brushing off bad feelings.

"General Mimosa, I am sorry. At the bar... I was at the bar, I mean I was... I had two glasses of wine and... Well, not really... I mean, I am not sorry and I can handle my... I'm not a bar girl..." Then she started to let go of the rail.

"You do that on purpose, don't you?"

She paused. "Do what?"

"My name." He studied her olive eyes. "You know it's Minosa."

"Oh, it's a mental block. I once had a customer named Rose, and I called her Linda. Never got the wrong name out of my head even if I practiced saying Rose over and over. I'm sure she didn't appreciate it." Ava rambled, as she felt nervous from his penetrating stare. "Sorry. You don't want to hear my stupid story. I was just leaving."

Ava could have kicked herself. She felt delirious. It was surely the wine.

His strong fingers lifted from the bar and touched her small feminine hand. "No..." He released the word as if issuing a command. Ava shivered from his touch. Luckily she hoped he thought it was his voice because he restarted in a much softer tone. "I mean, would you like to see Diesel closer?"

Ava could only nod, once again speechless in his presence, watching him open the door. She eyed the red card and touched it. "He's the only horse that has a red card pinned to his door under his name. Does that mean he's special, like a king?" She waved her fingers in the air in a nervous move.

"King? He might believe that." Remy smiled. "No, but you could say he has a derrière fetish. You can usually find a red ribbon in his tail, also as a warning. So, we will stay at his front."

He slid the door open with a sound like a train. Diesel snorted and faced the open door. He was massive and stepped forward.

"Whoa, Diesel," Minosa called, gripping the halter. "You have another admirer."

He motioned Ava to come closer, and she inched forward, but not without blushing. The wine was flowing through her veins, rushing her body with warmth. She raised a hand and stroked Diesel's soft muzzle.

"Your daughter rides him extremely well. She is a very proficient equestrian."

Ava only nodded.

"Why didn't you tell her... tell her I was here... that I rented the barbershop? You had the perfect opportunity."

He ceased stroking the horse, and his hand landed on top of her fingers. His forearm tensed. "It was your responsibility, I guess."

"Well, thank you. Although it didn't go over well." Ava looked at his strong hand pressing on hers lightly. "The second time I had to thank you." She gazed up at him and his hand lifted to her cheek.

"Please, don't..." Remy began to say something but stopped.

Diesel nudged out his nose and pushed Ava against Remy so hard she swore she could feel his heart. His other arm quickly encircled her waist.

He checked the immense horse back and for a moment stayed with her encapsulated within his arm. Ava could feel his heart beating through the light t-shirt and could feel his warm breath on her forehead. She closed her eyes and the woodsy aroma soaked her senses—the same aroma that enveloped her the night she'd danced in his powerful arms.

"Don't what?" she asked. His cell phone interrupted, and she anxiously tucked hair behind her ear. Still close, his hand slipped against hers to reach into his jean pocket. Regaining himself he cleared his throat and released her.

Ava could hear a panicked voice, but the words were inaudible.

"Where?" he asked. "Break-in at the barbershop? On my way."

"What?" Ava moved two steps away from him. "My Private M's?"

He nodded.

"I'm going with you. What happened?"

"No idea. Come on. My Jeep's right outside the barn."

Remy opened the door of his black Jeep, and Ava jumped in. She wanted to ask him questions but knew the phone call was too short to indulge in a wealth of information. The shop was literally a minute away, and she zipped a text to Jeffery asking him to meet her there.

CHAPTER 13

Remy glanced over at the small-framed woman sitting next to him in the passenger seat as they were about to rush to the barbershop. Ava was texting on her phone, probably to Jeffery, her hair wisping around her face in the warm summer air. Remy reflected, hesitating as he held the key in the ignition. Unfortunately, Ava had played right into his plan. Showing up unexpectedly had saved him a trip to her condo.

Ava turned her attention to him. "Let's go, General! What's the hold up?" He said nothing and obeyed.

Remy stopped at the gate, flashed his tags, and the MPs perked up in salute. *What the hell am I doing feeling this way?* She had no clue that Remy's covert operation was about to devastate her. He wished nothing more than to pull to the side of the road, tell her the truth, and ask her to play along.

My career, my career... He started the mantra in his head. Why was he so obsessed with this woman? She was like a bad drug.

They pulled in front of the barbershop, which was lit up like Times Square. Two MPs were waiting in front of the door next to the broken window. Shane Blevins, the owner of JW, positioned himself inside, examining the damaged door latch, a detained person visible on a waiting room chair, dressed in a black sweat suit and hoodie.

Remy parked the Jeep and touched Ava's forearm, stopping her from opening the door. "Ava, stay here. I want to make sure all is safe before you enter."

She hesitated, examining his hand on her arm, then glanced back at the scene with a nod. Ava waited at the car door. Remy passed the two MPs who saluted him. He feigned concern for Ava, though he knew there was nothing real to fear, ordering them to keep an eye on her until he secured the situation.

Shane Blevins, like Ava Kennedy, had no clue that the robber and Remy were in cahoots, and it had to stay that way for the sake of investigation. Remy hoped both he and Rhya could achieve their intention of fooling everyone.

Upon entering, General Remy Minosa shook Shane's hand and studied the person detained in the waiting area of the barbershop, fully aware Ava would be watching with anticipation and fully aware who was the suspect.

"Well, General. This young cadet, here, she was breaking into the barbershop," Shane explained. "Triggered all the alarms. Good thing I have them. Lit up the entire area like a light bulb. I can't get a word out of her."

Remy stepped toward her. "Stand up, soldier." The female rose. The MPs had her handcuffed, and she remained slumped forward until Remy tugged back her hood. "Kennedy?" He knew Ava would recognize her daughter by profile alone, and he tensed, prepared for her to bust in the front door.

His instincts were correct. He already heard the commotion from behind. The MPs at the door blocked Ava who was now rustling between them.

"Let her in," Remy commanded. One MP slowly released his angled weapon and allowed the woman to slip past.

Ava rushed in by her daughter's side. "Rhya, what are you doing?" She clutched the girl's elbow.

Remy watched Rhya shake Ava off. The cadet flashed her an angry look, so full of disgust Remy was even fooled. Then he remembered Rhya told him she comes from a line of strong Italian women.

"You know her?" Shane asked Ava.

Ava cupped her mouth, clearly flabbergasted, and simply nodded as Jeffery flew in the door in his tight workout shirt and bright yellow pajama pants. When the MPs blocked him, he let out a shriek, his hands flying in the air like he was in a western holdup.

"Rhya!" He immediately saw handcuffs binding the girl. "Remove them now!" He pointed his hand through the two MPs' weapons, to the cuffs.

"Yes, please," Ava pleaded, advancing to a mere inch from Remy, so close he caught a whiff of her sweet musk. He almost couldn't resist her plea.

He turned to the MP and motioned for him. "Take the dynamic duo outside."

"Oh, but this is my shop. You are not removing me." Ava started to thrash her hands in the air at them. Jeffery encircled her like a bear. Ava wobbled in her heels, reaching down into her purse and pulling out the clear sandal Jeffery had given her at the bar. "I have a weapon and I know how to use it." Ava pointed the heel in the face of the closest MP. He froze.

The other MPs struggled to control the two until the one snatched the shoe from Ava's hand. Remy shot a momentary roll of the eye to Rhya and shook his head, knowing Shane was engulfed in observing the scrimmage. Rhya squinted as if apologizing for the duo's behavior.

"Okay, okay," Remy's voice rose above the fray. The MPs were almost no match for the so-called dynamic duo. "Sit over there," he said to Ava and Jeffery. "Mind your manners and keep your mouths shut." Remy practically lifted Ava onto the chair, she was so tiny.

"Yes sir, Ma...mo...sa." Ava raised her hand in a sarcastic salute.

Yup, he thought, she was messing with his name on purpose. Damn her. He turned to Jeffery. "You want me to pick you up, too?"

The barber skirted to the chair like an obedient puppy with its tail between its legs, his oversized PJs flapping like fins.

"Now you see these MPs." The guards were gathering their disheveled selves, and Remy thought they seemed like a sorry pair. "They have weapons, too. And I have the most deadly weapon of all—your shoe, Mrs. Kennedy. So you are now disarmed." Remy grabbed the clear glass slipper from the waiting area chair. "So don't move or I will order them to poke you with a heel." He tapped the shoe on his other hand.

If the scene hadn't been so traumatic for Ava, it would almost be comical, Remy thought. The truth was, Remy was wasting time as planned. Keeping Shane Blevins occupied was of utmost importance.

Ava and Jeffery huddled together in the waiting room chaos, with Rhya standing before him and Blevins to his right.

"Kennedy, do you have an explanation?" Remy asked.

"Yes, General. I do, and I apologize for the commotion."

"Well, that's not good enough. I will need the group of us over at the commandant's office. Someone get a hold of him, now. Tell him the situation and we will be there at 2400. He is not going to be happy about being woken to this mess in the middle of the night."

"Just remove her hand—"

Ava rose in anger. Instantly the MPs moved toward her. Remy waved the shoe as a threat. "Oh, no you don't, Mrs. Kennedy."

Jeffery pulled Ava back.

"Kennedy's restraints stay on... and she better have a good explanation."

"I needed something from the barbershop," Rhya snapped. "I was not about to ask my mother or Jeffery. You know the tension, General. I made a mistake when entering the door, and the alarm went off, so I broke the window and thought I could get out quickly before anyone arrived."

"All of us, everyone in this room, are headed to the commandant's office, and we can formally press charges," Remy ordered.

"Charges?" Ava questioned. "I own the barbershop, and I am not pressing charges. Who's pressing charges?" She scanned the room. The MPs both shook their heads as if intimidated by her.

Ava had played right into Remy's hands. Now his only goal was to persuade Shane Blevins to go with them to the commandant's, and once there, to keep him occupied and hopefully convince him not to press charges.

"Shane, we will need you there... at the commandant's office. I think it might be a good idea to consider pressing charges." Remy emphatically suggested. Ava let out a gasp, followed by Jeffery's second. Even one of the MPs sucked in air as if sharing in their shock. Remy nonchalantly shook his head again as if disgusted at the MP, amazed how Ava Kennedy appeared to have the entire campus eating out of the palm of her hand.

Shane Blevins hesitated. Was he under Ava's spell too? Remy almost held his breath waiting for an answer, knowing Cadet Blade needed time to infiltrate the surplus store after this diversion.

Shane finally conceded, but never lost sight of Ava.

Remy breathed a sigh of relief internally. He anticipated Rhya would walk away from this with only a slap on the wrist and a little tarnish on her goody-two-shoes record. And hopefully tonight, Cadet Blade would confiscate the information Remy needed, what this entire dramatization had all been set up to accomplish. All without anyone being hurt—except Ava Kennedy. If she understood what he'd asked her daughter to do... and that he'd lied to Ava... she would never speak to him again.

Career is all that matters, career is all that matters...

When Remy entered the commandant's office, he knew Ava and Jeffery were already an issue. They were both hovering at the desk speaking simultaneously, pleading for Rhya to be set free. Shane Blevins's head was shaking as he sat in a metal folding chair next to Rhya.

Rhya looked to Remy, appearing relieved that he entered the room. The commandant's head was resting on his fist his arm elbowed on the desk. He yawned, acting slightly bored until he caught sight of Remy and immediately stood, banging his hands on the desk. "Enough! I got pulled out of bed for this mess?"

Jeffery leaped an inch off the ground and squeaked in shock. Remy apologized and explained the situation once the MPs plopped Ava and Jeffery down for the third time that night.

Everything had progressed to plan. And the meeting in the commandant's office followed suit. Shane Blevins, whether from believing that Rhya had accidentally tripped the alarm or that he was plain exhausted of the scene, agreed not to press charges.

Rhya would walk away almost unscathed, and Shane Blevins would have no clue what was happening next door in his surplus store while he had been side-tracked by the bizarre break-in at the barbershop. Ava had no idea her daughter didn't loathe her with every muscle in the girl's body. For that Remy felt heartsick as he witnessed Ava cry to the commandant, "Rhya has never done anything like this in her life. Something isn't right." When her petite frame started to teeter, Jeffery lurched forward and kept her from toppling... him in his yellow pajamas and her in an off-white satin skirt, both glaring at Remy with utter disdain by the end of the interrogation.

The meeting wrapped up well past midnight, and Remy arrived home to his townhouse anticipating a delivery. But no envelope of any kind could be found on the foyer floor under the mail slot. *Where could Blade be?* He paced the living room for over an hour. Scarlett was spread out on the lazy-boy watching his back and forth motion with her eyes.

"You have the life, dog." He stopped and acknowledged her.

Her tail whacked the chair several times.

"Tell me, was I wrong to ask these cadets to execute this mission?" Scarlett thumped her tail again. "Am I questioning myself now because of these feelings for Ava Kennedy? Why the hell does she keep popping in my head, lingering, replaying every time she trips in those heels?"

He eyed the second Cinderella Lucite heel on the coffee table and carried it to the fireplace mantel. Remy rested the shoe next its mate, the pink envelope containing Ava's card, and his son's graduation picture—all symbolic of things he would never have again.

The chime of his phone severed his thoughts, and he snatched the device up from the coffee table, hoping it was Blade. Remy sighed, recognizing Jeanie's number. He didn't have too much tolerance anymore for her drunken ramblings. Each of her phone calls had been the same over the last years. She'd razz him, repeating that Jason's death was Remy's fault for allowing their son to join the Army. Then her mood would snap, transforming to tears of sorrow, asking about the ceremony for Jason at Arlington. Then Jeanie would scream again, *"I will never divorce you! It's your punishment for taking him and never loving me. You will have to take care of me for the rest of your life."* He had to admit she was right about everything. Remy would never have the heart to divorce her even though they hadn't been together in years.

He laid the phone back on the coffee table and let it ring. Jeanie could leave her typical voicemail.

The clock struck 0100 hours, and Remy's concern for Blade festered until he heard the mail slot open and shut on the front door. Exactly what he'd been waiting for—the light sound of a manila envelope that landed on his foyer floor. He picked it up, and tried to scoot lazy Scarlett off the chair. "My turn, sweetness." She moaned, refusing, so Remy opted for the sofa. "You are so damn spoiled."

Remy woke an hour later to a bump on the porch. He stirred, the contents of the envelope strewn across his lap where he had been examining them. His reading glasses were half-cocked on his face and his shirt and shoes had been thrown to the side. He looked at Scarlett but her head merely tilted when the doorbell started.

"Really Scarlett? Not even a warning woof?"

He rose bare-chested, wondering who might be at his door at this hour, cautiously concerned considering the current situation. He reached for his sidearm in the drawer next to him, a small pistol just in case this whole deal was heading sour. He tucked the weapon in the back rim of his pants and peered through the peephole in the door.

He saw no one. Nothing. Except a hand, a small feminine finger with pink polished nail, one finger pressing on the ringer, repeatedly, and he knew who the finger belonged to.

Remy inched open the door, seeing Ava visibly tipsy.

They both froze. Ava had been about to say something when her eyes landed on his chest. Clearly she was caught off guard. Remy was positive the fact he had no shirt on interrupted her chain of thoughts.

He noticed her uneasiness as she pushed by him, slipping under the arm that was holding the door open. Remy raised an eyebrow, scanned the sidewalk and up and down the street. Only the streetlights at each corner were aglow, and a symphony of locusts chattered in the late summer eve. This wasn't going to go well. Her alone with him… and him without a shirt on. He shut the door, cautiously concerned.

Ava already found the living room, standing by the fireplace, facing the doorway when he entered. He stayed in the archway. "You, Sir Mimosa, have tarnished my daughter. Why? I want her back. The way she was in my nice little hometown… my beauty shop…" Ava took a breath. "My daughter was lying."

Scarlett moaned. The dog must have been thinking the same as Remy. Ava was cute while she was ranting there, tipsy in her heels. Scarlett's tail was practically vibrating on the chair.

"She likes you." Remy pointed.

Ava noticed a manila envelope on the sofa marked with black lettering, *Surplus Inventory, Blade.* "I know my daughter, Mimosa. She's lying. Something is very wrong over there, and really I've been watching that military store and something is very fishy there too. Deliveries coming late in the night. People sneaking out the back door and that Batman…. Something is not…" Ava tilted her head and a tear streamed down her cheek.

The tear gnawed at Remy's heart. "Where's Jeffery? Let me call him." Remy was impressed how well she could read her daughter while everyone else was fooled.

"Jeffery is not my husband." She wiped the tears and turned hard to face the mantel. "You and your heartless stare, stealing children away from mothers who have raised them from babies to be strong loving women. You can be very proud you've destroyed another family."

Ava swung around, the tears now trickling to the top of her perched lip.

Remy stood like an iceberg. He was not going to break. Perhaps those tears could've persuaded him until he realized the display on the mantel. He had to 180 her before she discovered the shoes and the card. Hopefully, she was a little too inebriated to pay attention.

He touched her bare shoulder. "Ava, you can't go back." He tried to slip her around. He was finding difficulty controlling the urge to passionately kiss her. That would surely catch her off guard. But the phone rang again instead.

Ava's eyes darted toward the caller ID. "Jeanie Minosa? Hmmm, Jeanie Minosa wants you. My daughter's future is in your hands, and you're trying to seduce me while your wife is calling."

Remy dropped his hand from her shoulder and stood tall.

"First off, your daughter will be fine, and I was not trying to seduce you at all... or Pam Waverly, for that matter."

"Answer it, why don't you?" Then she faced the mantel dead on and Remy's heart sank, running his fingers through his cropped hair.

The phone stopped ringing, and Ava stooped closer, squinting. "This is the card I sent you," she whispered in surprise. "And these are my slip-on heels—the ones I love. You did have the missing one... and now you have them both. Who's this in the other— oh... your son. Why are parts of me here on your mantel?"

Remy squeezed his eyes shut. When he opened them she was standing in front of his face shaking the letter under his nose.

"I don't know where to begin..."

"You stole my family, my life..." Ava stormed past him then stopped. She pivoted, glaring at him from behind.

"Ava..." he swung around.

"A pistol?" She pointed to his waist. "Were you going to shoot me, arrest me, scare me?"

"Ava, stop." He fingered the pistol jammed in his pants. The phone was ringing again, and Scarlett kept on moaning. He wanted to wrap the petite woman up in his arms.

Ava bulldozed back to him, and Remy prepared for a blow but she brushed by and reached up on the mantel to snare her shoes. "These are mine. To think you kept them from me. You stole my daughter and my shoes... I bet you have a strange fetish with woman's shoes. Ha! Well, you can keep the card!" She pulled it out of the pink envelope and slung his keepsake through the air, accidentally hitting Jason's picture. As if in slow motion, he could only watch it crash to the floor.

"Ava... first off, I do not have a shoe fetish." he said. "It's not what you think." Then she rammed the pink envelope into his chest, hitting him between the pecs. When the door slammed,

Remy was left staring down at her card and Jason's picture amid the leftover glitter dancing to the floor.

"I have a fetish for Ava Kennedy," he whispered, and Scarlett sank her chin into her paws.

CHAPTER 14

A va stopped at the corner across from the general's house, rummaged through her purse, and tried to clear her head. Taking a deep breath, she organized her thoughts about what had just transpired. She and Jeffery had shared additional glasses of wine at the house after Rhya was crucified in the commandant's office like a terrorist.

Jeffery had sat at their table to console her. *"Ava, you have to get some rest. We can think clearly tomorrow morning,"* he'd said. *"Here, take one or two of these. You will relax. And boom. Out like a light."* He handed her the bottle and she'd tossed it in her purse.

Then he tucked her in her room, closing the door behind him. *"Now out of that adorable little disco diva outfit. We'll have a fresh look at the situation tomorrow."*

She nodded, and he kissed her cheek.

That was when she'd decided to have some fresh air once again—to think, alone time to reevaluate her life. Jeffery would have never allowed her to walk by herself. It was too late, so she made a makeshift body with pillows under her bed covers and sneaked out with a glass of Merlot and her purse in hand.

The block next to her condo was named Officer Way, because all the officers and officials lived there, their names painted in black on the front step risers. As Ava passed each house, she read the names aloud.

"Well, it's Master Sergeant Dave Andrews... A toast to you and your lovely family."

Sometimes a lonely dog would bark or a porch light would pop on, and she would move to the next house.

"Dean Amy Ironside. Old Ironside, here's to you," and she raised her glass again.

Never thinking she would inevitably discover it, she read, "General Remy Minosa. Well, looksey here!" She bravely walked up the sidewalk, glad she always carried a thick black Sharpie in her purse. "Oh my, your name is spelled wrong. *Tsk*... Never fear."

She chugged her wine and set the glass on the top step while she replaced the *n* with an *m*.

"I can go to Army jail with my daughter. How's that?" Ava stood back and admired her work.

Just then, Ava managed the courage to ring the buzzer and wake him up. She could see a low light in the front room off to the right. But when the general had opened the door and she ogled him shirtless, every muscle in his chest and abdomen rippling and tight, she was taken aback. Ava never expected the specimen of the man—his speckled grey hair slightly ruffled, eyes sparkling in the moonlight.

Stopping at the corner, she remembered her discovery from the living room mantel. Her shoes, the card, and the manila envelope on the sofa marked: *Surplus Inventory—Blade.* He hadn't realized she saw the envelope. Ava knew Blade worked at the surplus store. Her keen hairdressing and motherhood ESP was most always right; something was transpiring in that surplus store.

Too much was tossing and pounding in her head, her heart racing like a freight train, and at this moment all she wanted was to calm down, so she found the bottle Jeffery handed her. She only meant to take one, but three pills fell into her hand just as a rush of warm summer air blasted her. A van barely halted at the corner stop sign. Ava looked up and caught Batman in the driver's seat. She blinked. She was ninety-nine percent sure she knew the cadet in the passenger seat too.

Ava had been cutting Blade's hair since first grade. Blade and Batman zipped by in the white military vehicle, the same van from the surplus store with the scratched bumper. The direction they were headed in was a dead end to one thing—the airstrip. Losing her concentration, she tossed the three pills in her mouth and started running toward the airfield. Realizing what she'd done, she thought to go back, but so much adrenaline was coursing through her blood that she dashed on. Ava was even running like a track star in stilettos.

Those pills were certainly not making her sleepy. The moment she reached the airstrip she was empowered like a superstar. The airstrip was located not only behind gates but surrounded by chain link fence and barbed wire. Ava noticed a sliver out of the fence at the corner. By luck if she applied some muscle, maybe her tiny body could manage to wiggle through.

As she dodged behind trees to avoid being noticed, she eyed the white van. Batman and Blade were exchanging crates like the ones she'd eyed that first day she ran into Batman at the back of the barbershop. Two other soldiers in uniform eyed a clipboard and then signed a document as they stood under the blades of a Chinook.

Ava struggled fifteen minutes to bend the wire enough to squeeze through. She managed, tearing her satin skirt, only praying the van was still at the helicopter.

Funny, when she finally reached the Chinook, the aircraft seemed to be wobbling. There was no white van and all the other helicopters appeared exactly the same. Her body was starting to feel heavy, her legs like cement, and her eyelids like locked doors. Even the lettering on the side of the massive Chinook was vibrating, jumping up and down.

Ava held her finger in the air as if touching each letter to read the name. They looked like the letters when a computer asks if you are a robot:

GG I l bra

Ava started to converse at the machine. "Why, you look like a big whale. Mouth open. I'm Jonah. No, not Jonah, but like Jonah walking into the mouth of the whale." Ava raised her arms in the air, parading up to the huge helicopter, humming, wobbling, indeed promenading deep into the belly of the fish. The back end was lined in crates. *MREs,* she recognized. *Good, I'm hungry.*

She tried to explore the inside, but everything was vibrating.

"Whoa, whale. This ocean must be rough." The Chinook swayed and she grew ever more seasick. "Lordy, I need something to eat." She eyed a small toolbox and armed herself with a screwdriver. "Aha!" Ava tried to head back toward the crates but felt so loopy she had to cling to the walls to stay upright.

Reaching the crates she fell across them, then gathered herself together and pried open the top. She fingered her way through the stacks of MREs, reading the labels which made her even more nauseous.

"Meat loaf and bread, no. Dried beef, yuk. Rice... *Mmm*, rice is good." Ava clutched three of the green and tan packages. Her head started to ache as if hit by a constant hammer, her eyes blurring even more. She slid down between the crates, stretching her body out, lying on the MREs as a pillow. Only her stilettos peeked out between the row of crates. Her heavy lids fluttering shut, she whispered, "Sweet dreams," until everything went black.

The rumbling in her pocketbook tickled her side and she smiled. "*Hmm*, that feels good." She could barely open her eyes. Her face was lodged against splintered wood, scratching her cheek. The phone continued to rumble against her. She was lying on cold metal in her outfit from the night before.

Ava tried to sit up, but the pain in her head only thumped harder as she rose, and she scraped her elbow against the crate. She attempted to read the package she'd been resting on. *Meal replacement?* Her phone vibrated again, but she was too tightly wedged in to claw open her purse.

Ava scantly could recount the previous evening. *How did I even get here? And where is here?* Turning, she managed to shimmy her body back through the crates and free herself, though still face down on cold metal, her skirt up over her waist, her pink thong visible, her shirt strap hanging loosely, and the blouse hardly covering her breasts. *Lordy!*

Faint memories diluted her head, remembering the commandant's interrogation and the wine at the house with Jeffery. Ava was awake enough to inspect her surroundings, which were still very hazy. She reached for her purse but stopped. "Remy.

I went to Mimosa's house." She slapped her forehead with her hand. Cursing, she hugged her legs into her chest, "What an idiot." Able to dig in her purse, she detected the bottle of pills. "Super idiot." Then she nabbed the phone. "Jeffery."

She pushed the callback button, but her phone flashed *low battery*. She hammered it again. *Shoot*. Ava dropped her head between her knees, her stomach aching in need of food. The sound of a click opened her eyes to two black boots positioned in front of her. Ava followed the pants legs up past the pelvis of a man with a pistol aimed right between her eyes.

"You think you have a headache now, lady?"

In his other hand he held a walkie-talkie. "Bruiser, we have a problem back here. Better start her up."

Ava heard the powerful rumble like an earthquake and stared out the enormous open area, daylight hurting her eyes. She was contained in something that was starting to move forward, the room shaking even more. Suddenly coherent enough, she realized this was no room—she was in the Chinook. Tapping her finger to her knee, Ava recounted entering the aircraft the night before. She squinted harder out the rear opening, increasingly aware quite a commotion was developing outside on the tarmac.

"Oh my. Can I please... Can I please get off? Where are you taking me?" Ava tried but the man holding her hostage stepped forward and shoved her down.

CHAPTER 15

Remy was up at the crack of dawn heading to the airstrip for the routine morning inspection. When he walked off the front porch he noticed a half-filled glass of red wine on his bottom step. He thought about Ava, who had been visibly tipsy. *Wow.* He'd traded a glass slipper for a goblet.

He bent over and retrieved the glass, placing it on the porch table until he could return. That's when he noticed the black *x* in his last name over the *n,* replaced with a scribbled *m.* He raised his dark sunglasses so he could examine closer. Sure enough, *Mimosa.* No question who the vandal might be.

"That little criminal," Remy grunted under his breath, wishing he could laugh if the situation were different. He proceeded to the airstrip with thought and smell of Ava in his head.

His inspection continued until he reached the Chinook *Gibraltar,* being saluted and greeted by soldiers and airmen at the large opening.

"General." Two men stood at attention.

Remy momentarily studied the airmen—extremely large and buff. He glanced briefly in the open cavity of the Chinook and eyed loaded crates lining the back.

Remy snatched their clipboard and rolled his finger quickly down the inventory sheet.

One airman cleared his throat. "We okay, General?"

Remy knew his position could be intimidating and sensed the soldier was uneasy. "All good. Safe flight."

He paced away in meticulous steps, shot a glance back at the Chinook and hesitated. Something didn't feel right, but he wasn't quite on his game today, probably because of last night's events. He needed to focus on today's mission—back to the house to spend the rest of the day comparing the inventory sheets Blade had discovered. A large piece of the puzzle was still missing... and that piece included more than inventory control.

Remy opted for a quick ride on Diesel, which would help clear his mind and allow him to reassess the facts. Sunday mornings were quiet in the indoor arena. The only cadets present, if any, would be the barn help. Plus he could verify whether Pam Waverly had heard about Rhya's indiscretion the night before. Hopefully that incident would strengthen the bond between the two of them. She'd certainly appeared to enjoy the drink with him at The Bulldog Den, at least after Mrs. Kennedy's accusations.

He was positive Pam Waverly was involved in whatever wrongdoings were being entertained on school premises, but how involved or expansive her activity, he had no idea yet. The inventory errors were probably just a cover-up for more elusive criminal activities.

As Remy maneuvered Diesel through his gaits, he pondered about the two soldiers loading the Chinook. A sick feeling flooded him. Why were MREs being shipped to an undisclosed compound in upstate New York? He knew of no army compound in that region. As a two-star general, he was informed on a vast amount of top secret data. Also, those two soldiers had appeared disheveled and particularly uncomfortable.

Remy nonchalantly opened the gate to the arena and headed Diesel outside to the athletic field, then down to the airfield. He couldn't stop dwelling on the soldiers' demeanor. If only he could put his finger on it.

His cell phone rumbled in his pocket, and Remy halted Diesel. He leaned back in the saddle, removed the phone, then stroked Diesel's shiny black shoulder with his free hand and let the reins dangle.

"It's Amy Ironside, and we have a problem."

"What's up?"

Remy could hear Col. Pendleton in the background. His familiar voice ordered into the call system: *Bring that Chinook back to the dock. You are not cleared for take-off.*

"What's going on?" Remy's mind ravaged through images of the soldiers. "Is it the *Gibraltar*? Is that the aircraft the colonel is asking to turn back?"

"How did you know? And there's another issue... but you're not going to like it."

As she spoke, Remy kept staring at Diesel's black mane. *Black.* The thought hit him like a cinder block. How had he been so stupid? He was a fanatic about uniforms.

"They aren't in uniform," Remy said. "I was there this morning, and something was wrong. They had on black boots when they saluted me—that's not regulation. Detain them until I arrive." Remy snatched up the reins, cueing Diesel to prance forward. "I'll be there in three minutes."

"Listen, there's still another issue. Jeffery the barber is here."

Remy heard a rise in her tone. Amy wasn't called *Old Ironside* for nothing. She could keep her cool. Something was drastically wrong.

"Jeffery? Okay, this is not the time. You lock him up, and throw away the damn key."

Remy all but cut her off until Amy's voice shouted over his, "Remy, he swears she's AWOL on the plane."

"*She?*" Remy stopped, circling Diesel to hold him back. "Who do you mean?" He heard Jeffery frantic in the background.

"Ava," Amy said. "Ava is on that plane."

Remy wasted no more time. "Put Jeffery on."

"Sir, sir," the barber's voice quivered. "Ava, she never came home last night. She faked me out... put a line of pillows in her bed."

"Why the hell would Ava be on that plane? This is no game. Get out of there before Sgt. Ironside has you arrested."

"Her phone," Jeffery said. "I have a tracker on it, just like she does on Rhya's... in case she ever gets lost or kidnapped, or... Ava doesn't have anyone else but me, you know..."

"Are you suggesting her tracker is on that Chinook?" Remy didn't wait for the answer. There was no more time to waste. He spurred Diesel to action, and asked Jeffery to put the sergeant back on the phone. "Amy, have troops down on the field immediately... weapons drawn."

Remy knew he had no time to dismount and race to his car. Diesel's gallop would be faster anyway. He cut across the campus, out the sliding barn doors, headed down the causeway at a flat-out run, only slowing to a lope in order to cross the street at the gates.

Diesel's metal shoes sparked on the pavement as Remy ordered the cadet to open the campus gate.

Remy didn't have much faith left after his son Jason was killed, but he started praying as fast as the wind was rushing at them across the athletic field. When he hit the airfield, the cadets already had the gates open in anticipation, and he blasted through at a gallop.

The *Gibraltar* was on the tarmac, propellers at full rotation, the hatch still fully open. Remy slid to a stop at the lower terminal to assess the situation next to an officer with binoculars. Diesel continued prancing in place, invigorated by the rumbling of the powerful Chinook.

"General. They are refusing to answer, but their hatch is open and they've begun to hover. Sgt. Ironside has several vehicles locking on in formation so they can't lift. But General..." the officer paused. "There's a civilian woman on the lip of the cargo deck."

Remy grabbed the binoculars. "Order someone on that front line to yell to her. Tell her to leap off."

"Jump?"

"Yes, tell him to instruct her to jump," Remy ordered.

The man with the walkie-talkie appeared confused.

Remy commanded again, "She needs to exit now."

"It's the pretty one with the really high heels. Looks like she was out last night."

"Did you hear me? Tell her to jump. It's an order!"

"I don't think she can, General."

"Why the hell not?"

"The gun."

"*What gun?*" Remy squinted through the binoculars trying to locate the hatch.

"The one the man is holding at her head."

Simultaneously as he heard the answer, Remy spied Ava fighting against her kidnapper, confirming a gun aimed at her head. His heart sank to his gut.

Remy threw the binoculars back to the other officer and spurred Diesel. The horse lunged into action.

Remy and Diesel raced down the strip after the *Gibraltar*, now hovering a foot above ground. The pilot appeared blocked by vehicles that strategically circled the aircraft; unfortunately Remy knew Chinooks were made for such tight situations. If the person at the controls was any kind of a pilot, it was only a matter of time.

As he neared, Remy could see Ava struggling to stand and free herself, but the massive man behind her held her in his grasp.

Diesel's hooves beat a record time across the macadam runway, stretching out like a thoroughbred in the last quarter of a race. Remy seated himself up in his stirrups, hands on Diesel's neck, urging the horse harder.

Remy could see Ava on the deck, gun still pointing into her temple. The Chinook danced so irregularly it made it difficult for Ava's captor, desperately trying to hold onto her.

"Lady, you're our ticket," Remy heard the man yell. "You're not going anywhere, unless it's to hell."

"Let me go!" Ava hollered.

"I will... once we're a hundred feet in the air," the man yelled.

Remy side-passed multiple soldiers pointing rifles. "Hold your fire!"

The fierce wind tunnel from the Chinook blew at them like a wall of cement almost shoving the two back. Remy was fully aware the familiar change in sound meant the machine was about to lift off. He had only one choice—leap onto the deck of the chopper if he wanted to save Ava.

First, he needed to back Ava safely out of the way. He loped Diesel close enough for her to hear him call, "Ava, your shoe," against the wind.

She looked at him confused. "My shoe? I don't care about my shoe. I'm about to die!" she screamed back.

Remy released his hold on Diesel and galloped closer. He squeezed the horse with the might of both his calves as if taking a barrel in a race, straight for the hovering craft.

The kidnapper shoved Ava down, freeing his hands. He spread both legs, and aimed the weapon dead center at Remy and Diesel.

Remy flattened his body down on Diesel's neck, hoping any gunfire would spare him and the horse. "Your weapon, Ava!"

Ava was in a kneeling position and suddenly appeared to understand what Remy had been trying to tell her. She ripped the stiletto off her foot.

The Chinook rocked, and the man with the gun was having trouble standing. The gale force winds would make every movement difficult for Ava as well, but Remy watched her raise up, slamming the heel of the shoe into the man, hitting him in the neck instead of his face.

The damage was done. He hollered and retaliated by swatting Ava with the pistol, knocking her back on the metal floor.

"Move this Jeep, now!" Remy ordered. "I need a path." The soldier immediately sped backward. "You judge it, Diesel. You can do this. Pop it high and just pretend it's a moving jump."

At that moment, Remy released the horse straight on, trusting him to gauge his leap. Diesel normally jumped higher than needed in a rush of adrenaline. Today the horse paid no attention to propellers, noise, or wind. He plowed straight on like a bull after a red scarf.

Remy knew there was a grave chance they wouldn't make it, but he encouraged Diesel forward. A chance he was willing to take.

The man removed the gun from Ava's temple and turned it at Remy as Diesel soared in his direction.

A rush of searing heat hit Remy's side and he grunted. Too fueled with exhilaration to stop, he spurred Diesel onward. His body clung to the horse's neck to avoid the upper deck while he heard a series of gunshots. He squeezed Diesel a final time, now airborne, like the craft...

They just cleared the opening, one tip of the powerful steed's rear hoof tickling the edge with a clang. Diesel's neck arched as if in battle, focused on a direct plunge, landing on the man in the cabin of the Chinook.

The man lay sprawled underneath the horse, grappling and moaning as Diesel continued to slide with crystal fireworks across the steel deck.

Remy didn't rein him in, but slid to the side over the horse's back, clobbering the man and knocking the gun away. The weapon spiraled across the floor to land at Ava's side.

Remy belted the man with one powerful blow, knocking him down.

CHAPTER 16

Ava was lying face down, planted on the metal floor for the third time. A taste of blood lingered on her lips. Remy finished sliding off Diesel who had managed to not only make the leap and clear the opening, but come to a complete stop before colliding into any of the crates filled with MREs in the back of the Chinook. The horse was now panting and snorting, nose to floor.

Remy dropped the reins as his feet touched down without a second to spare, pounding his body right on top of Ava's captor.

Her entire body ached. Ava regained her senses. *Grab the gun.* Her body didn't feel like hers, but she mustered the strength to control her fingers and reach for the weapon.

Something was happening to Remy. She could see it—he was weakening, his shirt darkening with red. Then the man kicked him hard in the chest, crashing Remy back against the cold fuselage. Her captor lunged forward at Ava and confiscated the gun before she could manage to move a muscle. Scrambling to stand, he aimed the weapon directly at her and yanked her to her feet... but she stumbled back to her knees.

"Get up!" He tugged harder.

Ava moaned.

The movement of the Chinook finally steadied. Ava could see the airstrip in the distance below. The Jeeps maneuvered in circles, soldiers and cadets dashing around. To no avail. They were in flight, no turning back. The back mouth of the helicopter was closing, and the powerful wind force settled.

Remy propped himself against a wall of the cavity, gripping his wounded side. Ava watched him raise his hand. "Let her go," he said. "She had no part in this. I'll do whatever you want."

The man searching the deck flipped a container across the floor. "Where's the walkie-talkie!" He jammed the tip of his gun into her head.

"I don't know..." she whimpered. "Please." His hand was squeezing her waist so hard she couldn't catch her air.

"There..." Remy pointed. He reached for the device. "You must have lost it in the shuffle—there. There it is." Ava could tell he was trying to defuse the situation with a calmer tone.

The man cocked the gun. "Stop moving."

Remy raised his arms forward to the avenging warden. "All good. I'll just shuffle it over to you. Easy on her, easy."

"So help me," the man warned. "One wrong move and those doors will open and the bitch, she goes out the back. Or better yet, you will."

"Understood," Remy said steadily. "Where is this plane headed?"

"None of your business." The man stepped forward toward Remy, loosening his grip on Ava. She observed Remy eye her, then look to Diesel. The horse was tight in the aisleway of the crates, blocking the door to the cockpit. The steed snorted, his head arched back, nibbling at the wooden crate tops.

"Damn horse is in my way," the man muttered.

The walkie-talkie vibrated as a voice echoed... *"Hey, Wood? You there? What's the status?"*

The man aimed his pistol at Diesel, and Remy leaned forward instantly. Ava grabbed the man's chest to distract him. "Please, no," she cried.

Remy tried to stand. "You need the walkie-talkie to speak to your buddies. I'll get it. Let me pass it your way," he pleaded, trying to draw the man's attention away from the horse.

The man the pilot had called Wood focused on Remy. "Buddy," he said. "It's just one guy and myself on this mission. Marcus can man a helicopter like no one else. But your horse is in my way, and I need the walkie-talkie."

Wood froze, trigger cocked and still pointed at Diesel.

Remy stretched his leg slowly in the direction of the walkie-talkie. "See, I can slip it right to you." He continued very calmly.

"You know, if you fire that gun in this chopper, there are a couple of scenarios you should consider." He acted almost as if he were trying to befriend the guy. "One, if you blow the airflow, we'll crash. Two, if you hit a vital part of this flying machine, we'll crash. Three, if your buddy hears it and loses concentration, we'll crash."

Remy waited. But all Ava heard was the word *crash,* so she shuddered, grabbing the man's arm. "Please don't shoot."

"Stop it, lady." The massive man shook her off.

"Let me just send the walkie-talkie your way. No funny business." Remy tried to interrupt the man again. "Look. I know she's quite annoying. Please don't shoot the horse. I'd rather you shoot me... or throw the girl out... but not the horse."

Ava immediately regained some composure at the *throw the girl out* line and stopped crying. She mouthed, *"What?"* at Remy, followed by *"Thanks a lot."*

"Annoying is an understatement," the man snapped. "She's been a live wire."

"Oh, I'm sure." Remy blew out a sigh as if finding a connection with the man at Ava's expense. "I've had issues with her, and so has the entire Army. I can help you reach your location. I'm a respected two-star general."

"I don't see any stars," Wood snapped.

"Back on my uniform, before I changed to go riding," Remy said. "You saw me this morning. Saluted me when I checked you in the queue."

The man scratched his head with the end of the pistol.

"You will have a problem," Remy shrugged. "The Army is going to be crawling all over you. You'll need me and the horse to lead you out of that situation." He added, "But the girl? Well..." Remy paused, rubbing his chin. "I only have a derrière fetish when it comes to her. What you do with her... that's up to you." Remy enunciated the words *derrière fetish,* and Ava scorched Remy with a pair of bug eyes, hoping he had a plan for making such a lude remark.

The man smirked, pulling the gun off Diesel. "That was you, this morning?" he said. "I swear you make one wrong move, I kill the horse first and then the girl."

Remy nodded and reached for the walkie-talkie, wincing. He retrieved the device and sat back up. Holding his side with his other hand, now wet with blood, he said, "You hurt me good, son. So I'll try to send this as hard as I can muster."

Wood looked at him. "Just fling the damn thing over here," he said curling his fingers in a rapid motion.

Remy grunted and slid the device across the floor like a puck, with only enough energy to shove it halfway. The man stared at Remy before bending over. "This gun is cocked." He waved the weapon.

Remy acknowledged, placing both hands in the air. "You have us detained. We certainly are in a real mess, you know."

The man glared in his direction. Remy was staring at Ava. "This woman about drove me over the edge. Three tours in Central Intelligence and no one quite irked me like she does. You know what I mean?"

Wood glanced back at Ava and slipped his grip on her a little more.

"Needs to let go of her child and get a life of her own, you know what I mean?"

The man grinned. "Glad I don't have one at home."

"You are a *red card*, full of accidents, Mrs. Kennedy. Just like Col. Pendleton said—one big accident." Remy exaggerated the sentence.

"Sounds like you should have listened to him, lady, and let your daughter grow up." The man was leaning further down, barely touching Ava.

The walkie-talkie had come to a stop directly behind Diesel's rear. Finally, Ava understood. *Derrière fetish.* Remy was trying to remind her. *The red card on Diesel's door.*

When the man reached for the radio, Ava resisted.

Diesel stopped nibbling on the boxes and immediately cocked a leg. Wood stretched for the device. Clearly irritated, the steed whipped his hindquarter into action with such force that Ava went flying as well because the man held her tight. Again she found herself shimmying across the cold metal floor.

The gun splayed from the attacker's hand, and he was thrown several feet in a flip. Ava peered up at him from the spot where she landed. He appeared unconscious, blood dripping from his mouth.

"Ava," she heard Remy. Within seconds she was being lifted to the side bench of the Chinook. Remy kneeled down in front of her. "You okay?"

She nodded, noticing he'd already confiscated the pistol.

"Stay here," he said. Remy headed to the man called Wood and placed two fingers on his neck. "You're alive." He grabbed a long cord from a red chest on board, knowing exactly where to look. He bound the attacker's hands and legs in a jumbo knot, then hooked him to a parachute clip on a line running to the ceiling. "That should hold him."

Remy walked carefully up to Diesel who was now wedged in the aisle between crates in line with the cockpit. Diesel cocked his leg again.

"Whoa boy, I owe you twice," Remy said. "You are a hell of a soldier. Now, let's see you back up." Remy clicked, staying off to one side, stretching across the crate for a loose rein. "Come on back, Diesel."

Ava regarded his gentle hand coaxing and patting the horse's neck until Diesel repositioned.

"Thanks, boy." Remy led him over to the same ceiling cord, then loosened the bridle and made a rope halter instead.

Both he and Ava froze when the man on the floor stirred. Remy waited briefly, easing when he realized the tied deviant was too weak to be a threat. Then he hooked Diesel to the line in front.

"You awake, buddy?" Remy asked.

The man grunted.

"Good, because now it's my turn to make the threats. Here's the walkie-talkie, Wood. What's the pilot's name?"

The man mumbled, "Marcus."

"Okay, you tell your buddy Marcus that you're just fine back here... or you'll see that rear again." Remy pointed to Diesel who whinnied. "Plus it's my turn with the gun." Remy aimed the pistol at Wood's privates. Diesel whinnied again. *"Comprende?"*

The man conceded and spoke into the radio Remy held out. "All good, Marcus. The woman is contained. Knocked out cold." Remy released the button.

"Good," the pilot answered. *"I didn't want to leave the cockpit to check. Now get up here and help me out."*

Ava rolled her eyes. "So glad he doesn't want to leave the cockpit."

Remy hammered the pistol against Wood's cheek, knocking him out.

Ava let out a gasp.

"Now, you listen to me," Remy said, limping over to her.

She could only lock on to his injured side.

He must've seen her concern so his voice softened. "It's okay, but I need you to help me."

She agreed. Her hair was a mess, her stained skirt ripped up the other side, her shoulder bare from a torn strap and her body dotted with cuts and bruises.

Remy carried the first-aid kit, laid it at her side, and popped the lid open.

"I'm sure you were a great nurse when your daughter skinned her knees riding her bike or horses. Plus you're a hairdresser, right? They deal with a lot of crap, I'm sure." He rummaged through the contents and stood in front of her. "I need you to pour some peroxide on this wound, and then cover it good and tight with this gauze." He pivoted sideways in front of her and removed his shirt.

Ava shuddered.

"You can do this," he said. "Trust me, it's going to hurt me more than you."

Ava said nothing as she slipped on a pair of oversized rubber gloves and opened the peroxide bottle. She told herself this was just like when Gwendolyn at the salon had a tick on her head. She was already feeling nauseous from the ordeal, but now she had to nurse his bleeding black-and-blue side.

"This looks serious." She wiped a tear with her wrist. Ava doused the gauze with peroxide and waited a minute, shifting her hands in the gloves.

"Come on," he coaxed. "There's no time to spare. My main focus is the cockpit. Take a deep breath and do it. We aren't free yet."

Ava inhaled, examined his side, then exhaled and stabilized the bottle above his wound.

"Just go a little easy, please." Remy's muscles tensed, and he raised his head as if preparing.

"Really, go easy on you?" Ava said. "You lured my daughter into this dangerous mess and tarnished her record! I uprooted my entire life. Now, I'm stuck at Jefferson Washington. I can't go back because of a contract. If she stays in the brig, I guess I could become a prison barber. If, that is, we live to return home!"

She continued rambling, first, because his comments earlier had sliced her like a knife. Second, and more importantly, she had to distract herself so she didn't throw up on the spot.

"And Rhya, she was an amazing girl. I thought she could be an archaeologist or marine biologist. All we had... all we worked for... all I worked for! Now she's going to prison. I liked my life before, my little beauty shop, in the same little town where I was born."

Remy slumped his shoulders as if surrendering in battle. "She's not going to prison, Ava. She has nothing on her record, just a slap on the wrist. I made sure of that. Now come on." He directed with his hand motioning her to nurse his side. "Besides, the way Col. Pendleton explains things, you were a lonely pain in the derrière long before you met me." He glanced at Diesel. "No pun intended, buddy."

The horse whinnied.

"Oh, yeah!" She poured the peroxide, now unconcerned for his pain. "Rhya admired you. You think you cleaned her record? All she'll be lucky to get is some clerk job at the door of a recruiting office." She roughly pressed the gauze.

He moaned, gritting his teeth. Ava wallowed in his pain.

"You have no..." Remy slurred, "...about Rhya. Please, gently."

Ava poured more peroxide, and Remy growled.

"I know my daughter," she said, almost relishing his pain.

"But you don't know the truth. And why are you smiling?" Remy muttered in a low voice. "Your daughter is fine. Just let her be."

"You're a jerk." She compressed the gauze against him, touching his bare skin with her fingertips.

"I just saved your life," he insisted with a grunt. "Could you be somewhat kinder?"

"You did not," she replied. "Diesel did. Do you even know what it is to be a parent who loves a child so much..." She stretched out the gauze, wrapping it tighter around his abdomen.

"Ouch, a little looser! Could you stop talking?"

His arms were in the air as she spiraled around complaining. "No clue whatsoever. Thank God. You would have been a horrible father. Maybe you're a..." Ava sensed him glaring at her.

"Your daughter... it was a set-up, Mrs. Kennedy." He moaned. "Damn you, you drive me crazy."

She froze and her head tilted up at him. Remy squeezed his eyes shut as if he'd just revealed top secret information by mistake.

"Set-up? What did you just say?"

He snatched the tape from her hand and sealed the wound himself.

"What exactly do you mean, set-up?" she repeated, still not moving an inch. Her hand rested at the edge of his belt and skin.

"Don't worry about it," he winced, moving back so her hand released him as he started to put his shirt on carefully.

"No, stop. What are you saying?" Ava touched him to retain his attention.

Remy glanced down at her hand. She immediately realized her palm was resting on his bare hard chest. Clearing her throat she slipped her hand away.

Remy grabbed her shoulders. "Look," he said, and Ava's slight cry seemed to stun him. He pulled her close, ensnaring her for what seemed only a second, before he released her, except for her eyes. "Sorry, but you landed yourself here. I'm going to divulge something to you. After that, let it go. I will not—I repeat, not—speak about it again, okay?"

She nodded, still captivated by him.

He picked up the peroxide and dabbed some on a bit of cotton. Ava was unaware what he was about to do so when he touched her shoulder to clean the cut, she shivered and let out another soft wince.

"Your daughter was part of a mission," he said. "It was a set-up. She did nothing wrong."

Ava watched him dab her skin, touching her lightly, then cup her chin.

"Rhya is on a mission to investigate who is behind the corruption involving some cadets and staff at the college. I needed a loyal soldier I could trust. You can be damn proud of her. And now because of your helicopter-mothering—maybe we should call yours Chinooking, because it's so intense—you're in the thick of the operation."

Ava felt as if she'd been stung by an entire hive of hornets. "You mean... everything she said to me on the field... it was a set-up?" Ava wearily eyed Remy as he pressed his shoulders back, ready to take his punishment. Her heart sank deep into his brown eyes and she studied his chiseled jaw, then watched him nod in affirmation.

"What's wrong with you?" she yelled, coming alive, rising up and shoving him backward. "I was heartbroken. Do you know that?"

He looked away and finished buttoning his shirt. "I confessed," he said. "That's all you get." His hands went up in the air. "Now, I'm ordering you to stay here, and if I don't come back, you take this gun and shoot whoever comes through that door once you're on the ground. Shoot to kill." He pointed at the cockpit and held the pistol butt toward her.

"You've got to be kidding! I never ever shot..." Ava refused to take the gun.

"You're a hairdresser. No doubt you've wanted to kill a few clients. Practice on whoever comes through that door," he said, grabbing her hand to demonstrate. "Safety, trigger, aim and fire. It's loaded."

Ava's hands were shaking.

"Oh, and him..." Remy pointed to Wood on the ground. "If he wakes up, kill him. And do not, do not leave this area. Here, put this on," he said, rummaging through another large chest, lifting out what looked like an oversized backpack.

"What are you doing?" She tried to resist him but he was too strong.

"This is called a rig." He spun her around and strapped an oversized pack on her back, pulling her arms out of the harness as if dressing a child. He stretched the straps across her chest.

"Excuse me. Are you purposely touching me in an inappropriate manner?" Ava's cheeks flushed as his fingers scaled her skin.

He didn't respond, instead buckling the harness, locking it dead center against her cleavage, almost preventing her lungs from inflating. Her breasts were smushed like pancakes.

"I can't breathe!" He ignored her as she gasped for air. "Tell me, do you hate females?" Ava grunted from the weight, but quickly changed to a horrifying yell when she felt an intrusion. "What are you doing?"

Remy's hands were fondling between her thighs, under her crotch, back up from her rear, and to her lower front where he maneuvered the leg straps. "Don't flatter yourself, Mrs. Kennedy."

Remy reached under her, once more brushing her lower body. Ava felt a fire ignite and she sucked in deeper, feeling faint. He tightened another strap from the back, crisscrossed to her left side. Leaving him square in front of her pelvis, between her thighs. "Never hurts to be prepared," he said. "It's a parachute and this just may save your life."

"I can't do this," Ava resisted. "Until eight weeks ago I never even left my dear beauty shop. My dear, friendly, amazing clients, and my small, lovely, did I mention small, country town... And my Jeffery, oh my dear, devoted Jeffery." She let Remy have his way with her as she rambled and dreamed of her old life.

"Things changed, Private M, when you insisted on being in the Army," he said, as he tightened the straps.

She was like a zombie.

"This, Ava, is called a Hoo Hoo." He pointed down.

"I know where my Hoo Hoo is, you idiot," she fired back as he tapped a ball on the back of the rig.

"Ava," he raised his voice over the hum of the Chinook. "It is slang for your deployment handle. It's here on the top of your apex.

For the pilot chute." He spun her around. "You grab the Hoo Hoo and throw it out away from you. This will pull the pilot chute away from—"

Ava slammed her hand on his chest. "I could care less, because I will not be leaping out of this aircraft."

He ignored her, almost speeding up his mini lesson. "The pilot chute will go into the airstream. This is attached to the bridle which looks like a strap. As it deploys, a pin will pull out which opens the parachute…"

"Stop. I don't care! Because I will never ever leap out of this aircraft!" Ava slapped his chest again.

Remy grabbed her hand and placed the gun in her palm. "End of lesson." He plopped her down. "Don't you leave this area. Got it! Sit on your tiny little derrière and don't move." He hinged his body toward the horse. "Diesel, she's all yours."

CHAPTER 17

Ava sat shaking like a withered leaf in a hurricane. Her insides swirled. She touched the gun and tried to breathe. The weight of the parachute was suffocating.

Don't know what he is thinking! I am not jumping out of a helicopter.

Motionless on the metal bench, the back of her thighs were freezing in her little satiny ripped skirt. Ava pouted, stamping her feet. The roaring of the propellers mesmerized her. It had been at least thirty minutes since Remy entered the cockpit, yet she'd heard nothing. Zero. She was doing exactly as ordered. Clearly something was wrong.

Just then the man named Wood stirred. Ava hopped up at attention and pointed the gun at him, her hand trembling. *What good was a weapon if she couldn't even aim straight?*

She sidestepped to Diesel's head. She knew enough about horses to back this one closer to her attacker. Ava didn't doubt she could pull the trigger if needed, but what about all those warnings Remy told Wood. The plane could crash. Had he meant it?

Or maybe he'd given her the gun just to scare the man. With her luck, the bullet would ricochet right off the metal walls and hit her or Diesel.

Fortunately the delirious man sloped back into the abyss of unconsciousness. Ava relaxed slightly as Diesel started nibbling on her half torn shirt. She ran her fingers down his muzzle, and he whinnied, seeming to like it.

"No more damage to my clothing, Diesel. I'm already falling out of this tattered outfit." She tapped his nose and he flicked his head, nudging her back against the crates. The cumbersome backpack cut into the skin of her neck, and Ava turned to relieve the pain. She noticed Diesel had gnawed the wood all across the top edge.

"Bet you're hungry," she said, fingering the splintered crate, then gazed along it to the aisle. She shuffled her way between the crates up to the door of the cockpit. She tried to reach the handle, but with the pack she became wedged, finally shifting herself around. Ava leaned her ear tight against the door. The only continuous sound was the tandem propellers rotating as they streamed through the air. She peeked to the floor and eyed where she had slept after taking the anxiety pills Jeffery suggested. *Wait until I see him!*

It suddenly occurred to her that might not happen.

Oh God, I pray I see him again.

Ava bent her head forward, a tear streaming down her cheek as she caught sight of the three MREs she'd used as a pillow the night before. Ava could not imagine how she had fallen asleep in such a confining space. She was paying for it now. Her entire body ached. She kicked the MREs around with her foot, only to discover her purse laying under them.

My purse!

Ava tried to lean down too quickly. Her body screamed with pain under the heavy pack. Again she found herself wedged between the crates and stretching her fingers out to nab the handbag. Once she had hold of its strap, the struggle was even more difficult to swivel around. Finally, she stabilized herself and rested her purse on a crate.

Ava began to tear through the contents and discovered her phone! She gasped in excitement, reclaiming her hope at the same time. But the screen remained black as she frantically pressed all the buttons.

Ava tossed the phone aside and continued ransacking the bag. A collection of stuff was jammed in—a small can of hairspray, lipstick, a metal-pronged teasing comb, tissues, credit card, and the anxiety pills. Pills she was not about to take again. She clutched her stomach, her nerves whirling inside. Well, she had taken three. Maybe one more wouldn't hurt in this very stressful situation.

Ava managed to gulp one with a wad of spit, then spread all the contents on top of the crates. She decided to apply the lipstick. Might as well look good if she was going to die. As she dabbed on the rose color, she now felt as if hours had passed since Remy stepped into the cockpit.

Ava extended her hand once more for the latch. Diesel whinnied as if he sensed the need to stop her.

Ava frowned at him. "I was warned, wasn't I?"

Diesel apparently understood because he flicked his head up and down followed by a whinny and a nudge of the crate.

"You're hungry, aren't you?" Ava fingered the open crates and pointed. "I bet there's something in here for you to eat." She laid the gun on the edge of the box and talked to Diesel like a waitress reading a menu. "Hmm... On the exquisite menu today we have fresh farm-raised carrots, honey-roasted peanuts, or hand-picked by Barbarian Monks French beans?" Diesel must have enjoyed the attention because he neighed. "Voila," she said. "Freeze-dried carrots, it is!"

She wavered back to him. "Dang parachute." Then she shimmied herself to a crate marked Water. "Let's see. You need some of this, too." She examined the corner where earlier she'd eyed an empty bucket and poured some for the horse. While he slurped and gulped, she tried desperately to open the package of carrots. "Wow, these are sure child-safe." Her nerves were settling from the anxiety tablet, and she made a joke to Diesel. "Guess those pills really work."

She pulled with all her strength, pinching each side of the plastic until finally the top split and the contents—a white powder—flew into the air. It dusted the crates, the floor, and her hands. Ava looked at Diesel then back.

"These don't look like any carrots I've ever seen." She reached for the string beans. "Guess you might have to settle for greens today, Diesel."

She once again pinched both sides of the next bag and yanked, only to discover the same white powder clouding everywhere. "Hmm... must be ancient. It's turned to dust. Sorry, Diesel. This last one says 'chipped beef.' Do horses eat meat?"

Ava tried a third in a panic, flushed with a bad feeling. To no avail, another mushroom puff of white powder plumed her hands and the air. Ava stormed to the cockpit door carrying the last MRE bag she'd opened. Ava was sure Remy would want to be aware of the contents in the crates.

Ava jarred the door cautiously and inched her one eye to the crack. Luckily, the propellers were even louder than the noise she made opening the latch. This was good because it masked the slight gasp released from her mouth. She immediately covered her mouth as to not alert the cockpit about her presence. The pilot was not Remy.

She could see the general passed out cold on the right seat, his head dangling. Ava clutched her mouth, imprisoning her scream. The pilot to her left was concentrating on flying the helicopter, in uniform and wearing full headgear, including headphones. She shut the door and rested her head on her fingers, gripping the edge.

"Oh my God, Remy. Don't be dead," she whispered.

Ava surged with panic, finding herself in an explosive dilemma, because right at this moment even if she knocked out the pilot, no one could land the helicopter. On the other hand, if she didn't act, and the pilot became aware of her, she might as well consider herself dead.

Perhaps her best bet was to somehow barricade herself in the back part of the fuselage. She had a gun that she would probably shoot her foot off with. *Not good.* Better yet, she had hairspray and a teasing comb, which she was a pro at maneuvering... plus the best weapon of all, Diesel.

Ava peered into the cockpit again. Slowly, she stepped back with a plan, but the weight of the backpack unbalanced her, especially while wearing heels. She wobbled with a scream, forcing the door open wider.

Breathing a sigh she had not been noticed, Ava regained herself and slowly attempted to push the door shut. Unfortunately the man named Marcus caught sight of her. He burst to a stand, his robust body more massive than Wood's, his stance like a WWF weightlifter cursed by fury and hate. He rushed the door like a linebacker.

Ava released a second scream, which stirred Remy. "Thank God, you're alive," Ava hollered, even though he barely moved. The backpack kept her body from maneuvering, and she blindly fingered the top of the crate where she knew the contents of her purse were scattered behind her. She needed something, anything for defense. Her hand touched the can of hairspray and the pointed metal prongs of the teasing comb.

The pilot slugged open the door with fury. Ava reacted by stabbing the pronged comb in the direction of his eyes and sprayed in terror, waving the can like gale force winds.

Marcus belted out a cry and tumbled back into the cabin. Ava slammed the door.

"Oh my! The gun. Where's the gun?" It was nowhere in sight.

Ava couldn't think straight. First, she tried dodging left then right, only her head moving because of the apparatus on her back. Until she saw Diesel. She angled a crate as best she could to delay the ability of Marcus to open the door further. Then she raced toward the horse.

"Okay, boy. It's just you and me."

Wood moaned. Ava accidentally backed the horse two steps, and Diesel kicked him again.

"Oh my. Whoops, so sorry." Ava shrugged at Wood who once again fell over like a tree, knocked out cold. Ava could hear the pilot swearing, rattling the crate. He was coming.

Ava massaged Diesel's nose with fast strokes. "Please cooperate," she whispered. "I need you."

Apparently once again, the horse understood because he let her position him in the tight narrow aisle between the crates.

Ava tucked herself under Diesel's massive neck and clung shivering to his broad shoulders. As soon as the door began to slide open, she witnessed Diesel cock a leg and she squinted.

Ava waited, but the door ceased opening. Then she saw the head and shoulders of Marcus fall out of the doorway over the crate, out cold, before Diesel swung his leg and nailed him right between the eyes.

"Whoa, boy. Whoa, it's me." Remy voice caused Ava to perk up from her cradled position. "Ava, Ava," he called.

"I thought you were..." She screamed to be heard over the engines.

"I thought I told you to stay put. Now, move Diesel forward. We don't have much time."

"You need to see these MREs," she said, inching Diesel ahead.

"This is no time to eat," Remy complained. "We're currently on auto-pilot with only enough fuel to last about ten minutes."

Ava seemed to not comprehend what he had just said. "They're not MREs," she insisted, using her pointer finger to tap hard on the packet in her hand. Ava gazed into the cockpit, and focused on the horizon through the windshield as Remy gathered up Marcus and dragged him next to Wood.

The Chinook was heading right for a forest-covered mountain. When she turned Remy, he was connecting the two avengers to one parachute rig, his face bleeding, along with fresh blood staining the side of his shirt.

"What are you doing?" Ava asked, pointing to the window up front. "We're going to crash into that mountain. Excuse me." She stared at him as he opened the back door release, and the mouth of the fuselage opened. Wind rushed her and the sound muffled their voices even more.

"Excuse me?" she hollered louder than before. "What are you doing?"

"Taking out the trash," Remy answered, right before shoving the two men off the end of the deck connected by one parachute. "Don't say I didn't give you a chance," he hollered as the two soared to the ground.

Remy did an about face to Ava then continued moving. He snagged another parachute, ignoring her holding the MRE, so she started to gather the contents of her purse.

"What are we doing, please?" She took Diesel's tether. "And what about Diesel? Is there a parachute big enough for him?"

He gave her no response.

"You know I can't do this..." Then she saw him connecting a crate of MREs to a parachute. "That's not food, I told you. What are you doing?"

"It's our guarantee," he said, dragging the crate to the edge of the opening, Remy grasped the ball he called the Hoo Hoo and shoved the crate off. He spun around to Ava and called her to him with his index finger.

"You're kidding! I cannot and will not jump. I mean, I refuse!" Ava screamed.

"Ava, we can't stay in this helicopter. Next stop is that mountain you were talking about." Remy pointed to the horizon. "Not to mention we only have five minutes of fuel!"

Ava shook her head violently, but Remy wasn't taking no for an answer. He reached out for her.

"No!" She wrapped a leg around him but lost her balance falling into his arms. "I can't!"

"Mrs. Kennedy, you must." He plopped a helmet on her head and snapped it tight. "You are leaving."

"We can't leave Diesel behind. He just saved my life."

Remy secured the parachute on her. "We are not leaving Diesel. Listen to me, count to twenty then yank the Hoo Hoo. Once you do, remember belly to earth."

"What?" Ava screamed. "Belly to earth, what?"

Remy spread his arms out as if in a holdup, shoving his chest forward. "Like this, otherwise you will spin and tumble. It is crucial. Count to twenty. Pull, then belly to earth. Got it?" He patted the Hoo Hoo.

"Are you kidding? I can't even remember what you said. I'm a screw-up! I drop bobby pins everywhere! I leave a mess behind wherever I go! Besides, we're not leaving that horse?" She was not really listening, instead trying to unsnap the helmet.

"You are leaving. I'm not leaving."

Diesel arched his neck back.

Ava studied Remy perplexed.

"You have a daughter, Mrs. Kennedy. I'm just sorry we did not meet under other circumstances. I think I might have liked you, very much."

The wind, propellers, and helmet were making it difficult for her to hear. She was trying to read his lips. "Did you say he's staying? I won't let that happen."

"I am staying with Diesel, but you, Mrs. Kennedy—"

The Chinook bumped like its heart skipped beats.

Remy gripped her arms above the elbows. "Ava, there's no time to explain... Remember what I said—count to twenty, pull, and belly to earth! That's all you need to do." He raised his hands to her helmet to place her goggles securely over her eyes. "One more thing." Remy gripped her biceps, and now she was having trouble both hearing and seeing him.

Ava tried to escape, but when his lips touched hers, her body fell limp. Her wiggling to be free stopped. Her body surged with warmth. The kiss wasn't wet, or French or luscious. His lips simply touched hers, drew her closer, tighter, and captured the essence of a softness she hadn't experienced in a long time. Forgetting about the terror and fear in her soul, she never opened her eyes to see him draw away. Ava only felt the bump of his nose against her goggles. She savored the moment, until she realized how strong his grip was on her arms. Her back was now facing the open hatch of the Chinook when the machine bounced again.

"Goodbye, Ava Kennedy. Remember—count to twenty!"

Remy flipped her body to the open door, and Ava felt air hit her when her feet left the metal floor of the *Gibraltar*. She only witnessed Remy standing on the edge for one second until she faced the clouds, then wind flipped her into a whirling somersault. His last words, "Belly to earth," were barely audible over her blood curdling scream!

She had no choice but to expand her arms as if she was attempting to grab something to stop her from twirling violently. The arms helped, and Ava splayed out like someone nailed on a cross, free-falling to the ground below.

The earth.

The earth was advancing closer every second, and her heart was racing. She choked on her panting breaths. Remy had only distracted her thoughts in order to toss her from the helicopter. Wait until she got hold of him. He would be dead meat. Oh, St. Joan of Arc, would she ever see him again?

She tried to locate the Chinook, heard the tandem rotors fading in the distance, but the pressure around her was so debilitating her body wouldn't respond to her commands.

Ava's lips extended like the Joker in *Batman,* bubbling into her cheeks. Her clothes were flapping, and air rushed up her thighs under her little satin skirt to her pink thong. Her petite body hit the waves and streams of air, thrashing her like a rag doll. What could she do? What was she supposed to do?

"Count," he'd said.

What number was she supposed to count to? Should she already have started? A guesstimate put her at well over twenty seconds. *Pull now?* She patted her chest for the dang Hoo Hoo. Ava panicked. *Oh my God, no tab.* It must've come off in the fall. She began to scream until her fingers touched her lower backside, never so happy to feel her Hoo Hoo in her entire life. Ava yanked and as Remy said, the parachute's bridle released.

The sound of the chute extracting and its forceful pull on her body took her breath away. The canopy held her like a safety net, streaming across the sky toward a corset-covered mountain. She no longer could see the helicopter, but as she closed in on the forest, the sky behind her lit up like a fireball, and she prayed with all her heart it wasn't Remy.

The dark plume of smoke that followed in the horizon swirled into the blue sky. Definitely not a good sign.

Ava's chest hurt, her heart sore from the aching both physically and mentally. Her mind panicked. The grove of trees was about to suck her into an abyss. She was lost in her own darkness... Then all went black.

CHAPTER 18

Remy was educated on flying helicopters, but not an expert. The Chinook was his least favorite. Not because of the machine's flying capabilities though... this beast was built for amazing feats. The tandem two-rotor helicopter could carry and unload cargo in remote locations of the world. *Including humans.* The Chinook could place artillery or men in perilous places sometimes inaccessible any other way. They were invaluable at rescuing casualties including other military machines. Remy especially despised them for one reason—because Jason's last mission had taken him to his death on a Chinook.

He stationed himself between the two seats in the cockpit gathering his thoughts, examining the gauges. The radio was purposely shot out by one of Marcus's flying bullets. And at this moment, there was little time to escape. The coordinates revealed he was somewhere in northeastern Pennsylvania. Calculating the time since takeoff, Remy identified the rolling mountains below as the Poconos. He had eyed the terrain where he dropped Ava near a waterfall and lake bed, then flew over the mountainous area in a circle, searching. Now he aimed for a hollow gorge, fast approaching. Maybe there would be a place to land this beast... or at least dismount.

The gorge was immense—a hundred-foot drop into a rocky crag with a rushing river curling down the bed. It was too tight to soar down with this beast. Not to mention too windy, like a double s-curve. Maybe a very experienced pilot could've managed, but not him.

He checked the fuel gauge... way too low. The soldiers at the airstrip had fired a few shots and must've nailed the tank. The Chinook was leaking fuel for sure.

A sudden jolt of pain caused Remy to glance down. Breathing was becoming difficult. There was no time to tend his wound, and his stamina was dissolving. He knew the moment to land or exit this bad boy was imminent, and even though he'd placed a tracking device on Ava he still had to find her before she delved into trouble as usual.

Remy concocted a plan. He was calling it "hover and pray." He turned back to the cabin area and hoped he and Diesel both had the courage and energy to make a leap of faith.

He set the coordinates on the Chinook, a craft that could suspend itself and hover on the edge of a cliff to unload or load troops and supplies. Usually though, there were three pilots. This mission would employ only one—the auto-pilot.

Diesel appeared to sense the escalated need to move ever since Remy threw Ava overboard. The horse clanged his hooves on the metal floor, snorting in between. Remy stuffed a bag with supplies and first-aid, plus another with some extra fake MREs—assurance, if he couldn't locate the crate he'd dropped. He was positive someone would be searching for the missing MREs.

Remy bridled and loaded Diesel. There was no time to throw a parachute on his back as security, plus the rig could offset his balance even more. Besides, if Diesel were plunging to his death, Remy intended to join him.

"Not sure how we're both standing, boy. Must be adrenaline. But I need your help again." He tossed the bags over Diesel's back. Remy scrambled to the cockpit to finalize the coordinates. Lowering the machine to the edge of a cliff, he locked her on hover, and dashed back to the horse.

"One more leap is all I ask." He turned Diesel to face the open fuselage. "We're headed that way." He mounted cautiously. He could not sit straight up without hitting the ceiling of the Chinook. And because Diesel's jumps were always high, it was vital Remy stayed low. The key to riding this steed off the chopper was to mount and hang off the side. Remy would swing his leg over when they hopefully made landfall. He just hoped he didn't set the horse off-balance and still had strength to maneuver the dive.

Diesel was stamping to move. Remy released the reins and clicked, surging his steed forward. The horse lunged three strides, but suddenly stopped at the lip of the deck. He pranced in place, as if dancing on a high wire.

Diesel lost concentration and sucked back, reaching the mouth of the opening. The Chinook wavered then began to ricochet like a bullet off metal. The roaring flushed Remy's ears and the wind tunnel blew them back like a tornado.

Remy grimaced in searing pain, then flew forward clutching the horse's neck. He was left in a side position, eyeing his death by plunging into a hundred-foot drop, visible as the pair vaulted over the three-foot chasm to the edge of the cliff.

Remy immediately checked the reins and swung Diesel around, plastering his nose to the horse's face. "Listen here. Know one thing... I am not about to let a Chinook take your life or mine. Diesel, we are doing this for Jason."

Remy had such force in his words Diesel must have sensed the terror. Remy hardly had to touch him to spin 180 degrees to face the deathtrap opening.

"Now, use that pretty ass of yours and get us out of here," he yelled. "We've got about three seconds before this baby starts spinning in a free fall."

Diesel followed Remy's command and instinctively plowed toward freedom. Remy crouched low, barely avoiding a head scraping as they lunged airborne. Remy had never experienced a horse so strong and powerful... or capable. He just hoped they both had the stamina to clear the open-air hurdle.

"Leap of faith, buddy!"

Remy jammed his fist into Diesel's side without release. He wasn't going to let go. He couldn't.

Diesel had to stretch out to be able to clear the three-foot break from the Chinook to land... and now the gap was growing wider. Remy's fist would anger him, compelling them across the open air grave.

Remy closed his eyes tight, hoping not to see the earth closing in below.

Diesel soared, stretching as Remy prayed. "One, two, three!"

They hit the earth hard like stone, with Diesel's front two hooves pounding, almost collapsing him to his knees from the shock, and his left back leg missed landing completely. Diesel had to scramble like a cat scratching and clawing for its freedom. Finally he found his footing on the flat ledge.

Remy mustered every inch of his strength to gather himself astride the saddle. Once on, he galloped forward, no time to spare. They were both injured, but that beast behind them was roaring in pain, too. The Chinook was going to blow!

They galloped ahead of the massive explosion, a rolling ball of flames biting at Diesel's tail. Remy felt a surge of blistering heat until the horse's speed finally won.

Remy sidestepped them to a rolling stop, pausing to listen to the burning explosion and the fall of water below, dark smoke pluming above. Both rider and horse dropped their heads as if thankful in prayer. Diesel's sides inflated and deflated in sync with Remy's heart that pounded through his chest.

Remy offered Diesel time, glancing at the steed's back leg cocked, trembling and bloody. He needed to find water, a stream. He studied his tracking device. It showed Ava about five miles into the thick woods, and the parachuted MREs off to her left.

First point of contact would be to locate and gather Ava. Once he knew she was secure, he could locate the crate of MREs for evidence and collateral. Because he was concerned—not about the two attackers he'd dropped first. They would have enough to deal with worrying about their own survival. He was most concerned about the likely fact someone knew that cargo was coming, and they were waiting for their drugs on the other end... which represented an awful lot of money.

Once he reached the woods, Remy made the decision to dismount and ease Diesel's journey. He'd burdened the horse long enough. Even walking would be a struggle for Remy, but there was still time before dark. Once they reached Ava, hopefully they could rest, dress their wounds and hydrate. Then he could venture out to the other packs.

Remy glanced again at the tracker. Diesel pushed into him. "Listen," Remy said. "Is that water?"

Diesel's ears perked up. Indeed they were headed in the right direction. A refreshing waterfall splashed in the background. Then they heard a screeching sound echo from the valley. Diesel erected his head, twitching his ears as if it hurt.

"Well, we don't need the tracker for Ava anymore." Remy shoved the device in his pack. "Her chilling screams will suffice."

Reality surfaced as he scanned the treeline and eyed Ava. She was flailing her legs and arms like a fish out of water. But nothing was working. She'd been captured, her parachute snarked in a grove of trees. Relieved at first she was alive and in one piece, Remy reveled in the thought of leaving her hang.

The two slowly trekked down through the thick underbrush, serenaded by her screams. "Ouch, *eww*, ouch!" The tree limbs were scraping and scratching her until a branch gave way and she dropped another foot.

Remy halted, squeezing his eyes, hoping another branch would snag her before she could hit the ground.

Luckily one did, and Diesel appeared to shake his head in dismay that she continued her ranting. Her body now dangled about twelve feet from the earth, the satin barely covering her. For a minute when he'd tossed her from the plane he'd watched that little skirt flip over and bare her sweet pink thong, revealing a tattoo he could by no means make out. He'd prayed he would see her again. And his wish came true. Only Ava Kennedy was moaning and screaming, talking to herself. Complaining about him.

"Why did I ever let him shove me out of a helicopter? Why did I ever follow Rhya to school? Come on, Ava. What's the matter with you?" She shimmied, tugging on the shoulder straps of her pack. "Help!"

Her cry echoed, almost shaking the trees imprisoning her. Remy stopped. Diesel shook his ears. "Could you please keep it down, Mrs. Kennedy? But why did you even follow your daughter?"

His voiced silenced her. She turned her head in all directions. "Remy? I thought you were dead!"

"No, I can assure you from the pain I am feeling right now, I am quite alive."

"But... the plane crashed. It made such a loud noise in the distance... *poof*... a ball of fire. And all that smoke," Ava fearfully explained.

Remy stopped and gently removed his backpack, then dismantled the other packs and saddle from Diesel and set them on the ground. He whipped out the locator device from his backpack.

"Oh, you don't have to tell us. And a Chinook is a helicopter, not a plane."

Diesel nudged Remy.

The general ogled the lake, a few yards below them, the sparkling waterfall. Refreshing thought. The temperature was in the high eighties, but at this point it seared like a hundred. Exhausted, in pain, and thirsty, Remy decided Ava could hang a little longer.

"I think Diesel's tail was singed." Remy knew they needed water. "Okay, boy," he said, sidestepping toward the water, past the trees where Ava still dangled.

"Excuse me? Me, Ava, tree removal?" she yelled at them. "Where are you going? Excuse me!"

Remy said nothing, just continued trekking to the water with Diesel. She could swing in that tree for some time as far as he was concerned. She'd landed herself in this mess for her own selfish reasons. At least Remy knew where she would be, safely in the tree, out of trouble. Plus, he wasn't quite sure how he would manage to cut her down.

"You always unearth trouble, Mrs. Kennedy," he bounced back as they neared the water. "God forbid you ever find a way out of trouble yourself."

"Hey, get me down," she ordered, seesawing her legs.

"I saved your life and I believe Diesel did too. So give us a break."

When the two reached the shores of the lake, Remy thought the best way to clean Diesel's wound would be to wade him in, then let him stand and soak in the cool late summer water to rinse off and drink his fill.

Remy opened his shirt and laid it on the shore. He untethered the makeshift bandage Ava had created earlier and examined his side. Luckily, a flesh wound. He cupped some water in his hands and let it ooze across the wound, wincing some. Evening was approaching and he still needed to retrieve the other parachutes—his guarantee—and return to Ava. This would be a good spot to camp for the night because all three needed rest.

His body thumped in pain. None of this was new to him, as he had been in remote and desolate places many times. But he'd never had a Private M to worry about before.

Ava had been swaying her legs, higher than a ride at an amusement park and sounding off cries. But when Remy turned he noticed she was now quietly dangling, observing him as he dripped water over Diesel's leg and buttoned his shirt back up.

"Mrs. Kennedy, I will release these straps under one condition. You simmer down. Well, there will be two conditions."

He trudged back up the terrain after letting Diesel cool down. He waited, eyeing her.

"What?" she snapped.

"Do you promise to do whatever I ask from here on in?"

"Whatever."

"Okay, I'll cut you down as soon as we pick up the other parachuted pack with the MREs. Be patient. We shall return. Maybe you can think about your actions. And we will be camping here for the night."

"Mimosa! What if someone kidnaps me?"

"Kidnap you? Here in God knows where? They would most likely run the other way."

"Mimosa, come back here! That's an order!"

"Remember, Ava. You are only a Private. I'm a General. Oh and there's a third condition… no more Mimosa. My name is *Minosa*. General Remy Minosa."

CHAPTER 19

Ava ranted as Remy and Diesel left. "I'll call you Mimosa if I want to," she hollered at his back as he disappeared through the thick forest.

She couldn't believe he'd actually left her. Hanging from the trees. She even thought she could hear him whistling as he and Diesel weaved a path into the mountain terrain. She thought about the last three months. She had gathered herself up and moved in two weeks, opened a new barbershop, led a yoga class, made new friends, flew in a Chinook, and parachuted out—maybe not by choice, but she was counting it as an accomplishment. Maybe the time had come to free herself... and not just from a tree.

Ava studied the situation. Her body was suddenly electrified, bound and determined to untether itself. If she could swing enough, maybe she could reach the branch in front of her and shake hard enough to break the limb which held her prisoner.

Her entire body screamed for a warm shower and a shampoo. Come to think of it, a massage, a manicure... a pedicure. *How about I just aim for a dip in the lake?*

She lunged into a swing, higher and higher with her strong yoga legs, until it was like that ride at Dempsey's Park that Rhya was always trying to make her go on. How Ava missed those days. She swung higher, stretching to the next branch, wrapping her legs, and then she heard the limb above her crack.

"I did it!" She smiled.

The branch cracked again.

"Oh no!" Ava let go of the other limb, her body bouncing off the tree until she landed on a soft cushion of mud from a previous rainfall. She crashed to the ground, tented and wrapped in a twisted mess of parachute, "Ugh!" Every muscle wept in pain, but at least she was breathing and touching the earth. She'd never been so elated to fall in her life.

Ava struggled, puffed, and moaned. The heavy weight of the parachute billowed around her body, entangling her in a mess. Finally she discovered a pocket of fresh air, and her head and shoulders popped out. She gathered up the parachute as best she could. The canvas would make a great tent if they had to sleep here. Once free and organized, she retrieved a cup from Remy's pack and raced to the water as best she could still wearing her heels. They were strapped so tight, and she was a proficient runner. They of course were not the best shoes to have in the forest, but at least they were shoes.

She started dipping and refilling the cup, gulping down the fresh water. Then she went back to her landing spot. "He says I never save the day. He'll see. I'll prepare camp. When Rhya was in JROTC I followed her everywhere as a chaperone."

The backpack had all the tools she needed. Ava toiled extensively. She found a knife, cutting the parachute and peaking it on an angle between two trees. The remainder she laid on the ground as bedding. She then gathered sticks for a fire and found an igniter in the pack as well. The sun would be going down soon, and she wondered if Remy and Diesel were okay. What if she had to spend the night alone?

She found the pistol stuffed in the pack. But it wasn't until she found the bar of soap that she decided to head back to the alluring lake to rinse off the dirt, sweat and blood. After a bath she could start a fire and maybe find something other than cocaine MREs to eat.

Ava reflected on the rocky edge at the waterfall. The moist pine aroma filled her senses while the echo of the roaring water called, inviting her aching body to savor in a refreshing dip. The temperature was still very warm, and her skin was smeared in sweat and dirt. The only way to properly clean her wounds was to strip, and succumb to temptation.

She scanned the surroundings. Remy had said they landed in a remote area. If someone was returning or lurking, they would have an eye full. Even so, she had a beautiful body for forty. She could run fast and she'd just been through hell—worth the risk.

Remy was headed back toward Ava, exhausted. Surprised he hadn't heard Ava's screams yet, he grew concerned and stepped up the pace with his last morsels of energy. He felt both thankful and guilty as Diesel's head drooped by his side, limping back together. Diesel had given more than he ever expected.

When Remy crested the ridge, he eyed the parachute first, tented over the trees, the rest made into bedding. The makeshift fire and two logs set like a campsite...

He freed Diesel, tying him loosely to the parachute cord, even though the horse clearly had no intention of leaving. Diesel began to nibble contentedly on the foliage around him.

Remy examined the tree, Ava nowhere to be seen. She freed herself? *She did it!* Remy perked up when he heard sweet humming and followed the alluring sound. He cleared a passage through the wild laurel, vines and thistle, eventually reaching a stained, ripped satin skirt and the one-strap little top marked with droplets of blood splayed out on a boulder to dry. The pistol, from the Chinook, lay at his foot. At the sound of light splashing, he peered through the thicket, seeing Ava bathing in the lake.

His heart fluttered, spying her sculpted body, firm but bruised. His desire to go to her masked any pain or exhaustion. Instead Remy swelled with an overwhelming urge to blanket her body in safety. He was mesmerized as she dipped her head back in slow motion, submerging into the water directly under the cooling waterfall where she had found a clear wading cavity. The streams of drenching water cascaded over her topless body as she rose like a flower searching for the sun.

Ava's bare back was exposed, sculpted in thin muscles to the tip of her rump that creased at the edge of the water. Unexpectedly, she turned her upper body, glistening in wetness down her abdomen, below her navel, until the water crested, rising and falling in a gentle wave as she walked. She inched toward him, emerging from the water and ringing her hair, dressed only in a pink thong.

Remy became immobilized, examining her tiny but well-defined body. His eyes locked on a motorcycle tattoo on her upper inner thigh until he was awakened by how close she had come. Quickly he buried himself amidst the bushes to return to Diesel.

Remy rushed back to her makeshift camp, lit the fire she had prepared, and rustled through the pack for food. He discovered two bars and a bag of trail mix. God knew the MREs were not edible—they were at the heart of this entire mission. Ava had accidentally discovered the underlying reason for the covert investigation. MRE containers stuffed with drugs. Now he only needed to determine *who* and *why*. No doubt, the *who* would be on their trail in no time. A lot of money had just exploded in the gorge. And it wasn't just the Chinook.

Remy observed the area Ava had prepared. He laid the bars on large leaves like he was setting a table for a family meal. Something deep in his heart longed for a family, but he managed to block it—Sunday suppers after church, baseball games with the grandkids. He chanted his new mantra. *"It's all about the mission. Get her out of your head."*

Ava froze. Leaves and branches rustled on the edge of the lake where she had left her clothing and laid the pistol. She slowly turned and dipped her body down into the refreshing water. Ava peeked out with just her eyes, ready to dive and disappear under the water if threatened. She was a good swimmer as well as a runner.

She waited a few minutes until she was positive it was just a bird or bunny hopping through the woods. Then Ava rose from the water. The sun would soon be headed down, and she prayed Remy would return. Concerned and shivering as she dressed back into her skimpy skirt and torn top, Ava didn't even have a sweater. The forest would surely drop in temperature quickly at night even though it was late August.

Her tiny frame hiked back to the makeshift camp, thankful to be clean, even though she was sore and bruised. She was alive. Ava scrunched the wetness from her hair, draping it over her strapless shoulder to the one side. Wet blonde wavy locks tingled her skin as she walked up the hill through the bushes, sending goosebumps up her arms. The water had soothed her body, but now she was feeling the evening chill.

As she crested to the campsite, Ava was ecstatic to see Diesel and sped up, ignoring briars scratching her calves. The horse's head was down munching on foliage.

When she whispered, "Diesel!" he raised his head and neighed. Ava wrapped her arms cautiously around his sleek muscular neck, slipping her hands away when she sensed a presence. She pressed her cheek against Diesel and turned to find Remy.

Ava became overwhelmed with the desire to run into his arms, to tell him how elated she was to see him, and how she savored the kiss he delivered before throwing her off the Chinook. But she knew he'd only tried to swoon her in order to catch her off-guard so he could toss her out of the helicopter. Neither stepped closer.

He was the first to speak. "I'm surprised you were able to free yourself."

Ava said nothing.

"I found some trail mix and bars," he said. "If you're hungry?"

Ava nodded and followed him to sit next to the warm fire which now crackled, puffing tiny cinders into the air. They sat beside each other on the edge of the bedding. She shivered, the evening air continuing to drop in temperature.

"You lied to me." Ava shivered again, this time from his closeness.

"It had to be that way. You weren't supposed to be involved. This isn't a joke." Remy rose and combed through the pack. He brought a thin blanket and the first-aid kit. "I did try to apologize with a kiss and save your life." Remy lightened up as he wrapped her shoulders in a blanket, then began to remove his shirt, to try to change the dressing.

"Is that what you call it?" Ava asked squarely as she watched. The sun was almost gone, and the chill moved even quicker into the campsite.

"What do you call it?"

"A typical man and a brush with death."

He exhaled quickly with a smile, but winced when he touched his side.

Ava let the blanket fall and touched his hand to release the gauze. Their eyes met and he obeyed.

This time Ava nursed with a gentleness in her touch. Remy went silent, just looking into the darkness as she finished wrapping his bruised side.

"It really should be looked at by a doctor," she said. "The wound is tender and looks bad."

"No doctor here," he joked.

Ava couldn't smile, she was so scared.

"You found the MREs," he said. "They're at the bottom of this. We can rest here tonight, but we'll have to move tomorrow. Appears the Chinook was headed to a drop-off location somewhere near this coordinate."

"Who's involved in this?"

Remy seemed reluctant to continue. "At the college, I'm not positive who all is involved. That's why I needed a cadet's help. Two, in fact... One in the equestrian area, because that is the front— selling military equestrian equipment, which is already illegal." Remy was shuffling to find his sleeve.

Ava touched his arm and directed him. "I hope the other cadet was Blade?"

Remy nodded.

"I saw him with Batman the night I left your house. They were in the white van... the one from the military surplus store owned by Shane Blevins."

"Yes," Remy said. "The same Shane who owns the school, which is about to file bankruptcy."

Ava thought then spoke. "Shane Blevins would have a motive. Do you think Batman knows what's really in the MREs?"

"I can't be sure about Batman's involvement. He might just be a scapegoat. But I'm positive Pam is involved. I think she might even be in a relationship with Shane."

"You know..." Ava knelt in front of him like he was her child, unaware she was even caring for him in such a manner. "I noticed that a while back when I went down to give Pam the shampoo for her and the horses. Shane was in her office, alone with her, and I felt... awkward."

"The fruity stuff?"

Ava tilted her head when he smiled, and suddenly realized she was buttoning his shirt for him. *That's why he was smiling?* She ceased and awkwardly turned to sit down on the bedding.

"It's okay," he said, seemingly recognizing she was blushing.

"You mean the shampoo."

"Yes, Diesel still smells like a strawberry." Remy stood, then stoked and fed the fire a good serving of sticks and leaves, finishing with two more logs until the flames were bursting with warmth.

"Someone will be looking for the drugs, eh?" Ava asked.

Remy continued stoking and merely nodded. He seemed reluctant to answer.

"Then we have to get out of here. Get help. Let someone..." Ava leaped up on a mission to leave, rolling up items to stuff in the backpack. She was in such a panic she never realized Remy had moved closer.

"Ava," he said, brushing her shoulder. He confiscated the blanket from her and snuggled it once again around her shoulders. His shirt dangled, still partially open to reveal his sculpted abdomen. "You have to rest. I have to rest. Diesel has to rest. We'll head out in the morning. The terrain is rugged. The people that will be after us hopefully will find it difficult moving in the dark."

His hands remained at her neck, tightening the blanket to keep her warm. Her own hands somehow inched forward, found his waist, and fingered the rim of his jeans.

Remy sighed and his hands scaled her neck to her chin. He hesitated and leaned down. His thumb dusted across her cheek, sending vibrations through her body that he had awoken since they met. His lips brushed hers, lingering only for a brief moment.

She sensed he desired more, but he simply pressed her head against his chest, embracing her in both arms.

"Ava, it will be okay. Come, we need to rest." He encased her hand and led her under the parachute that canopied the trees, resting on the tarp. They both fell back, their heads facing the open edge and the stars.

Ava admired them. "They are so beautiful... the night sky."

"They certainly are."

"If only the situation was different."

"Another time maybe," Remy answered.

Ava laid motionless, unable to relax, almost imagining the touch of his hand even though he was inches away.

The moment was broken by a scream—like a cat on fire.

Ava rolled toward Remy. "What was that?" She shimmied closer still.

"That would be a fox."

A low hooting followed.

"And what was that?"

"That... that's an owl."

She rolled over onto her belly and inched closer, so close she could feel a slight touch of his hand and shoulder. Suddenly, a low yelping and harmonious howl drove her to a breaking point. Ava didn't even have to ask.

"And that... that would be the big... ferocious... evil... bad... wolf." He demonstrated a clawing at her. "You better move closer. You only have a mere quarter-inch to go," he teased. "I'm not going to bite." Remy patted the earth, urging her to move nearer. "Ava, nothing will happen to you on my watch. You are safe with me tonight." Ava gazed over at him. "I'm a good pillow," he added.

Convinced, she shimmied across with a slight smile and slipped in under his strong bicep. She rested her head on his chest and covered both of them with the blanket. The sound of his beating heart rocked her to sleep, but it was his hand rubbing her bare arm that sweetened her dreams.

CHAPTER 20

A symphony of chirping birds awoke Ava at the first slice of light. She searched for the shoulder that had pillowed her safely. But Remy was gone. She could hear his familiar voice talking to Diesel and looked out over the campsite to locate him. Ava was shocked she'd slept so soundly and never heard him rise. She hadn't slept in days. Taking a few deep breaths, she tried to sit up but a tsunami of pain rushed her sore muscles.

After hesitating a few minutes more, she ruffled her hair and crawled out from under the tent. Cautiously she stretched, a few yoga maneuvers, eyeing her work—the makeshift tent, the fire pit that was nothing but sparking ashes. She wanted to pat her own back, proud of herself.

"I'm like a real Private in the Army," she whispered, admiring her toil, hands on her hips.

"Okay, Private. I have a job for you."

Remy's commanding voice caused her to jump. A heat surged her cheeks. "Yes, sir."

Remy grinned. 'Take these containers and fill them with water."

"Aye, aye, sir." Ava slipped her heels on with an ouch.

"That's the Navy, Ava. We're in the Army."

"Yes, sir." Ava saluted and took the jugs, whining as she walked, her shoes rubbing the raw blisters. "I mean General."

"Are those the only kind of shoes you ever wear?"

She smiled. "Let me go look in my closet and I'll be right back." She raised a jug in the air and trekked away, realizing he was ogling her rump in that little satin skirt.

Actually her feet were really starting to hurt like hell, but she wasn't going to let him know. When she reached the lake she scanned the beauty. The waterfall, the morning sun shimmering across, and the birds resting on the lake. She bent over at the water and filled the jug when she heard a similar rustling to what had scared her the evening before.

"Oh, little bunny. I'm not afraid of you," Ava spoke to a line of bittersweet entangled in a thicket of laurel. "I'm a Private in the Army."

A click sounded in her ear at the back of her head, and she swung around, never expecting the barrel of a semi-automatic to be planted at her face.

"Get up!" a man with an accent ordered her.

Ava was too sore and scared to rise quickly, but he wasn't willing to wait.

"Get up, I said." He grabbed her, and she wobbled to stand with a moan.

"Ouch, please..."

Another man was firmly stationed to her right off the shoreline. Both were armed with automatics and packing a pistol at their waist. Ava stared down the metal barrel, again paralyzed.

The first man nabbed her hair, motioning his gun in the direction of the campsite. Ava trudged along slowly, with him prodding her in the back in a two-count beat. She needed to create a scene in order to warn Remy.

"Do you really have to be so mean? Stop poking me," she complained loudly. She turned and stared at the man pointing the gun at her.

He had just popped up his ball cap to wipe the sweat from his brow. Ava wrinkled her crooked nose, taking notice of the man's thick hair that waved out from underneath in a long pompadour. The color demanded her attention and a double take—haircolor was her specialty. This man's hair was the shade of freshly picked navel oranges or carrots at the open market on Saturday mornings. Which might have looked okay on a younger person, but she saw the hair against his dark skin, along with his black eyebrows.

Clearly he was orange as the result of a professional dye job gone awry… or a nonprofessional kitchen attempt.

Ava scanned the other man. He too sported a ball cap. He was seemingly quieter and nervous when Ava examined his hair. Once he cleared his throat, he remarked in a low tone, "Looks bad, don't it?" He curved a frown.

Ava nodded in shock.

"Jimmy, get over it," the other man said. "It's the in thing. B.C.'s daughter says so."

"Alright, Bossman," he responded.

Ava glared back at the embarrassed man named Jimmy. "No, it's not," she said softly as he seemed to bow modestly away from her. "Orange hair is not in style."

The thug called Bossman tried to swing the gun at her, but she quickly blurted, "Why is your hair that color?"

He ceased, gritted his teeth, and raised the gun higher to swat her.

"Okay, I'm going, I'm going." Ava pivoted and headed up the incline singing the only camp song she knew. "Kumbaya, my Lord. Kumbaya." She hoped Remy would receive her Army code for help.

"Hey, I know that song," Jimmy interjected and started singing along.

The more the merrier… and the louder.

"Knock it off," the Bossman ordered.

Jimmy reluctantly ceased and eyed Ava. "I liked that song. My mother used to hum it when she put me to sleep." He mumbled the hymn quietly in defiance as they continued.

The man behind Ava again nudged her forward with the tip of his gun on her bare skin in rapid two-beat taps. She was about finished with the brutality she had experienced the last two days. She belted the words to Kumbaya louder.

Remy was bent over packing the sacks to saddle on Diesel. He turned around when he heard Ava enter the clearing. Unfortunately, the gunman angled the weapon in his direction.

Remy's smile deadened as if stung with a taser. He slowly raised his arms in the air and shot a disapproving look at Ava. "You always manage to find trouble."

"I did not find trouble. They found me," she defended.

"Check out those MREs," Bossman commanded Jimmy.

"I tried to warn you," Ava cocked a hand on her hip as she grunted to Remy.

"Next time, try something a little more foreboding than a Girl Scout church tune."

Jimmy sliced open a meal replacement bag. "This is it, boss."

"Where's the rest?" the man in charge confronted Remy and Ava.

When Remy refused to answer, Bossman stabbed the rifle into his wounded side. Remy crashed to his knees with a gasp.

Ava fell to the ground next to him. "Stop. This man needs help," Ava cried. "We haven't done anything to you."

The man ignored her. "Let's finish packing this up. Use the horse," he pointed to Diesel.

"B.C. isn't going to be too happy. Nope, not happy at all." Jimmy was shaking his head, mumbling.

"Be careful with the horse," Remy cautioned. "He has an injured back fetlock."

Ava held the inside of Remy's shoulder, aiding him to rise.

Bossman ignored Remy and threw more on Diesel's back. Then they strapped packs to both Remy and her.

"You in the front," he pointed to Jimmy. "The woman follows you." He pointed his rifle back to Remy. "I'll hang next to you. And no funny business." Bossman passed the reins to Remy.

The four weaved in and out between clusters of different foliage and thickets beneath an aged forest of trees. Ava's legs and arms were defenseless against the slapping branches and stabbing thorns of wild berries and brush. She had not recovered at all from her soreness and could only imagine how Remy must be feeling in this daunting trek. She checked on him frequently, that is when her captor wasn't egging her forward with a shove.

They wrestled the wilderness for over two hours. Ava's feet paying the price for sexy shoes, the blisters on her heels now raw. "Can we please stop? The horse needs water, and my feet are killing me."

"She's right, boss."

Jimmy removed his cap to wipe his head with his wrist. He realized Ava was gawking and slipped the hat back on. The sun was rising in the sky, and although the trees offered shade, the temperature was also heating up.

Bossman was reluctant, but clearly by the sweat dripping at his temples he could use a break too. "Just a minute, then back at it. We only have an hour or so to go." He pointed to a log for Ava to sit. He placed Remy several feet away.

"Who's B.C.?" Remy inquired. "And where are we headed?"

Bossman threw him a canteen. Remy cupped his hand and poured some for Diesel first, letting a bit trickle down his muzzle, then bending to the injured leg.

"This animal needs rest," Remy said. "He isn't going to go far."

"Well, if that's the case, who needs him? We'll just put him out of his misery," Bossman scoffed.

Ava gasped and watched the fire rise in Remy's eyes. Ava almost back-talked, but something led Jimmy to touch her arm. He leaned into Ava and handed her his own canteen after opening it. He seemed to be smitten with Ava, and she was going to use his attraction to her advantage.

"B.C. is short for Big Cheese," he whispered. "No worries. We'll be there soon. Bossman just has a bad temper."

Ava slurped water, letting it drip down her neck on purpose, realizing he was ogling. "Maybe Bossman is agitated by his hair and appearance," Ava snarked. "What's up with your hair?"

"Sore subject. B.C.'s daughter is a beauty school drop-out. Well, you know. With the situation, she has to stay underground. It's too dangerous to be out in public. Especially if your friend doesn't produce the rest of the goods."

Ava clenched her teeth and shrugged. She noticed Remy was listening. "Oops, that might be an issue." She tilted her ear into Jimmy, letting her hair dangle on his shoulder.

"We're all guinea pigs," Jimmy grunted. "Not by choice. The daughter wants to be like some famous hairdresser. B.C. has his hands full with that chick. But it's his own fault. He lets her do anything. Spoiled bitch makes us all look like freaks."

The arduous journey continued. The only sound was the crushing of leaves and cracking limbs as Ava's new friend hummed Kumbaya. Soon after they had rebooted with water, Remy broke the silence as if fueled with a burst of adrenaline.

"Kennedy, what exactly did your husband die from? Death by nagging? Or your clinging like you do to your daughter?" Ava's heart sank to her blistering feet, as he added, "Or was it death by a helicoptering wife that made him crash his Humvee?"

Why did he always evoke this conversation? Make such accusations? Ava burned.

"And those shoes, waddling around in those heels. Get a life."

Jimmy hollered back, "Knock it off, I think she's nice!"

Ava thanked Jimmy in silence.

"I have survived the nastiest corners of the world, faced the vilest evil bastards, yet this Mrs. Kennedy puts me over the edge. I can only imagine what she did to her husband."

Ava's eyes began to swell with tears. She was sore, tired, hungry, scared and filling with rage. What was he doing? She turned back to flash Remy an eye of disgust, but he only continued.

"She has a weapon, you know," he said, meeting her stare. "She managed to win the war with me, I'll give her that. I surrendered last night. Almost had my heart. To think I was about to lay one on her."

Ava's anger boiled. "Lay one on me? Are you a lunatic? You... you... self-centered, cold bastard. No wonder no one ever loved you. No wonder *Jeanie* is out there and doesn't care what happens to you. You are a nasty, ignorant man, and someday you will die a lonely death. I feel sorry for your tiny little soul that has melted away! No... it's withered." Ava made her index finger mirror the idea of dying away.

"Are you suggesting I have an issue?" Remy inquired. "You're probably withered yourself after twelve years."

Ava fumed, clenched her fist, and met Remy's gaze. He winked. "You and those stupid shoes. You use them like a weapon when you walk in that little skirt, swaying, teasing." Remy winked again and angled his head, lifting a brow.

Ava swiftly understood the code. "My feet hurt so bad," she said. She raised her arms in the air as if nonchalantly stretching, then bent to remove a shoe. "I'll just walk barefoot. I can't continue in these."

"See." Remy made eye contact with Bossman again as if chumming. "What a flake."

Jimmy grinned and spun her around. Even if it was accidental, Ava had her heel pointed in the direction of his face. It poked him right in the eye like Joan of Arc was by her side.

Remy swiveled and walloped the other man who flew back. He stole Bossman's weapons and searched his pockets for a phone.

Ava followed suit. "Sorry, friend," she kept apologizing to Jimmy.

Remy tied them both together, dragging them at a cumbersome walk, tethered just far enough behind Diesel so they would maintain best behavior.

"Take us to this B.C.'s fortress, or Diesel will take matters into his own... um... well... you'll find out."

CHAPTER 21

Remy handed Ava the reins and pointed the rifle at the two men. He had tried their phones repeatedly, but there was absolutely no reception in the forest.

Diesel's head was low at her knee. He needed another good day's rest, a check on the leg, some fresh grass and water.

Before they peaked the next ridge, Ava ceased the lead and sucked in a deep inhale. "I'm not sure I can keep going."

Remy neared her. Neither had talked much since they tied up the idiots. "Ava, you've come this far. When there's no way out the backdoor, you have to forge forward."

Ava thought about his remark, remembering when Rhya was small and they were headed into a haunted house on a boardwalk ride. Rhya became frightened and cried to go back. Ava had coached her, *"In order to go out you have to go through. Forge ahead."* Funny thing, she hadn't thought much about Rhya lately, just her own survival.

Reaching the pinnacle, Jimmy spanned his arms out and hollered, "Behold, the estate below!"

The panoramic view snatched Ava's breath. The scene below clearly was not just a working estate but a mini fortress with cattle and sheep on grasslands to the west. Orchards, grapevines and gardens rimmed the east side. The stone mansion and numerous buildings sprawled out in multiple levels, with bell towers and turrets. The enormous barn and riding ring were around the back, just below an Olympic-sized swimming pool. Even a lake next to a skateboarding ramp were contained behind iron gates and stone walls too numerous to count.

As they neared, she recognized the white stone statues because of her Catholic upbringing. "St. Francis, the Blessed Mother Mary, Roman knights, even Joan of Arc..." Ava was positive she was in Italian territory. Her crooked nose would fit right in. "It's breathtaking."

"Sure is," her tied up friend agreed. "Thousands and thousands of acres in the middle of nowhere. Just an airstrip to come and go. But once you're here... you don't come and go."

"What's the plan?" Ava asked Remy. "Leave them here at the gate and scram? Maybe we can trade them or the drugged up MREs for a ride."

"Lady, what you are is plain stupid," Bossman cursed. "You ain't getting no ride out of here. You might as well do yourself in before you get any closer."

Remy scanned the horizon, studying the airstrip, making mental calculations perhaps. He loosened his pack and said, "We're going in."

"What?" Ava jumped.

Remy started down the hill, and Diesel was already whinnying, seeming to sense the horses on the hill had been alerted to strangers. They were dancing across the lush green pasture, stirred by their presence.

The four and Diesel reached the twelve-foot iron gates locking together a massive stone wall that surrounded the estate. All the way down, Ava had tried to talk some sense into Remy. "Did you hear what that guy said? We might as well take the gas pipe instead of entering this fortress." A few minutes later she said, "This is a terrible plan. It's worse than pushing me out of the Chinook. Don't you know, we're waltzing right into a death trap?"

"Ava," he calmly stated. "I remind you, you survived."

Remy untied Jimmy's hand. "Ring the buzzer," he commanded.

"What are you doing?" Ava tried to assert. Remy ignored her.

"Tell them to let you in and that you've brought company." Jimmy hadn't even touched the buzzer when an alarm sounded, and Jeeps and Hummers carrying men with machine guns zoomed in from all directions. They were instantly surrounded.

"Look what you've done, so dang stupid!" B.C.'s army—Ava was sure.

Immediately a voice began ranting and raving through the gate intercom to Bossman who was now freed and had shoved Jimmy aside.

Remy dropped his sack and coaxed Ava to do the same. "Arms up, Mrs. Kennedy. This part isn't going to be a welcome committee at one of your reunions. More like special forces at a desert raid."

Once again guns were poking and prodding them. Quickly they were forced forward and thrown in the back of a vehicle. Someone took Diesel's reins, and she heard Remy quietly say, "Please go easy, he's hurt."

Ava's own body was so beaten and tired she just obeyed the commands given as they drove up the long concrete-stamped driveway to a fortress of stone and cedar. Wood shutters and iron rods were on every window. "What is this place?" Ava whispered to herself.

They drove around the back. A massive garage door opened and the Hummer entered into darkness. She could feel them driving deep into the earth led only by headlights until, as if someone tripped a switch. Suddenly, bright lights—as if on a Friday night football field—lit up. Ava could hardly see without her sunglasses. They were definitely inside a bunker, as the smell of concrete and damp earth hit her when the car door opened.

Several men shoved her into an elevator where they pushed "G." Ava was alone with Bossman and three other men. Smashed in a small elevator, her tiny body cried in pain. She began to teeter, as a nauseous feeling swirled in her gut. Her face felt flush and she weakened.

"I'm going to be sick!"

The four men moaned. Thankfully the doors opened, and none prevented her escape as she clenched her waist. Ava found herself in the middle of what appeared to be a game room and workout area. She strengthened her body and already felt better when a cooler air rushed her. One of the men scooped her up by the elbow.

Two massive bodybuilders stopped lifting weights and gathered around the plush sofa where Ava was tossed. She felt the cold cherry leather and gold inflated buttons against her thighs. Her satin skirt made it hard to keep from slipping off.

The elevator closed and reopened a few minutes later. She was never so glad to see Remy. He didn't look good at all. The gash on his forehead had reopened, and his body appeared drained.

Ava rose but someone from behind reached onto her shoulder and weighted her down. Jimmy followed Remy, obviously embarrassed and pissed. He shoved Remy to another chair facing Ava. The general glanced at her, saying nothing.

The elevator opened for a third time, and a short robust man was ushered out. He wore a pinstripe suit and gold pinky rings. Oddly he also sported a straw hat that was no style match with his formal suit. Clearly Italian, she noted his tanned skin and bushy black eyebrows with some wiry grey pinnacling out. An entourage surrounded him, and that's when Ava observed the odd commonality. All the staff had one trait in common—the same orange hair. Boy, someone definitely was a beauty school wannabe.

"You are bleeding on my floor," the man said to Remy. "*Tsk, tsk.*"

Remy said nothing.

"Where are my drugs? And might I add, the incorrect answer would be in the helicopter that crashed in the gorge."

"Then I failed the test," Remy answered bluntly.

One of straw hat's lackies made a motion to hit Remy. "Now, now. We don't need to be so aggressive yet. There is time for that. They call me B.C.," he said. "But do you know who I am? My real name is Ferdinand Garbozzo."

Ava gasped. "Garbozzo? You can't be? A member of the Regina and Ferdinand Garbozzo's clan? Impossible!"

Ferdinand pivoted toward Ava, his cheeks round and blushed. "You are spicy." His belly inflated like a beach ball. "Stand up," he commanded Ava. He touched a lock of her hair. "What is your name?"

"Ava Garbozzo Kennedy."

"Garbozzo, eh? You have such beautiful blonde hair. Ava Garbozzo." He shook his head. "The Garbozzos from Sicily are known for their hair, their beautiful... ebony hair?" He muttered the last part almost inaudibly.

"Well, my mother's grandmother's father's father," Ava shrugged as her voice weakened.

B.C. was trying to do the math with his fingers in the air.

Ava started to twitch, her feet throbbing and stomach whirling. "Can I please sit? My feet are so sore, and I don't feel well."

B.C. was still trying to calculate the generations, ignoring her. Ava held her stomach while glancing down at the coffee table planning how she would pass out without hitting her head on anything. That's when she spied the magazine resting next to an old-fashioned crystal ashtray. "Hey, you have *Hair Bloom*."

Garbozzo squeezed his bushy eyebrows together as if answering, and Ava read his mind, *Yeah right, lady. Tell me something else I might believe.*

"That's me! Ava Kennedy."

All eyes in the room fixed on Ava. She pointed to the magazine. "May I?"

Remy rolled his eyes. "Ava, stop. It's not..." But Jimmy bumped his head with a fist.

"Stop hurting him," Ava pleaded. "Please stop beating on him. How much can his body take?"

Garbozzo raised his closed fist, except for the little pinky sticking up in the air. Briefly, he stared speechless as if her message was cryptic. Suddenly, he delegated, "Go find my Gina." Bossman nodded, throwing Remy an evil look before he left the room.

Then B.C. studied Ava. "Your blonde hair, it is lovely. But if you were a Garbozzo, it would be dark."

Ava arched her back to build courage. She noticed a slice of brassy hair peeking out from under his hat. "I would be, but thanks goodness for bleach upgrades in the twenty-first century. If I might say, sir," Ava wished she would have swallowed the words with her big gulp, but it was too late so she continued. "You are not really dark either." She muttered. "Really not sure what shade you might be, but not dark, for sure."

"More like a ripened cantaloupe," one of the bodyguards blurted out.

Garbozzo snapped a head toward the men in the back, taking a moment to glare. He turned back to examine the magazine. "Ava Kennedy, indeed you have the same crooked nose. You sit. Maybe kneel. Pray this is true." He hinged his oversized belly to face Remy and waddled toward him like a penguin. "Let me deal with you first. I want my drugs. The small amount you returned to me, they are nothing. I have a lot of people waiting."

"Well, I guess you have a problem. You'll have to reach out to whoever was responsible for the drop-off. They might have messed up, and I had nothing to do with that. In fact, I saved the merchandise I could. And even brought it here."

The man rubbed his chin and placed his hand in his vest like Napoleon. "Ahh, a martyr. What will I do with you, because I am very pissed off?" He tilted his hat back and the same orange hair peeked out.

One of his entourage snickered.

"Pipe down, it's not that bad. I am tired of the comments," Garbozzo hollered. "Next man that makes a remark is going to be shot."

"I can fix that." Ava spit out the words so quick she could have slapped herself silly.

Remy blinked again. "Ava, this is not the time."

Garbozzo pivoted to her rather quickly for his size. "It's bad. I get no respect around here. All my daughter ever wanted to be was this woman from the magazine. And you say you are her... and three times removed from the Garbozzos of my homeland? If my daughter agrees, I can't kill you."

"Kill?" Ava questioned horrified. "Why kill anyone?"

Jimmy leaned over in the direction of the leather couch and mumbled, "Bossman told you no one ever leaves this fortress."

A bell rang, letting the room of people know the elevator was about to besiege them. Clearly the Big Cheese wanted Remy out of sight from whoever was coming. He snapped his fingers, and two men grabbed Remy's arms and hauled him through double doors next to an elaborate wooden bar.

A pain shot through Ava's gut. She wanted to call out his name, order them to stop.

"This elevator will be bringing my daughter, Miss Ava... if that is who you are. I allow Gina to practice and practice on anyone's hair... as you can probably tell. However..." He shuffled to the bar in heavy breaths and poured a glass of red wine. "...she does not improve. She begged to attend a beauty school in New York City, but it was too dangerous for her with my, let's say, job title. Now, she locks herself in her room crying, so I allow her to practice on every head on this estate, but she still hates me." He was panting now, trouble catching his air, clearly out of shape.

"You don't have to tell me about your daughter's practicing. I see someone is..." Ava said in a low voice.

The elevator opened, and he scurried to the door like a king greeting his queen. But the twenty-year-old dismissed him and brushed right by his arms. Gina was short and robust like her father, with the same thick wavy, pumpkin hair.

"Gina..." Garbozzo chased after his daughter. "This is Ava Kennedy." He waited then added, "From *Hair Bloom*?" He left his remark standing as a question.

Gina froze, studying Ava.

"That's me," Ava cued shyly toward the magazine. She realized she looked like heck, probably unrecognizable.

"Hold this up." The girl had Ava hold the magazine next to her face. A silent anticipation filled the room, waiting for the princess to comment.

Gina clapped her hands immediately. The entire army of Garbozzo's men seemed to inhale. "It's her! Daddy, it's her."

"Yes, yes?" He savored her joy.

"What happened to you? You look awful. How did you get here?" Gina touched Ava's arm. "Daddy?" Gina slapped her sides. Everyone was searching for a response to Gina's questions.

Ava ransacked her mind for a remedy. If her captor had been right, Garbozzo's daughter meant everything to him, and he would do anything for her to reciprocate. *Boom*, Ava had a way to get them home. Now to figure out how to execute.

"Why, your dad-dy..." Ava enunciated the word slowly. "Your dad-dy brought me here and... and..." Ava searched her brain. "And..."

"And her plane went down," Garbozzo added, and they both nodded in collaboration followed by the orange-headed army.

"Went down? Oh my gosh!" Gina shrieked. "No wonder you look like death."

Ava raised an eyebrow. "Yes, that's it, the plane went down, crash, boom..." Ava demonstrated a plane in the sky with her hand crashing to the ground. "I jumped..."

"You jumped? Daddy, was that the big boom earlier?"

Garbozzo could only nod. Apparently, he was stunned he'd actually made Gina happy and clearly wanted more than anything to keep the momentum going.

"I had a parachute, of course," Ava quietly added.

"You did? Daddy won't let me do that either." Gina locked evil-eyes on her father. "Daddy, she parachutes. Can I keep her? I want to keep her."

"Oh, that's nothing, my friend," Ava said. "Wherever your *daddy* took him, the pilot is here on the compound too. He taught me everything I know." Ava emphasized the word daddy again.

Garbozzo choked on his wine. "Compound? This is her *home*, not a compound."

Ava looked at Gina. "You can't keep me, honey. I have my own home." She slapped Garbozzo with a flick of the eye. He seemed to enjoy her scolding.

Gina ignored her. "Can your pilot friend teach me to parachute? Daddy? Please? Where is he?" She circled the room in search of the so-called pilot.

"Probably out. He may be at the barn checking... on his horse," Ava added. *Oh, I think I have a plan!*

"I love horses, too, Ava. Daddy, please let Ava stay and teach me hairdressing, and her friend can teach me parachuting. All my dreams, Daddy. Please, pretty please?" Gina batted her almond eyes, folded her hands in prayer, happily jumping up and down.

Ava thought a twenty-something woman jumping up and down for her dad looked like a spoiled brat. *Ridiculous.* For a moment she did think of Rhya and how responsible her own daughter had grown up to be.

Garbozzo nodded. "Let's let her get cleaned up. And then... I will meet you at dinner, my dearest daughter." He pointed to Gina. The room was silent until the girl skipped over to the elevator.

When she was out of earshot, he ordered everyone to exit the game room immediately. The last bodyguard was reluctant to follow orders, but he insisted. When the room was completely empty, he plopped his round body and skinny legs next to Ava on the glistening leather sofa, and offered her a glass of wine. He breathed heavy heaves as he could hardly lean forward on his girth to set the wine glass on the table.

Ava accepted, her body crying in pain and her mind a ball of nerves. Perhaps a drink might help. "Clearly, you need me."

"I want my drugs."

"You want your daughter to be happy?"

"Of course. She lost her mother three years ago and it has been a tragedy. She's been confused ever since. Her mother loved the *Hair Bloom* magazine... wanted a daughter for a hairdresser."

Ava sighed. "I know that feeling." She slid closer, changing her demeanor. "Okay, B.C., here's the plan." Again he seemed to almost enjoy her ordering, smiling as if enchanted in being bossed by a woman.

Ava laid out her request. She would agree to educate his daughter and complete the needed color corrections to make this estate beautiful again—in exchange for her safety, along with Remy and Diesel. Both the latter needed medical attention that B.C. would supply immediately. They agreed to discuss the drug issue. If all the so-called clients were satisfied with their hair, she, Remy and Diesel would be home in twenty-four hours.

"I will need supplies," Ava said.

Garbozzo immediately picked up his cell phone. "You are using a phone? Your men had no reception in the forest." Ava instantly thought of calling for help.

"I'm calling for Jimmy. He will retrieve your supplies." He ignored the reception question.

Garbozzo handed her a pen and paper.

She listed foil, combs, shampoo, color supplies and capes. "I also need to know how many clients I will have." Ava stopped writing just as the elevator rang.

"On that thought, there is something you should know though, Mrs. Kennedy."

Ava tilted her head, confused. When the elevator doors opened, five girls from the estimated ages of about twenty to thirty-something stumbled off, all with not only orange but multi-discolored and chopped hair. Their slumped shoulders and dragging walks revealed their embarrassment.

The one that appeared to be the youngest uttered in a sudden outburst, "Sweet Kennedy lady, can you help us?"

Garbozzo rubbed Ava's thigh. She experienced a powerful rush of negative feelings from his palm planted firmly against her skin where her ruffled skirt was torn. "I have six daughters," he announced. "These are the other five."

"Really?" Ava attempted to remain cool, a light perspiration collecting on her neck. "That might up my ante, increasing my demands, and I surely will need to update my list." Ava started scratching the pen on the paper again. "I'll need one more thing."

"What is that?"

"A Jeffery."

"What's a Jeffery?" Garbozzo asked. "Some kind of tool or product?"

"My assistant. I need your phone."

Chapter 22

W hen Jeffery heard Ava's voice, he broke out bawling.

"Jeffery, calm down, please," Ava said. "I am fine, but I need your help. And by what I am looking at right this moment, it's going to be some serious revamping. I will need lots of assistance." Ava was staring at the five girls analyzing the situation with wide eyes.

Ava knew Garbozzo was monitoring their call even though he walked back to the bar, so she had to be discreet. He had agreed she had twenty-four hours to work her magic, but with twenty-plus clients, she couldn't handle that alone. At the same time he insisted she teach Gina some styling knowledge and techniques. Garbozzo promised her if she accomplished everything asked, they would talk. And Ava trusted him—it's all she had.

Her perfect plan had evolved. She even told Garbozzo about her daughter Rhya, though not that she was in the Army, but how Ava was widowed like him. He appeared to sympathize in her pain and agreed she could leave a message for her only daughter. The plan would provide Remy and Diesel time to heal for a future escape. They were getting off this compound somehow, some way.

"Ava, what... where have you been? Where the heck are you?" Jeffery cried.

"Listen, Jeffery, there is not much time to explain, a private helicopter will be coming for you early in the morning hours."

"Lord, how much time do I have to prepare?"

"Tomorrow morning first thing," she answered.

Jeffery went into an anxiety attack. Ava imagined his hand fanning himself like a hummingbird.

"The arrangements will be handled after I hang up. Can you please get a message to Rhya? Tell her I love her, and be clear when you tell her the old Garbozzo family from Italy is amazing. I met a relative on our visit here to northeast Pennsylvania." Ava was speaking very deliberately hoping Jeffery would pick up on her indiscreet coded language. "We dropped off the MREs right on the airstrip at his home and all went well and blew up to a regular family reunion. Believe that?"

Ava prayed that her hunch would be right. Jeffery would instantly involve Rhya, and hopefully repeat exactly what Ava said. As long as he could remain calm and remember the information. But Jeffrey was never very good at repeating messages, like in the game Whisper Down the Lane. Last year at her salon Christmas party, Tula refused to talk to him for a month after he repeated the words *"Tula has a big butt and slept with her neighbor in the afternoon,"* when really what was whispered was *"Tula has a big mutt and is kept with her neighbor in the afternoon."* Jeffery was only second in the line down the lane that night.

At this moment, Jeffery was an emotional wreck. She could hear his sniffling and blowing, and she imagined tissues flying all around. "Jeffery, I hope you are listening." Ava prayed when she hung up.

After the mafioso boss verified through Gina that Ava was indeed the hairdresser on the cover of *Hair Bloom* magazine, he treated her like a queen, actually toying and flirting with her. He made the remark, "You remind me so much of my deceased wife. She ordered me around... the only one that could. And I loved it."

This made Ava somewhat edgy, but Garbozzo kept his promise and led her to a luscious suite overlooking the orchards. He vowed both she and Remy would be his guests for twenty-four hours, promising to bring the man to her suite that night.

When Ava first entered the ornate room with gold and mahogany, an open veranda overlooking the valley and the oversized canopy bed, she should have felt like Cinderella. But all Ava desired was a warm shower and to fall across the king size bed... and locate Remy.

Garbozzo stated he hand-picked clothing that was arranged next to Ava's purse across the mattress. She was relieved to see all the contents of her bag intact. She touched the low-cut white silky nightshirt… a Ralph Lauren, the extra plush towels… from Neiman Marcus and champagne… decidedly French. She showered amidst stone ceramic tiles with gold fixtures like something out of *Architectural Digest*, but all her thoughts dwelled on Remy.

Everything she could have desired to feel fresh was supplied in her room, from makeup to a hairdryer, even a footbath. While soothing her feet in chamomile, she hoped Garbozzo would follow through on his guarantee.

At nine o'clock, Ava heard a light tap on the door. She clicked the knob, praying, and peered out while keeping her body tucked behind the door to block the low-cut satiny nightshirt clinging to her shape.

Her heart fluttered like a hummingbird when she eyed Remy standing before her, next to one of the massive bodyguards. Remy appeared better than when she had last seen him, weak and blood-stained. He wore clean jeans and a new shirt unbuttoned to his abdomen. Ava noticed stark white bandages at the edge of his pants rimming his midsection. His wound had been tended to, also as Garbozzo had promised. The slice on his forehead had been nursed and closed with three white butterfly bandages.

Ava leaned against the door, letting it drift open. Tears welled in her eyes.

"It's okay, I'm here." Remy touched her fingers as she held the edge of the door waiting for him to enter. "Hey, big guy. Don't wait up," Remy said to the man behind him.

"I won't be leaving this door, so don't try anything funny."

"No worries here, buddy. I'm sore to the bone." Remy shut the door behind them, leaned back against it, and seemingly had no patience to wait to hold her. He wrapped his arms around Ava's shaking figure and curled her into his body.

"What have you done, Mrs. Kennedy?" He rubbed her back and tucked her head under his chin.

"I bought us twenty-four hours. Jeffery is coming, and I have sent codewords to Rhya… hopefully she'll fully understand and send help."

"Ava, this is not a game," Remy said. "No matter what you think, doing some styling will not set us free. It's not going to happen."

Ava drew back, freeing herself as he gently released her and walked to the open veranda door. He had to be wrong. All she had was her belief. The night sky was clear and dotted with stars, the moon almost a complete round ball shining over the patio. A slight breeze blew her shirt.

Remy slid up behind her, and she tingled without a single touch of his hand, just like the night in the forest when she first lay next to him.

"I am sorry you think I am a flake, a helicopter mom," she said. "I'm just a mother who would do anything for her daughter."

"No, Ava. I'm sorry about my words earlier. I was only trying to defuse a situation. I do not think you are a flake. Far from it." He unexpectedly fingered her waist. "Actually I think you are cute and quite a success."

Remy spun her around, slipping his hands up to her face, and touched her lips with his. He gently encased them and opened his mouth slightly so she could taste his tongue and he could savor hers. They lingered for minutes and then he molded her to his body again. She contoured the hands that cupped her face until she touched the golden wedding ring.

Ava ceased and her forehead fell into his lips.

"Yes, I'm married," he said. "Jeanie and I have been separated for a long time—before my son Jason passed, even."

Ava's heart sank. She wanted to believe him, and did not want to pull away. "I'm sorry about my words," Ava softly spoke.

Remy encased her hand and led her to the bed. "You need rest. I'll sleep on the couch."

Ava patted the bed. "It's okay, you can join me. Remember we slept together once already at the campsite?"

He smiled. "I won't refuse. My body is aching all over. I promise I'll be a gentleman." He removed his shirt, and Ava followed the ripples across his chest.

"A gentleman you must be," Ava remarked. She cuddled up under his arm. "I need you to tell me it will be okay."

Remy was quiet for some time just holding her. Her head crested his smooth shoulder, and she fingered a scar on his chest, no doubt some military injury. He landed his palm atop her hand, and Ava brushed the gold band on his finger once more.

"We were married young," he explained. "Just graduated high school. She got pregnant. My son Jason was the pride of my life... and hers." Ava heard him breathe deep. "When I see you with Rhya, that's how I remember my relationship with Jason. I am envious. All he ever wanted was to make me proud."

Remy stopped and Ava moved her hand to his abdomen above the bandages.

"Jeanie—my wife, his mother—she was never happy with Army life. I went to school, graduated. All with the Army. Then several tours of duty, and I focused on moving ahead. I traveled and I was away a lot."

Ava shared a condolence with his wife. "I do know Army life, but I stayed put while Tyler traveled. I was always there, in our little hometown, my little shop, afraid to leave, raising Rhya."

"My wife Jeanie started to drink, had a few boyfriends on base. By the time Jason died in the accident, we hadn't been together in years." He exhaled. "Jason was the love of my life. I didn't care what happened after his death. He was in a Chinook maneuver. Hit by enemy fire... he saved many lives. But when the chopper blew, everyone got off except Jason. He died instantly. Jeanie vowed never to divorce me. She said supporting her would be my hell on earth. But she didn't have to threaten me. Of course, I would take care of her."

Ava's head nestled on his heart just like the night before. She listened.

"Jeanie's real pain is Jason's ceremonial burial at Arlington Cemetery. She won't do it yet... or maybe it's me. Says she can't face letting him go. It's been a knife in my heart for almost four years."

Ava lifted up to see him. "I am so sorry."

Remy pulled her up, bringing her toward his face. He circled her lips with his own in a fury, then pulled back, kissing every inch of her face.

She returned his passion as her hand encased his neck, slipping down to his shoulder. He stirred a sensitivity, a warmth that infiltrated her veins that had been lost since Tyler's death.

"Please, tell me it will be okay?" Ava whispered lying on his shoulder.

"*Hair Bloom* magazine... front cover. I had no idea. You are quite a star, Ava Kennedy. Quite the plan you devised." He'd diverted the answer.

"Just like you... good at what you do."

"Well, we will see. We certainly have our work cut out for us. I need you to do two more things. In the morning when you leave, you must divert that big WWF wrestler at the door away from me so I can escape."

"I can certainly try."

"I also need you to blow a fuse or something... in order to turn off the lights on this compound for just a few minutes."

"Blow a fuse? I run a beauty shop. I can take out an entire circuit board in seconds," Ava chimed.

Remy inhaled deeply. Ava had fallen asleep on his chest, and his lips brushed the top of the silky waves draping his skin. She smelled divine, like the card on his mantel she'd sent to him at Fort Knox. He could not sleep a wink even when burdened with exhaustion. First, his heart was burning with longing. After their goodnight kiss Ava snuggled into him. He could barely control the urge to scoop her up and make passionate love. It had been so long with anyone, let alone someone who stirred him as Ava did from the moment they met.

The second reason he couldn't sleep. Garbozzo. Remy knew Garbozzo was never about to agree to let them go... especially not him. He would be lucky to survive. Ava's plan certainly bought them time, but the Garbozzo clan were notorious mobsters. Notorious especially for murder. Remy had a suspicion who was the connection at school, but despite knowing this, he could not be a hundred percent convinced without more evidence.

He juggled the plan in his head. *Ava thinks she can depend on Rhya, but chances are the message will just be a garbled mess by the time she receives it.* And perhaps too late anyway.

He struggled all night devising his own plan, so while Ava was executing her magic, he would be doing everything in his power to call in the forces. He was, after all, a general in the United States Army. And his partner was Private M.

He smiled, for a brief moment. He could only dream of another time and place.

CHAPTER 23

*J*effery had raced around the Jefferson Washington campus for an hour in a full-on anxiety attack as if he were an erupting volcano until he finally found Rhya. He'd been huffing and puffing and crying. "I could hardly make out a word she was saying," he rambled to Rhya after she forced him to plop down in the privacy of the barbershop... and held his hand. Jeffery was utterly shocked, and Rhya, without warning, slapped his cheek.

"Jeffery, get a grip. You said something about Mom."

Jeffery sucked in air and hesitated in disbelief. "I thought you were sweet! I thought you loved me."

Rhya headed to the shampoo bowl and soaked a towel with warm water. She returned and pressed the towel on the back of his neck. "I do, for God's sake. Never in all my life have I spoken back or yelled at you. But this is not a game of Whisper Down the Lane, Jeffery! You must repeat Mom's words exactly. Her life could be at stake!" Rhya explained. Apparently she suspected he held crucial information about her mother.

"I have to pinch the top of my nose, there was so much pressure from that slap. You will miss me. I have to pack," he curtly remarked.

"Pack for what?" she asked.

"Your mother said there would be a plane..." He placed a finger on his chin. "No, a copter. Oh my God, a helicopter. I have to fly. I can't..."

"A helicopter, when?"

"I don't know. Army time. You know... 0400, 1300, 2000, 4035..."

"Jeffery, who the hell is sending a helicopter to get you?" When he didn't answer, Rhya raised her hand to nail him again because he was still counting hundreds.

"No, no... okay... Your mom phoned me and said the car-beanies, no... the bozos... or maybe it was the Carranza's. You know... the Italians you're related to."

"The Garbozzos?" she asked.

Jeffery felt a sense of relief. "You know them? I feel so much better then."

"What else?" Rhya latched onto both his shoulders.

"That's it..." His memory was nothing but a jumbled mess.

"This is Mom we're talking about!" In disbelief he watched as Rhya couldn't hold back, and for the first time in years she actually started to cry.

For her, he would do anything. He squeezed his eyes tight. "Oh my God! Yes, yes. I remember!" He was thinking straighter. "She said to tell you she met them, and they are great people. Up in northwestern... no, northeastern Pennsylvania. Northeastern."

Rhya grabbed him. "Jeffery, the Garbozzos are not nice people. They're lethal, murdering gangsters. What else?" Rhya released Jeffery. "You know what? She's sending a message. That's it!" Rhya had never ever manhandled Jeffrey. She always respected him thoroughly.

The shock brought him around like a soldier under torture. Jeffery began to spill his guts without another tear.

Rhya kissed him and apologized.

"Do you think I can go into the compound alone? I am so scared."

"Jeffery, you have been like a father to me. All these years when I wanted my own father, Tyler. I was so angry and today I realized you were my second father. I want my mother and my Jeffery to always be safe. So, I promise, no worries. I will have an army right behind you." Rhya encircled Jeffery with a bear hug like never before. "Now, go pack what you need."

Jeffery swayed away, proud of himself, making up for all the times he lost the Christmas party Whisper Down the Lane game. Today, he remembered!

He kissed Rhya back and held his arm in the air like a sword. "Forever *onward charge!*"

She just stared at him, a puzzled look on her face.

"They say something like that in the Army." And he rushed toward the door.

Rhya left Jeffery to pack up supplies. The private helicopter would arrive at 0400, and once in flight it wouldn't take long for them to reach the remote area of northeastern Pennsylvania. She needed to confide in the only two people on campus she could trust—Ironside and Col. Pendleton.

She met the two in the Dean's office. Both were calm, but something was different between them.

"We can't let them know we're coming. This must stay absolutely confidential," Ironside replied. "No one here on campus can know we're following that helicopter."

"I will go arrange the Chinook which is here for the week on display. Plus I will see who commanded this helicopter and whose name is on the billet," the colonel affirmed.

"Colonel," Ironside addressed him. "I know you're reluctant to allow Rhya to go, but Gen. Minosa has involved her from the beginning, and he has complete faith in her."

Col. Pendleton hesitated and eyed Rhya. "I know. I have complete faith in her too, no question." Rhya nodded, feeling a rush of pride. "It's her wacky mother we have to be concerned about." He winked and secured his cap. The colonel headed for the door. "It's nightfall and a good time to sneak down to the airfield, search out the information needed, and set the stage for the Chinook." He nodded to them both.

"Thank you, Colonel. I will make you proud," Rhya affirmed.

"It's been a long time since I've flown." The colonel glanced at Ironside.

"It's like riding a bike... one never forgets," she coached.

"I guess I will have the best pilot by my side, too." The sergeant blushed at his praise. "Kennedy, you'll man the back. Might as well make this one hell of a learning adventure."

Rhya studied the two of them. They certainly were considerate of each other, more than two officers talking. Whoever thought Rhya's retired colonel from high school would be on such a mission in one summer? She could tell the room was suffocating with adrenaline.

"We fly in at 1900, under the wire," Ironside ordered.

The next morning, the light streamed in through the veranda. Birds chirped and a sensual kiss on the lips roused Ava. "The waiter is here," Remy said softly, lingering over her head.

Ava desired more, another kiss. She wished to wrap her arms around his neck and pull him into the satin nightshirt molding her body. But he'd already walked onto the open balcony. The sun shone across his shoulders, his flecks of grey hair shimmering. Ava waited for the clanging cart being pushed by a man in white waiter's attire to unload the sterling.

Ava folded her arms and followed Remy to the veranda, the late summer sun helping to warm her. He started to offer her coffee. He froze, studying her in that nightie, then he ran his fingers through his hair and turned, firmly clenching the stone balcony. Ava watched every muscle in his back and neck tense.

"This could be so like a... a wonderful runaway vacation. Maybe another time," he muttered as he scanned the horizon.

Ava said nothing. She knew in her heart she shared the same desire.

She poured the coffee. He stepped up from behind and rubbed her arms, then bent to kiss her shoulder.

Remy commanded her to sit at the settee as if they were not two people half-naked with uncontrolled urges. "We have a lot to discuss." He avoided any connection with her eyes. Instead he stared into his coffee and a plate of scrambled eggs and fresh fruit.

A sound of rotating propellers closing in from a distance caused Ava to rise and rush to the wall. "It's Jeffery, I feel him."

"You feel him?"

"He's been my partner and saving grace for over a decade. We've worked together like two peas in a pod."

Sure enough, when the helicopter passed the balcony and neared the landing strip, Ava recognized his familiar figure gasping and clinging to the pilot. She heard him too, his yelps for help until he was flabbergasted at the sight of her and Remy. He pointed, screaming, almost distracting the pilot enough to cause an accident. She tried to read his lips... *My God, you're alive! But what are you wearing..."*

"Showtime," Remy announced softly. "Let the games begin. Get dressed, Ava. Let your stilettos do the talking."

When Ava came out from the bathroom, once again Remy tightened his chiseled jaw. "It's clear why the Big Cheese might have a crush on you."

Ava was wearing a skintight black top, cut low, with a pair of white jean shorts. She was standing in a pair of clear stilettos after having told Garbozzo she only works in heels and a pink glitter apron. Ava flipped the apron on next and performed a spin.

Remy smiled. Her sculpted yoga body hopefully would lure the man at the door into the elevator that would give Remy time to make an exit down the other side of the hallway, leaving the bodyguard to believe Remy was resting in this room.

Ava picked up her purse when they heard the knock. "My escort is here."

They both took a deep breath and moved closer. Ava let her head fall into his chest. Remy kissed the top of her head as he had the night before.

"I don't want to cry," she said. "Maybe we should have escaped down the balcony last night."

"You know the place was crawling with guards watching us... from the ground, in the air. No chance of that."

Ava snuggled in deeper.

Remy closed his hands on her chin and lifted her face up to his. "But today, Ava... Private M... is a new day."

"I better see you at the end because I am not leaving here without you," she affirmed. He kissed her. "Remy, I'm not joking. No more pushing me out of helicopters without you, got it?"

He encased her lips again, before holding her tight.

They were interrupted by a powerful knock.

"Let me in there, or I'll open it myself," the bodyguard grunted.

Ava looked at Remy one last time. "I made the bed like you said just like a body sleeping. I am good at that. I fooled Jeffery and he generally doesn't miss a trick, unless of course it's Whisper Down the Lane." She noticed Remy raise an eyebrow of confusion. "And around nine this morning, when the beauty shop is in business, consider those fuses and circuits blown!"

"You mean exactly 0900?"

"That Army time gets me so confused. But, yes sir, 0900."

"Good girl. Now go make the place look better. I'll see you later. I promise."

"Yes, General Mi... *Minosa*."

Ava couldn't guard against the one tear that drifted from her eye. She wiped it with an inhale. "You will always be Mimosa to me." Then she slipped away from his arms and opened the door. "Well, good morning, Mr. Bodyguard." Ava eyed her escort waiting for her by the elevator. "Jimmy!"

He waved and tipped his hat nonchalantly and then remembered the orange hair issue.

"It's okay, Jimmy," she said. "You will be my first client."

Ava pretended to trip, and she purposely dropped a lipstick right in front of the other bodyguard as she was about to go down the hall. With his back to the bedroom door, she felt his ogling. *Perfect.* Ava bent all the way over, tilting her rump in his direction as high as she was able. She purposely kept one straight leg in the stilettos, sure to cock the other, offering the guard a seductive tease.

"Whoops." Ava snagged the lipstick, staying in the bent position a moment longer, pretending to stuff it deep in her purse before swaying in a sexy walk to Jimmy at the elevator.

He reached out his hand to greet her. Ava thought Jimmy seemed like such a sensitive person. A shame he was walking on the wrong side of the tracks.

Jimmy pushed the button. "Nice to see you this morning," he said as they waited. "I've never known anyone famous, Mrs. Kennedy."

He was adorned in a black-and-blue mark on his temple from her shoe. "Sorry about that," Ava said with all honesty.

"Oh, that? I've had worse. I deserved it." He stepped into the elevator and practically fell into the corner.

Ava glanced back to be sure the stern-faced bodyguard was all eyes on her. Indeed he was. Time for action! Ava slid her stiletto slowly into the elevator, catching the heel between the metal strips on the floor... the one she always thought her keys might drop into if she didn't hold them secure. Once her mother managed to catch a heel in an elevator, and the doors closed, almost eating her foot. Hopefully these doors would have a safety provision.

Ava was about to find out. "Oh no. Help!" Ava yelled.

"What?" Jimmy exclaimed.

"My heel, it's caught in the strip!" The elevator started opening and closing about the length of a ruler in confusion. The bell was ringing nonstop now. "I can't get my foot out. There's a strap across my ankle."

Ava eyed the bodyguard. He only moved one step, but Jimmy was already hitting the floor to free her. Ava couldn't let that happen.

Here goes.

Ava performed a Downward Dog yoga maneuver over Jimmy, planting her palm right over his face so he couldn't see. They were both on the floor, as if entwined in a game of Twister, her butt cheeks peeking out, her yelping noise causing quite the stir.

Finally the ogre bodyguard left his post to assist. She looked down the hall, arching over Jimmy. *Where was Remy?*

The bodyguard hovered over them now, his legs in a wide vee.

"Get up, you goons." That's when she caught sight of Remy between the massive thighs and calves of the bodyguard. He winked and discreetly tiptoed out the back.

Ava let the bodyguard attempt to help her up, pretending to lose her balance and fall again. He clearly had enough when he grasped her wickedly in both hands and lifted her like a barbell. Placing her upright, Ava wobbled, gathering herself and fluffing her hair before stepping into the elevator.

"Really, do you have to man-handle me so!" Ava snapped.

Jimmy rose, brushing himself off then clearing his throat. Both he and Ava were like tiny mice next to the beast.

"Now, get going." The bodyguard slapped the elevator button on the other side of the wall.

Ava waved and mouthed, *"Thank you,"* but the bodyguard never flinched a facial muscle. "What a grump." Her escort just nodded in affirmation.

Jimmy steered her to another floor, and when the elevator door opened Ava's mouth dropped. A full-service salon complete with four hydraulics, a dryer, nail tables, and mirrors of which only the most exclusive salon could afford were arrayed before her. Every station had the latest electrical supplies and tools. A veranda skirted off the styling room with tables for coffee and lunch while maybe a client had their hair set. *Client*, she thought. The same clients every week. *Hmm... a lot like home.*

Then she saw him, folding towels just the way he did back home, ironing the crease. "Jeffery!"

"Ava." He forgot about the towels on his lap when he leaped up, scattering them in an unfolded mess on the floor. But for once he didn't care. Jeffery rushed to her. "Ava, Ava." He squeezed her so tight she thought her ribs were cracking. After what felt like an hour, he arched her away and studied every crevice of her body up and down. "Oh my, you are so skinny. This woman needs food." He snapped his fingers, and a lady ran to retrieve something from the kitchen.

"This place is amazing. I feel like a celebrity," he commented, flipping a wrist in the air.

"Jeffery, I am okay."

"But look at you."

"I was only gone two days. More importantly, did you see Rhya?" she whispered.

"She was a wreck and..."

Ava gripped his cheeks, pinching his lips together. "I meant did you give her my message?"

He couldn't move his mouth, instead affirmed with a nod.

"Thank you. Now, I guess you've seen the coloring blunder here on this estate?" Ava pointed to Jimmy, motioning him to remove his cap.

Jeffery cocked a leg in disgust, then released a high-pitched shudder and placed his hand over his mouth. "Oh my, that is putrid. Just nauseating."

Jimmy frowned and glanced in a mirror as if questioning Jeffery's condemnation.

"Dear Lord, have a seat." Jeffery swung the hydraulic around and tapped the back.

Jimmy immediately plopped in. Ava glanced at the wall clock. *Nine o'clock.*

"Since Gina's not here yet, let's test all the equipment first, Jeffery."

Jeffery eyed her questioningly, but she winked and called the bodyguard on the veranda to help. "On the count of three we turn on anything that's electric."

"Is that a good idea?" the bodyguard questioned. "Some of this equipment is pretty high wattage."

"What do you mean?" She looked at Jeffery for support.

"What if a dryer goes off in the middle of your color process? You would have... oh my, is that what happened to you, Jimmy?"

"Poor guy, I don't think the Big Cheese would be happy with any of us." Jeffery thankfully played along.

"That's why we need an electrical power check. We must hit the dryers and the curling irons at the exact same time. Now go."

Jeffery dashed around, flipping switches. Even Jimmy helped. "One, two, three!" Ava yelled. "Wait..."

They all froze. She looked at them both with concern. Suddenly she couldn't remember the time. "So, 0900 hundred is 9 A.M., right? Or is that 2100 hundred. For A.M. versus P.M.?"

Jeffrey shook his head, but Jimmy nodded, confusing her more.

By the time she said, "The hell with it," the clock on the wall froze at 9:10 precisely when the circuit blew.

"What the hell? The generator will take thirty minutes to flip on, lady," one of the bodyguards huffed.

That would be great timing for Remy. Besides, Gina was late. They waited.

At 9:50, Gina lumbered into the room, yawning with a donut in her hand. It irked Ava because this girl was quite spoiled. Ava was there to do a job, and if she were going to do it correctly, so was Gina. "The first thing you need to know about hairstyling is... you must always be on time!"

Gina stopped chewing, shocked someone would speak to her in such a manner. Surprisingly, she complied with a nod and plopped in a hydraulic chair.

"You are not the customer," Ava said. "The hairdresser is the last client to be served. Just like the shoemaker has no shoes."

Gina was spinning the chair like a child.

"Up and at 'em," Jeffery stirred. "Jimmy is awaiting." Jeffery held a smock for her and shot Ava a stare as if warning this was going to be a difficult student.

By lunch the room was cluttered with color corrections, new highlights, lowlights, color removal, color dying, and lots of re-cutting demonstrations.

Gina moaned several times that her arms were sore from holding them up. Jeffery allowed no excuses. "This is a hairdresser's life."

When Gina asked for lunch, Jeffery almost threatened her with the scissors. "Hairdressers don't have lunch. We work through the day. Straight through! We are on a huge time schedule."

Ava winked at Jeffery to go a little easy. She knew they had to keep Gina from running away in tears. They had to keep her happy. After all, Gina was the reason the Big Cheese was allowing leeway.

Garbozzo peeked his head in early in the morning, and again in the afternoon. Ava sensed she had an admirer. Which was both good and bad.

"I am saving you for my last client," she told him.

"We can have our little meeting then. I have quite the proposal for you, Ava Kennedy. No pun intended."

Ava shot an odd look at him. *Proposal? Pun?* What exactly did he mean? Ava checked around frequently, scanning out over the estate past the veranda. She wondered where Remy could be.

In the afternoon, the room surged with fumes and odors. The bowls rushed with water, and the dryers shut on and off. Jeffery patted himself on the back, then Gina. "Another amazing creation. See how it's done?" Then he would snap his fingers and order her to the next round. "This is how you make the big bucks," he announced. "We fold towels."

Ava pulled Jeffery to the side. "She already has the big bucks, go easy."

He listened for a time, but when Gina tried to collapse between "clients," Jeffery stressed, "I said no sitting. That's why they are giving me another position at Jefferson Washington."

Ava looked over as he folded towels. "You have a new position?"

"No worries. I am still the barber, but I will be teaching a class on folding. Did you see how some of those students folded their sheets when they arrived? Dean Ironside noticed my folding skill and said it's all mine. Jeffery's Folding and Fluffing Class. My card will say: *Make 'em full, fluffy, and wrinkle free. Pass all inspections.*"

Gina clapped. Even after all his forceful ordering she still liked him. "I will tell Daddy I want to keep you, too."

"Gina, you can't keep us," Ava insisted. "We aren't Barbie dolls."

"She looks like one, doesn't she?" Jeffery pointed to Ava.

"She does today. You should have seen her yesterday," Gina replied.

"Jeffery, Gina stop." Ava rolled her eyes. Those two were actually becoming chummy. "Now Gina, imagine if I could not return to my clients."

The two continued to joke as Ava drifted into her own thoughts, wondering even more about Remy. The staff at the estate was ecstatic over their new "dos." So far Ava's plan seemed to be working, at least from her end.

Gina appeared to be enjoying herself as she attempted to master twenty years of knowledge in a twelve-hour shift. But the toughest part of the mission awaited... the sisters would soon be promenading through the salon door for massive color corrections followed by a complete inspection from the Big Cheese.

CHAPTER 24

Remy escaped down the hall from the bedroom where he'd spent the night with Ava. A night of holding her. He was now driven by the power of a woman, inspired to love again. She was such a good actress, he wondered if most of her flakiness wasn't just a put-on to fool and win people over. Perhaps she was even acting about her feelings for him.

First goal, to find cell phone reception. His success on the mission was counting on Ava to blow the breakers that would turn off the cameras. Remy managed to duck into the outside patio for cover until 0900. He prayed Ava could do what he asked.

Although slightly late, sure enough, Remy monitored the red alarm lights Jimmy had pointed out to him in the garden the previous day, and at 0910 the entire place shut down. He scurried to the stairwell, managing to dodge into a doorway when several men rushed out of the game room carrying rifles.

Jimmy was a godsend. He had been an undercover agent for over a year with the DEA and was damn proficient at his job. He'd apparently deceived everyone as a doofus and dedicated follower, even the Big Cheese. He explained to Remy the team of ogres would not stay in the game room if the circuit blew. If Remy reached his goal and made it to the game room, Jimmy would leave a hidden phone and three keys on the bar behind the Crow's Whiskey bottle on the left. Again, luck was with him. Remy found the phone right where Jimmy said. And a ring with the keys.

Remy had not clued Ava in on the complete truth about Jimmy being an agent. He thought it dangerous to reveal too much other than he thought they had a friend in Jimmy. Jimmy had worked far too hard to infiltrate the Garbozzos, and Remy's intentions were not to blow the agent's cover.

Jimmy had filled Remy in on two other major issues—where the so called MREs were stored, and where Remy could find enough gunpowder to light up the sky.

The MREs, stuffed with drugs, were located in a compound wired better than Fort Knox... but Remy had been to Fort Knox. He'd met Jimmy by dumb luck, and they were both ready to torch this place. Jimmy claimed he would keep an eye on Ava, explaining that the explosives were also behind the barbed wire, next to the drugs behind locked doors.

Remy crouched low waiting for the perfect opportunity to ambush a guard about his size at the gate of the facility. Stepping into the other man's black pants and white shirt, cap and sunglasses, Remy stole two cans of gunpowder. He distributed the explosives around the MRE building and took a trail out through the back gate. All he had to do later when the time was right was hit that baby with an igniter.

He made contact with the outside via phone, and headed for the two facilities. This was no small undertaking. In fact, the mission to line the place with explosives took all afternoon. In the end, he walked off with two Rugers and a rifle. Every step panned out like clockwork. Almost too easy.

One last stop, he had to check on a friend.

"Diesel," Remy whispered through the barn. Finally he heard the familiar whinny. "Hey, buddy." Remy creeped into Diesel's stall, relieved to find him. Someone had taken the time to tend to his leg as Ava said she requested. Unfortunately, Remy was disappointed to see the horse still limping. "Well, you are not getting us out of here in that condition. At least not the way I planned."

Remy huddled in the stall with Diesel, hiding the weapons under the straw bedding, and spent the next hours evaluating their exit. How he intended on blowing the place to smithereens. Until a glance at his watch. 1700 hours... four hours to go. He rose momentarily to stretch his legs and slightly slide the stall door open to peer into the aisleway, never expecting to face a semi-automatic before his world went black.

At 8:00 in the evening, Ava stumbled off the elevator with Jeffery and Gina following. All three entered the game room exhausted, Gina most of all. She complained her arms ached, her legs ached, and she couldn't wait to talk to Daddy. That worried Ava. If Gina complained and moaned, that would not be the guarantee to ensure them leaving the estate that she needed.

Ava eyed the room, remembering what Remy had told her about there not being cameras in the game room. The two bodyguards were playing pool behind them. They were joking with each other as the clacking of the balls interfered with their ability to hear them clearly.

"This must be where they kill people," Jeffery whispered into Ava's ear.

Two pool balls cracked together, and Jeffery jumped, grabbing his heart. "I think I heard him say the word *kill*, '*I am going to kill you.*'"

"Jeffery! Don't even try to play that Whisper Game. You can't hear right. All the years of hair dryers have made you completely deaf." Ava grunted. Ava wasn't about to reveal her true thoughts, because she had heard the word, too. "Lord, I need a drink."

Jeffery crossed his legs, elbowed his thighs, and placed his chin in both hands, sinking into the oversized wingback chair. Gina sat zombie-faced at the bar, too much sniffing of hairspray on what was probably her first day of hard work ever.

Meanwhile Ava sat on the edge of the shiny leather couch wondering about Remy. Two of their previous "clients" were the ones shooting pool behind them, without ball caps. *Nice hair.*

The elevator dinged its warning that the Big Cheese was on his way down. Everyone in the room went on alert as if he were an Army general.

Garbozzo waltzed off like a Godfather, a stone-faced monster. Ava squirmed. He didn't look happy. Maybe Gina had already chatted with him, maybe one of the sisters complained, or maybe he'd killed... Ava couldn't think the last thought. Maybe Jeffery's imagination was right.

Or maybe it was the fact he was the only one left in the house with orange hair.

Garbozzo opened a gold box on the side table and lit up a cigar, then re-opened the box and aimed it at Jeffery. "You want a tote?"

Jeffery declined, only able to shake his head in an exceptionally polite decline.

Two pool balls clanged behind them. Jeffery shuddered, then leaned over to whisper in Ava's ear. "Maybe one last drag before he shoots us."

Ava shushed him while Garbozzo sucked in a deep inhalation, then blew several smoke rings with puckering puffs. "Well, here we are, twenty-four hours later. Sucking on cigars again."

Jeffery reached a hand to shelter Ava. The pool balls clapped together behind them. "We'll go down together," he said.

"Jeffery." Ava tried to shoo him again.

Suddenly, Garbozzo snapped his fingers to the bodyguards.

Jeffery was shaking so hard Ava decided to accept his hand. She could feel his vibrations zip up her arms.

The bodyguards came to Garbozzo's side immediately, pool sticks in hand. He looked from Ava and Jeffery to the two ogres. "End it," he ordered and puffed again on his cigar like he'd just completed a roll in the hay.

Jeffery screamed and landed on his knees in front of Ava. "Please, not the woman! She is a mother!"

"Jeffery, sit back in the chair. If they are going to shoot us, we go together," Ava declared.

He raised his head up from her lap. "Maybe they are going to bludgeon us with pool sticks? I saw it in a movie once."

The three men stared at him, confused.

"Shoot you? Bludgeon you?" Garbozzo laughed a hearty spell. "I wanted them to end the pool game. Those clanging balls were preying on my last nerve."

One of the bodyguards spoke, "And man, I was just about to win... murder him for once in a game of pool. I was killing it." He pointed to his partner and banged the pool stick onto the floor.

Jeffery and Ava both sighed, and Jeffery planked himself back up to the chair, patting his chest to see if his heart was still beating.

"My daddy, shoot someone?" Gina laughed a raucous laugh just like her father. Then she turned to the three men. They fixated on her, and after too long a minute, all three laughed an almost fake laugh for her to hear.

"Ava, my dear. Come here." Gina's father extended his hand. "You appear exhausted. But everyone here is so elated with their hair. Why would I shoot you? You have completed an amazing job. Gina wants you to stay."

Gina clapped.

"But you explained?" Ava looked at Garbozzo. "You explained why we can't stay."

"Oh, Mrs. Kennedy, you are a master. I do have a proposal." He kissed Gina and commanded her to turn in for the night.

Jeffery eyeballed Ava.

Ava shrugged back as they waited for Gina to leave. As soon as the elevator door closed, B.C. spoke. "Ava Kennedy," he said, and tossed the *Hair Bloom* magazine at her. "I need you."

"Sorry, B.C. I must return to my fans."

Garbozzo bent over to touch her hair. Ava leaned back and cringed.

"As I said, I have no need to shoot you. But I do have the need to shoot him."

Jeffery yelled out again, covering his face between his knees. "Please, no," he begged in a muffled voice.

"*Tsk.* Not you," Garbozzo announced disgustedly.

The bodyguards both rolled their eyes.

"Him." Garbozzo pointed to a door behind the bar. Remy appeared in the doorway, hands tied behind his back with Jimmy following behind pointing a gun at the general's head.

"Remy!" Ava acknowledged. She'd been so wrong about Jimmy. She glared at Garbozzo. "You are an evil man."

"*Hmm.*" He swiveled the cigar out in the crystal ashtray on the coffee table. "No, it's your friend here who is evil. He blew up my drugs. You know, you may have a chance to save him, Mrs. Kennedy. With my proposal of course."

Chapter 25

The room fell silent as Ava waited to hear Garbozzo's proposal. "Seems the two of us have a common thread. We are widows. I feel it's quite suitable that we marry. I find you charming, sexy and not to mention my daughters already love you. They are holding their heads high, walking with a spring, and I must say magnificent looking. The confidence of a Garbozzo. I can't wait for my turn! And you, my precious princess, can now live out your life as a very content, very rich woman." He smiled. "Imagine styling at a secret location... the world would be in awe of the mystery stylist... where she was hiding... all the money you could generate with the facade."

Jeffery let out an enormous sigh. Ava wasn't sure if it was relief or worry for her. *"Jeffery!"* she mouthed. He shrugged, his hand holding his chest. She was about to tell Garbozzo how much she detested him, and he could kiss that proposal goodbye when the elevator rang and interrupted them.

"Ahh. We have a guest," Garbozzo said seemingly unsurprised. The doors opened in slow motion as everyone waited in anticipation. Ava never expected who she would see strut off the elevator. Both she and Jeffery gasped at the familiar face.

Remy immediately perked up. "Shane Blevins. I should've known."

Jimmy conked Remy in the back with the pistol. "Shut up." Remy merely grunted.

"Well, well, the dippy hairdresser and her even dippier assistant."

Jeffery shrieked again. Everyone in the room focused on Jeffery. He cocked a leg. "I am sorry, I just despise being called dippy. Sounds like an egg at Sunday morning breakfast."

"Now, now, she is to be my princess," Garbozzo announced.

Shane Blevins ignored him and headed to the coffee table where he picked up the *Hair Bloom* magazine and stared at the front cover. Then he eyed Ava. "Wow, whoever thought?"

"The military inventory you're black marketing," Remy scoffed. "Just a front to offset the Feds? Underneath it all you're selling drugs packaged as MREs. How convenient. Your product can come and go on military vehicles and planes without anyone suspecting."

Jimmy whipped him in the back again, sending Remy to his knees.

"You know what? My head is about done with the abuse."

Ava and Jeffery wrapped arms around each other and clung tight.

Garbozzo slithered closer to her. "The way I see it, here is your only option. If all goes as planned, you will live as Mrs. Ava Garbozzo, and your Jeffery will get to stay alive and live here, too. You as my princess and him as my... court jester."

She heard Jeffery shudder a sigh of relief.

"Your friend over there who was caught by my good man, Jimmy... well, I'm sorry to say must be handed off to Shane Blevins."

"He'll kill him," Ava snapped. "Remy's a general. The entire U.S. Army will be after all of you."

"I hate to tell you. You don't know what Shane Blevins found in that Chinook crash, do you? Well, let me tell you. A lot of drugs wrapped in MREs and a dead General Minosa who turned bad. Like a Benedict Arnold." Shane walked over to Remy who was being held in a kneeling position. "Anybody else you want to add?"

"Don't you touch him," Ava glared. "I will tell Gina everything about you."

"Oh my princess, that girl's spoiled and loves her life." Garbozzo drew close and rubbed Ava's cheek.

Ava wanted to puke. "We don't own people, Mr. Big Cheese. Jeffery is not mine. And you will never own me."

Garbozzo laughed, about to bend in close for a kiss, yanking her back from Jeffery. His vibrating phone stopped him.

Ava could hear the panicked voice on the other side. *"Sir, there is an uninvited Chinook. Too dark for us to see who. But it's definitely Army. Out of nowhere, I tell you."*

Shane piped up, "What? Tell them to let it go. I'm coming. The aircraft could be the real deal, and we don't need trouble. They will be searching for their general." Garbozzo nodded. Shane motioned the two bodyguards to accompany him. They trailed him into the elevator before he thought to ask, "Will you be okay?"

Garbozzo waved his gold jeweled pinky. "Of course. I have Jimmy. Go, now!"

The elevator closed.

Ava glanced over at Remy who was still kneeling. He unexpectedly met her eyes and winked, sending Ava a confused message. It seemed like a victory wink.

Jimmy yanked him up and pushed him over to Garbozzo in one motion. "Hey boss, should I free him?"

Garbozzo raised an eyebrow as Remy's body collided into his own. The Big Cheese was caught off guard when Remy's arms surrounded his body and toppled the kingpin to the floor. No one had a clue Remy hadn't been tightly tied.

Ava gasped and once again Jeffery fanned his cheeks as if he was about to pass out. Once Garbozzo was on the ground, Jimmy aimed a pistol at the mobster's head while he flopped around like a fish out of water.

"B.C., meet Jimmy the DEA agent. He's been on your tail for over a year."

Jimmy handcuffed Garbozzo and stood him up while Remy faced him square on. "Don't you ever touch Ava again." Then he fisted Garbozzo on the chin, putting him back on the floor.

Garbozzo tried to sit upright, but Jimmy rammed a foot into his chest to lock him in place.

"You don't understand," Garbozzo said. "I can't go to prison like this! My hair will be the laughing stock. I will have no respect. Ava, I need you!" the grown man pleaded.

"Too late for that, B.C." Jimmy pointed an index finger at Remy. "You three be okay?"

"We will," Remy nodded.

Remy clasped Ava's hand and Jeffery's arm. "Let's go, you two."
He led them to the elevator.

Jeffery leaned over Remy to Ava. "I never wanna see another
elevator again."

Once the door shut, Ava reached her arms around Remy and
embraced him. Jeffery leaped in, over top, and encircled them in his
own bear hug.

"All right, you two," Remy said. "This isn't over yet. Your ride is
here."

When the door opened, Remy grabbed Ava's hand. "Jeffery, you
stay on our tail! Keep quiet, and no outbursts."

Jeffery appeared baffled. "Me? Outburst?"

Remy dodged in a zigzag path to the airstrip. Jeffery cupped his
own mouth to remain silent and followed after in high prancing
steps.

They stopped at the crest of the hill before the barn. Ava could
see Shane Blevins searching the Chinook but seemingly finding no
one. Suddenly all the lights in the fortress went out again. The
estate was black as night, just like the evening when Ava first met
Remy on the field behind Rhya's high school. Only the sound of
voices triggered by nerves raced around below.

Remy smiled. "Thank you, Jimmy. Good thing you taught him
how to blow circuits, Ava." He squeezed her hand.

Remy led them to the barn, keeping low to the ground to avoid
being spied.

"Diesel," Ava uttered his name upon seeing the magnificent
beast.

Once ducking in the stall, the three scaled the stable wall. Remy
searched the straw to find the weapons he had hidden earlier. He
loaded both pistols, tucked one on his waist and then handed the
other to Jeffery.

"Me?" Jeffery spoke in a higher octave than usual.

"You." Remy pointed down the barn aisleway. "A contact will
meet you at the end." Then he kissed Ava on the lips.

Jeffery cocked a leg waiting for them to unlock, shaking the
gun, stuttering, "N-no w-way... I c-can't... I will shoot my foot off."

Remy pulled away. "Listen, both of you. It will be okay."

"Remy, no," Ava cried.

He was done conversing, and crushed Diesel's lead into Ava's right hand. Remy proceeded to wrap his arms around her waist.

"What are you doing?" Ava's left hand snatched his belt and back pocket to resist. Momentarily, she latched onto something smooth and metal. Ava heard the clang of something hitting the cement barn floor, but the commotion took precedence. Before she could prevent him, Remy mounted Ava dead center on Diesel's back. He then faced Jeffery, making a stirrup out of his hands for the nervous man.

"You're next... up! Let's go!" Remy shook his interlocked hands, cupped together for Jeffery to use as a step to climb on Diesel behind Ava.

"Lord, no. I can't ride. Are you joking?"

"Jeffery, this is no joke. You step up on Diesel now... or you and Diesel will both be pureed into dog meat."

"Dogmeat...?"

Remy nodded.

Ava was shaking her head, only attempting to dismount, but Remy was pressed against her with his side.

"Yes, sir." Jeffery saluted.

Remy catapulted Jeffery over the horse and Ava's assistant almost plunged to the ground on the other side, but Remy gripped his thigh to drag him back up straight behind Ava.

"Good, I need you to take care of Ava," Remy insisted.

"I don't need to be taken care of," she snapped.

Remy ignored her and continued, his eyes now locked on Jeffery. "Someone will be waiting for you in the distance. Head straight out the barn and toward the Chinook on the airfield below." Remy positioned Jeffery's free hand around Ava's waist. "Keep her on the horse."

"How will we recognize the person who is waiting for us, sir?" Jeffery sounded like a soldier.

"Trust me, you will know. Now go."

Bewildered, Ava struggled with jumping off or staying with her beloved Jeffery. She wanted all of them to exit this compound,

Remy included. This was the second time Remy forced her to leave his side, and she wasn't going to stand for it again.

Jeffery squeezed Ava's waist.

"Jeffery, I don't want to. Remy needs my help." She skirted her body sideways, catching Remy headed out of the stable. Jeffery tried restraining her firmly with one hand by the waist as she leaned over, searching. That's when she observed the silver ring with keys lying on the ground. The keys must have fallen from Remy's back pocket when she tried to resist.

"He dropped something!" Ava exclaimed.

"Ava, he'll be fine." Jeffery squeezed again.

Ava lifted Diesel's lead forward and swung one leg over the horse's neck, a maneuver she was positive she could not perform unless she practiced Hot Yoga. Ava was sitting sideways on the horse's back.

"I want off. I must help Remy. I'm positive he needs those keys." She slid to the ground passing under Jeffery's hand. Before he could speak, Ava slapped Diesel's rump hard and sent him soaring. The horse trotted down the aisleway, in a loud clomping sound that echoed until they reached the end of the barn.

Ava reached down and nabbed the ring of keys. Three keys. Unfortunately Remy had disappeared into the dark opening at the other end, and she had no idea where he was headed. She had to follow her gut instinct.

Jeffery sank into Diesel's back, trying to muffle his voice as he hollered, conversing to the animal as if the horse could answer back. "There, I see someone waving at us, there at the end, Diesel." He clenched horse-hair and hide in his free hand, trying to stay centered. They trotted parallel to the fence heading toward the airstrip. "Look at that shadow of a person. See them? They're waving us on! I don't want to be eaten by a dog. Maybe a man, but not a dog!"

The lights of the Chinook were blinding, and the engine sound was deafening behind the shadow waiting for them. Diesel appeared to know exactly where they should head as he aimed for the person and the aircraft with a new vigor.

"What if it's a trap? I think we should go back," Jeffery mumbled. He was almost sprawled out on the steed's neck.

Diesel pricked his ears back and then focused them like antennas forward.

As they neared the motioning figure, Jeffery recognized a female. "No, it can't be?" he whispered.

Jeffery egged Diesel without realizing. One touch of his heel into the steed's belly almost catapulted him off backwards. Diesel followed the heel command and gathered up the pace. "It's Rhya. I see her. Rhya!" He waved his arm in the air frantically like an eight-second bull rider, the loaded gun flailing over his head causing Diesel to gallop faster. "Save me!"

Rhya spoke in a soft voice as Diesel neared.

Jeffery felt as if he was riding a freight train zooming off the tracks. "He's not going to stop!"

But when Diesel heard Rhya's calming tone, "Whoa, big boy," the beast buried his rear and stopped within a foot of her spread out arm. "Whoa."

Jeffery tumbled off and instantly jumped to his feet. "Rhya!"

She had to remind Jeffery of the loaded gun. She nabbed his arm and said, "I'll take that. Where's Mom?"

"She went back," he screamed between his panting.

"She went back?" Rhya blurted.

"Yes, to help Remy, I tried to stop her but..."

"Alright, come on. There's no time. We only have thirty minutes to fly out of here before this place blows! I'll think of something, but first, you and Diesel need to be safe. Hopefully the agent Jimmy will be keeping an eye on them until we figure out a plan."

"Jimmy the agent? He can save me anytime!"

"This is no time for ogling."

Jeffery cleared his mind. "Rhya, how did you get here?"

Rhya pointed. Jeffery was again blinded by the lights of the Chinook, and luckily the tandem rotors were still operating. An armed gunman stood watch, oblivious to the commotion.

"We have to get back on that helicopter. The colonel and Ironside are restrained on board. I'm just not sure how we're going to knock the guard out."

Jeffery examined Rhya, her beautiful eyes just like her father's. He pinched her crooked nose which was like Ava's. "I'll take care of him. I've seen it in the movies. You know all those Friday night movies we watched together were not for nothing."

"Jeffery, this is no time..."

He interrupted with a finger over his lips. "The man standing at the Chinook has a familiar face. I worked on his hair this morning. He likes me. Trust me, Rhya."

"What do you mean you worked on his..."

His voice seemed to hypnotize her, and after a slight hesitation she nodded.

Rhya and Diesel maintained position on the edge of the airstrip, hovering behind another helicopter. As Jeffery non-chalantly strolled up to the guard standing at the mouth of the Chinook, the man instantly angled his rifle in the air. "Halt! This area is off limits."

"It's me. I am Jeffery. Don't you recognize me? The new barber." Jeffery smiled. "Hey, didn't you have orange hair earlier?"

The man froze, still holding firm. "Jeffery, is that you? Man, what the hell are you doing? We have invaders around here. I could have blown your head off!"

"Lordy, the Big Cheese would not be happy about that now that he has a teacher to help his daughter style hair."

"Man, you're right. Spoiled girl. We looked like idiots. Sometimes I hate this job." He lowered his weapon. "But what are you doing out?"

"I heard a commotion down here, and I needed a cigarette and some fresh air."

The man placed his gun butt on the pavement and searched his pockets.

"I think I see them here, in your upper pocket. Let me hold that for you." Jeffery pointed to the gunman's shirt pocket and reached for the rifle. "Your uniform has a bulge in it right here."

The man bowed and followed Jeffery's hand which was between the gunman's two pecs. In a quick move, Jeffery tickled under the man's chin and then belted him as hard as he could muster.

To Jeffery's dismay and horror, the man raised his head, rubbed his chin and roared like a lion, seemingly unaffected by the slug. Jeffery dropped the gun and began a powwow dance in a circle to curb the pain zinging up his arm. "Ouch, what is your jaw made of—steel?"

"Now, why did you do that?" The man lunged forward, but a powerful jolt prevented him from reaching his rifle on the ground. Instead he fell to the earth, knocking himself into a trance on the macadam. Rhya had slammed him from the side with a colossal punch. And Diesel backed her up with a kick to high heaven.

Ava scanned the valley. Complete darkness. The only light was cascading from the moon and the Chinook. The engines revved and the craft was ready to take the sky while voices bantered and echoed in all directions. The evening was similar to the night Ava interrupted Rhya's mission back at Stayman High. This time though, Ava was determined. She wasn't about to trip or fall.

Her eye caught a shadow below. "I know where Remy is," Ava mumbled, and she burst out the stable door. Luckily the moonlight revealed the shadowy figure to her left heading toward the two large pole buildings barricaded behind gates and barbwire. "That has to be what the keys go to."

She flicked her head right, praying Jeffery made it to the rescue person awaiting him and Diesel.

Good thing Ava was a runner. She had no problem dashing in heels after Remy who was probably succumbing to his wounds by now. It had been a long day for them both. Dodging in and out of bushes, she avoided three gunmen by a hair, until she arrived at the back gate, where she discovered Remy fiddling with his back pockets.

"Are you missing something?" Ava asked in a low voice.

Remy made a quick pivot while reaching for his pistol. Clearly shocked by her presence, he said, "Ava? What are you doing?"

Ava extended the keys out to him. "You dropped something."

He wobbled toward her, barely able to lift his arm to reach for them. "Good job, baby."

The sound of the word *baby* melted her heart, and she rushed to him. "You need help. You're hurting."

Remy appeared delirious, wet with sweat. "Come on, we have a field to light up," he muttered, ignoring her and holding the lock. He slid open the gate after she worked the key.

Ava observed a band of men racing in the opposite direction toward the Chinook, which appeared to be slowly rising and holding a hovering position.

She gripped Remy's arm. "What are they doing? Big Cheese must've found out something is wrong. How are we making it back to the Chinook? It's already lifting off."

"We aren't. We have another ride."

He continued limping, while Ava attempted to steady his body, leaning into hers. With that, his phone rang. Remy raised the cell from his pocket, but was hardly able to push for the call. Ava pressed the button.

"Colonel," Remy spoke.

"It's Kennedy, General."

"Rhya, oh my Rhya." Ava sealed the phone to her ear.

"Mom, where are you?"

"She's with me." Remy's voice was clear as if he felt no pain.

Ava arched the phone between them. "Do you have Jeffery and Diesel?"

Rhya didn't have to respond. Ava could hear Jeffery in the background like Dorothy from the *Wizard of Oz. "I just want to go home,"* he was repeating over and over.

"We do, General. The troops are on the way, just minutes to the front entrance. Like you asked."

"Okay, then get out of here, this instant, before they reach you to prevent your take-off."

"Yes, General... and Mom? I mean Private M... I love you."

A lump hovered in Ava's throat like a Chinook. "I love you back."

She clung to Remy as he slid open another set of doors. A Kawasaki sports bike awaited them.

"The third key?"

He nodded, but as he straddled the bike, Remy wavered and the cycle fell to the ground. Ava grappled to hold onto the handlebars with all her might, aiding in standing the metal machine back on two wheels.

"You can't drive. You don't have the strength. You must have a full blown fever."

Remy let his weight fall into her shoulder, trying to maintain his stand and the bike at the same time.

"Who in the hell do you think is going to..."

"General," she said. "Get the heck on."

"What?"

"That's an order!" Ava spread her petite legs on the front of the motorcycle which luckily was low to the ground. He held his stance hesitantly as she turned the key in the ignition, pressed the starter and revved the motor. "I said get on. Remember that little tattoo on my inner thigh? Well long story short, I am very proficient at cycling. Just have those matches ready."

Remy straddled behind her, clearly too weak to fight, and the pair peeled out the door. Remy hung from the side, gripping her waist from behind as he tossed a fiery torch into a pile of what appeared to be black powder. Gunpowder.

Ava had no time to worry about the firestorm that erupted behind her. She had her focus on one thing—getting out of the compound.

Holding the clutch she changed gears and zoomed onto the cement driveway heading toward the iron gates.

"Ava, the gates aren't open."

She made a sharp turn and aimed for the lake, almost scraping against the ground as she laid the bike low to pivot.

"What're you doing?"

"Trust me," she yelled. "Don't you remember? There's a skateboard ramp by the lake where the fence opens, and a bridge clears the water. We can do it. I can do this. But hold your breath just in case."

"How long has it been since you scaled a ramp? Or rode a bike for that matter!" Remy hollered in her ear.

"Since I broke my leg trying!"

Ava raised her chin up, her body erect, keeping Minosa stable over the center. A long time was the truthful answer, and for one moment she thought of Tyler as she hit the skateboard ramp dead on and tore through the air aiming for the bridge.

The Chinook was rising directly in front, and when the cycle arched into the air Ava could momentarily catch a clear vision of Diesel hanging from the cargo hook in a sling soaring through the sky. Rhya and Jeffery were standing at the large back opening in the fuselage.

Jeffery screamed and fanned his face while Rhya was mouthing the exact words Ava prayed: *"St. Joan of Arc, please!"*

CHAPTER 26

The fall morning was chilly. Ava wrapped a cape tighter around her body as she tiptoed between white tombstones. Arlington. Three months after her motorcycle rescue, Ava was attending the funeral with Jeffery for General Minosa's son. It was the least she could do for the man who saved her life several times.

"Ava, I told you to wear the flat boots. We will be walking in the grass, I said!" Jeffery ranted.

"I am tiptoeing out of respect," she quietly replied.

The service was reverent and somber. Not the entire band or typical caisson used in the procession. Just one bugler, a three-rifle volley and Rhya leading the riderless horse, Diesel.

Ava broke when she saw Rhya leading the majestic black animal who also saved her life. Memories of Tyler's funeral were etched in her heart forever. Ava and Jeffery stayed back, out of respect, as she watched the flag folded and laid in Jason's mother's arms.

As the crowds drifted away, Remy touched his wife and whispered something in her ear. She gently nodded and pointed to the black car that awaited them. Remy saluted his son and headed toward Ava. Her heart pounded harder with each of his steps as he neared. They had not spoken since she told him he needed to repair his life, and she never expected him to respond today, of all days.

Remy was as handsome as ever in his full uniform. He removed his hat and nodded at Jeffery who bowed away. Ava caught a whiff of his woodsy aroma in the crisp air.

"Thank you for coming, Ava."

"It's the least I could do."

"Everything is wrapped up. I will be on a new mission, and your daughter will fulfill her time at the JW and go on."

Ava's body flooded with emotion as she eyed Jeffery, Rhya and Diesel waiting at the edge of the path.

"My wife... my wife and I... I would like to somehow see you again." He stumbled over the request.

Ava smiled and examined his wife standing by the car.

"My heart breaks for her... and my heart breaks for you," she said, ignoring his remark.

He pressed a smile together and let out a little air. "You are the best thing that ever happened to me."

"No, your son was the best. You need to console her right now."

"She's my ex, Ava."

"No matter. You shared a son, a glorious man. I wish I would have known him. So be with her," Ava advised even though the words went against every grain of feeling in her heart. She was overwhelmingly filled with a desire that Remy would wrap her in his arms and kiss her.

"I will find you."

She smiled, her blonde highlighted hair sparkling in the fall sun.

"You know, I will find you."

He reached to touch her cheek, but Ava stepped back, avoiding any hand against her skin. "You know where I will be, General Mimosa." Ava shrugged her shoulders holding back tears.

"That I do. Private Mom."

The day was sunny and almost summer-like for late March, too warm. Ava held the door open for a cadet as he strolled into the Jefferson Washington barbershop.

She had been cutting hair all morning next to Jeffery who appeared uneasy and frankly nervous. He continually glanced out the window. The electrician was rewiring the fuse box in the back, hopefully preparing for another summer of styling without blowing the air conditioning out on the entire campus.

"Who will take over the school now?" Ava asked Jeffery who was styling one of the officers. "After the temporary Dean steps down?"

"I hear the Army is in need of a qualified person. Now that the military has confiscated ownership of the school, Shane Blevins will spend a long time behind bars. Along with his girlfriend, the horse instructor Pam Waverly."

"I hear a potential candidate is visiting today," the officer remarked. "We are all to be on the field at 1300." Ava glanced at the clock. It was 12:45, almost 1:00. She was becoming very proficient at Army time.

The door opened and another client in uniform planted himself in the doorway. Jeffery screamed with a gasp. "Colonel and Sgt. Ironside. What are you doing here?"

Ava stopped cutting, confused.

Jeffery's voice was almost rehearsed. "Col. Pendleton with his new wife... Sgt. Ironside!" he exclaimed further in a long drawn out sentence.

"You're married?" Ava tilted her head. They both nodded and she rushed for a hug. "Sorry but I must, Colonel. I've missed you so!"

"Why, Colonel, I think you are blushing," Jeffery touted. "And what is coming here?" Jeffery pointed outside, once again sounding fakely surprised.

Ava recognized Diesel first, his black shining mane billowing in the sun, then she eyed the handsome general astride his back. She untied her apron and walked out of the barbershop as the colonel held the door open, removing his hat.

"Good morning, Private M." Remy halted Diesel. Jeffery was already standing behind with a prepared cart of champagne glasses and a pitcher.

"Mimosas, anyone?"

Ava began to tear. "What is going on?"

"Remember the movie *Officer and a Gentleman*," Jeffery asked. "When he carried her out? You know I always wanted to be the gentleman, but he's all yours, Ava." Jeffery handed Col. Pendleton a glass.

"Mom!" Rhya peeked her head out under Diesel's neck. In full uniform she took the steed's reins as the general dismounted. A chestnut bulldog nestled at Rhya's calf. Scarlet's tail smacked the macadam in repeated succession.

"Rhya?"

"Mom, this is our new Dean and horse instructor, General Minosa. General, this is our barber, I am proud to say my mom, Private M."

Remy inched closer and lowered his head for a long awaited kiss. Ava drew in a deep breath as he saluted her. "I think you are due for an upgrade in rank. Maybe Mrs. General M? For Minosa?"

Ava smiled, taking his hand. "Maybe I will, but you will always be General Mimosa to me!"

And he kissed her again.

Acknowledgments

A heartfelt thanks to JJ whose determination to forge ahead while parented by a helicopter mom is an inspiration.

Thanks to editor Demi Stevens, my dear friends Teresa Shaub and Rhonda Rodriquez who read and reread, and to Lori Browning, Darlene Smith, and Tabby Shury.

An enormous thank you to Kayla L. Chandler for her creative and artistic abilities. Her talents are highly recommended for cards, posters, and advertising at alyakdesigns@gmail.com.

Thanks to Peggy Selway, my skydiver and pilot expert with over a thousand lifetime dives. What a woman!

Finally an enormous thank you to all the men and women who serve, especially my father Joseph Stephens.

LEAVE A REVIEW

Loved *Private Mom?* Please consider leaving a review on Amazon, Goodreads, or other book recommendation sites!

This is one of the best ways you can help other readers find great books, so authors can continue to write more stories you want to read.

Discover more articles and fiction by Alicia, and be the first to learn about new releases by subscribing to the blog:

aliciastephensmartin.wordpress.com

About the Author

Alicia Stephens Martin has been a teacher and the owner of Rubee Z Salon in southcentral Pennsylvania for over thirty years. Her daughter, a Second Lieutenant in the United States Army, is an avid equestrian, holding many state and national awards.

Alicia holds a Bachelor's degree in Creative Writing and has published a romantic suspense, *Spurred to Justice*, and an interactive children's workbook for the salon called *Let's Go to the Hairstylist.* Her short fiction and non-fiction stories have been published in *Salon Ovation Magazine* and *PBA Progress*, and her non-fiction piece "Healing in a Pocket" won the prestigious Bob Hoffman writing award. Her articles have also been published in *PA Equestrian*, *East Coast Equestrian*, and *From Whispers to Roars*.

Connect with the Author

 Alicia.StephensMartin

 ASMartin_Author

ALSO BY ALICIA STEPHENS MARTIN